FRACTURED THRONE

LEE H. HAYWOOD

FREE DOMINION PUBLISHING

Story Consultant and Editor: Kerry Haywood

First Published 2018

Paperback ISBN 978-0-9970810-8-4

www.leehhaywood.com

For J.B.

THE CONTINENT

OF ELANDRIA

THE FOUR REALMS

TABLE OF CONTENTS

FRACTURED
THRONE

Their son they unbound, so splendid was he
But greed led his heart and he boiled the sea
He burned the forests, laid waste to the hills
The rivers he mired, the people he killed
The land, once pure, now tilled blackened soil
Calaban's folly brought brimstone and toil

PROLOGUE

Killing a god was never a pretty affair. It was violent and ugly, and rarely went as expected. Lillian had seen dying gods rip mountains in two and turn cities into craters. She had also seen gods plead for mercy with their dying breath, acting no different than the mortals they lorded over.

"My own death will be more dignified," said Lillian, trying to reassure herself. She leaned out over the edge of the precipice and considered how far it was to the base of the cliff. A league or more of unobstructed sky spanned between her and the valley floor.

The drop will suffice, she imagined, *that is, if my skull isn't bashed to bits against the cliff wall first.*

The wind howled up to greet her, twisting her hair and tugging at the feathers that sprung from her back. For a moment her balance wavered. Like the talons of an eagle, her toes hooked into the crevices that pockmarked the basalt ledge. She flung her wings wide, letting them hang on the updraft. A blissful smile creased her lips as she enjoyed this final sensation of flight. It would be the last time she would experience such joy while she wore this guise.

Bong. Bong. Boom. A bell tolled in the distance, calling the tribunal to order.

The smile faded from Lillian's lips.

"From this point forward all my actions will be out of necessity," Lillian whispered to herself. "My life will be hard and cold, but I will survive to continue the fight." She must survive. She had to.

It was an oft spoken mantra, yet no matter how many times she reassured herself of this truth, a nagging doubt remained. When she closed her eyes she saw other lives and other paths, and in them all the Shadow still lingered. "Maybe this dance is eternal." She scowled at the prospect.

"We did the best we could," said Lord Parius beside her, misreading the frown on her face. There was a resignation in his voice that had not been there earlier in the day.

He has come to accept his fate, realized Lillian with a degree of pity.

Lord Parius knelt, trying to display a degree of grace in his final moments. Both he and Lillian had been stripped naked; it was the Calabanesi's vain effort to shame them before the sundering. But Parius, god as he was, would not be cowed so easily. He stared defiantly into the crowd that had gathered to witness their execution.

"We'll do better in the next life," replied Lillian.

"The next life? Ha!" Parius curled his lips scornfully. "Perhaps you will fare better, but I only had this one chance. No, Lillian, I have failed in my purpose."

Have patience, she wanted to say. *Let the trial run its course. You will find a flicker of hope in the depths of your despair.* But she didn't dare say anything that would reveal her plan, not with so many eyes watching their every move, not with the Shadow so near. Instead, she turned away from the abyss and gave Parius's hand a reassuring squeeze.

The gaunt lines of his face drew into a strained smile, but the doubt within his eyes did not fade.

She didn't blame him. In truth, she didn't blame anybody. The malignant Shadow. The unflinching Secutor. The false gods. All were playing their part as fate would have them. It almost gave her pleasure to consider how orderly events had unfolded. Everyone and everything was in their place until now. *This is the part I did not foresee.*

For eons Lillian had danced with the Shadow,

3

and with each step she wove her web with care. Each string was as fine as gossamer; invisible to the eye yet as strong as steel. No one saw that she was weaving a noose until the very end. First she deceived, then she ensnared, lastly she destroyed. Unfortunately, she had faltered in the final step. Betrayed perhaps, or maybe she was simply outmaneuvered.

She scanned the crowd seeking the telltale symptoms of the taint; blotched skin, a yellowing of the eyes. The face of every onlooker was shadowed — they all wore hoods — and Lillian could see nothing of their complexions.

The Shadow creeps as it ever does, thought Lillian with an internal laugh. Now she would have to pay the blood price for her folly. She turned to accept her due.

The basalt ledge was encompassed on three sides by a crescent colonnade, forming a plaza that ended at a sheer cliff. Three splendid towers served as a backdrop. These were the Seeing Towers of Bel Atum. All the inhabited lands of Elandria could be spied from atop these pale steeples by the far-reaching eyes of the gods.

Gathered around the base of the three towers stood the winged-gods of Calaban. The Calabanesi had gathered to bear witness to the purging of the so-called heretics. The only characteristic that distinguished one of these gods from the next was the pair of wings that sprouted from each god's back. The wings were dyed a variety of colors. Some were garish — green, blue, and red. While others austere — jet black or pearl white. The colors represented membership in one faction or another, the ideological distinctions of which made little difference right now. Currently, all were unified for one purpose — to kill Lillian and Parius.

Parius sighed as he looked over this heavy-handed tribunal. The Calabanesi had already passed their judgment. There was little he could do, save look from one accuser to the next with a slow methodical stare. His piercing gaze settled lastly upon the one god, who besides Lillain and Parius, was separated from the rest.

In the shadows of the central colonnade, silent but aware, was Tiberius, supreme lord of the gods. He sat sullenly upon his copper throne, thrumming his fingers impatiently upon his armrest. While he was typically fair in all measures of beauty and grace, these attributes were lost to him on this day. His golden locks had turned brown, his vibrant skin was pale and sickly. And his eyes, which were usually so bright and warm, hung heavy, pulled earthward by the shame of his disciple's betrayal.

A father is never free of his child's sins, Lillian knew. Tiberius raised Parius, trained him and loved him like a son. But Parius had too much of his mother's spirit. He couldn't resist the impulse to do what was right; that was why Lillian selected him from the start.

"Maybe I should tell him the whereabouts of Shadowbane," said Parius, moved by the pain in Tiberius's eyes. "There has to be another way forward."

"There is not. The weapon is now beyond our reach," said Lillian, hoping what she said was true. "Take heart, Tiberius has already forgiven you. He would stop this madness if he could, but it has run too far. It is the Calabanesi's will and the Calabanesi's way. There is nothing else he can do, Fate has seen to that." Lillian smiled at her own part in this wretched affair.

Her grin seemed to set Lord Tiberius off. His anger boiled over, reaching into the physical world, and the sky became entangled in his will. The sun fell behind a wall of churning clouds and a tempest roared out of the north, filling the sky with lightning. Hail and freezing rain pelted Lillian's bare flesh, causing her skin to pimple.

A familiar croak sounded near the edge of the

cliff.

Lillian's eyes darted to the sound. She discovered a dragon whelp had crawled up over the lip of the cliff. She had to focus to keep track of the diminutive creature as it slithered against the surface of the basalt. It was hardly larger than a crow, and with its black scales slick with rain, it was difficult to discern where the body of the dragon whelp ended and the black stone began.

"You should have stayed hidden," she whispered from the corner of her mouth.

If the whelp heard her, it made no effort to reply. Instead, the whelp hopped a few steps closer and cocked its head sideways. It felt odd putting so much faith in such a young creature, but Lillian had known the dragon across a hundred generations. The whelp was as trustworthy and capable as every ancestor who came before.

The whelp clacked its beaked maw and blinked, flashing its black beady eyes, then it took to the sky, spiraling ever higher upon the updrafts. It perched itself atop the steeple of Bel Atum. From its indomitable aerie, the whelp idly watched history unfold. It was the only mortal, beast or better, to bear witness to the Sundering.

It is time, Lillian admitted to herself. *I can delay no longer.* She took in a deep breath and envisioned the world as it truly was. Not the world of flesh and blood, earth and water. The spirit world, the web eternal, and the One Soul that linked all living things together. In her mind's eye Lillian plucked one string, and like a symphony, the world played for her. The ceremony began.

Bong. Bong. Boom, tolled the bell.

A figure emerged from the row of cloaked gods, taking long haughty strides. The Secutor was a tall man with a stern, chiseled face. His hair and furled wings were as black as onyx. In one hand he bore a rusted iron chain that trailed back to the foot of Lord Tiberius's copper throne. In the other hand he held a dagger, the fuller of which was set with twinkling gemstones that were at one instant blue, at another green. Lillian scowled at the Sundering Stones; she did not relish the prospect of feeling their burning touch.

The Secutor rested the blade on Parius's shoulder, placing it threateningly close to his neck. He then took a knee, coming cheek to cheek with Parius so he could whisper in his ear.

"Lord Tiberius offers mercy, Parius," said the Secutor, "but you must tell us what you did with the weapon. Where is Shadowbane?"

"The tribunal has ruled, brother," said Parius, his voice wavering ever so slightly. "Nothing I say or do will change their decision."

"The tribunal be damned," hissed the Secutor. "I offer mercy. The blade or the chain? Mercy or damnation? The Shadow will take your soul, brother. Do not let it be this way. One path returns your soul to the web, the other makes you a slave to the Shadow. Is that what you want, to spend all eternity in damnation? Choose mercy, brother. What did you do with Shadowbane? Where did you hide it?"

Uncertainty filled Parius's eyes.

"It's gone," blurted Lillian, speaking for her master before his fear betrayed him.

"Silence!" The Secutor slapped her across the face, hitting her so hard she almost fell over the edge of the cliff. She immediately clawed back to her position beside Parius; he would need her strength.

Parius's eyes wandered to the blood dribbling down Lillian's lip and chin. All doubt vanished from his eyes. "Send for the Shadow, brother," he said sullenly. "I have nothing more to say to you."

Shaking his head with pity, the Secutor stood. Like a man girding himself to wrangle a bull, he looped the chain around his hand and grasped with all his might. For an instant Lillian detected a quiver in his lip. Uncertainty perhaps, or fear.

"Send forth the Shadow," ordered Lord Tiberius, as he ruefully ordered his own disciple's undoing.

The Secutor gave the chain a harsh tug.

A black shape rose from beside the foot of the dais, blotting out the sheening copper throne with its frame. If there was a shape to the damnable creature, Lillian could not detect it. The Shadow was nebulous, a well of pitch darkness surrounded by undulating grays. It inched across the courtyard on unseen limbs. Lillian's vision blurred as the Shadow drew near. The world seemed to dim. The howling wind became a mere hiss on the periphery of her senses. All she could think about was the wretched clangor of the rusty chain that dragged in the Shadow's wake. The Shadow stopped before Parius and rose to its full height, looming impossibly tall.

Lillian had forgotten what true fear felt like. She found herself short of breath, and an involuntary tremor worked through her body. She was so close, she could feel the bite of chill air emanating from the Shadow's invisible core. Her instinct told her to flee, to jump over the cliff and into the void. But the trap had not yet been set. She girded herself, resisting all urges.

"Strength, my lord," she whispered to Parius.

Have strength to bear the unbearable. Have strength for the both of us.

The nebulous shadow took form, and a hand clasped at the wrist by an iron fetter reached out from the gloom. It was dead, gaunt flesh, pale to the point of being translucent. Knobby fingers stroked Parius's cheek in an almost loving fashion. Parius grimaced as his mind became polluted by temptation. He leaned forward, slowly drawn into the abyssal darkness of the Shadow's cloak. Suddenly, a second hand grasped Parius's forehead, striking like a snake hitting its prey. The pungent smell of burning flesh filled the air.

"Mercy," moaned a terror-filled voice from amongst the crowd of onlookers.

"Mercy," echoed others.

"Bear it," chided Lillian sternly. Parius had to withstand the test. If his mind broke, there would be nothing else she could do. "Don't give in. Resist the temptation."

Billowing smoke began to emanate from beneath the Shadow's fingers, until finally the ghastly cloud concealed Parius's face.

One by one, the onlookers in the crowd looked away, sickened by the sight. "Have mercy, my lord," called more voices than Lillian could count. Each gasp of disgust and grimace of displeasure was another thread sewn, Lillian's grand army in the making. She smiled inwardly. The Calabanesi were finally seeing the devil they allowed to linger in their midst.

Lillian wanted to scream her condemnation. *You supplant a god by killing him. Only a fool binds a god in chains and believes they can turn him into a slave.*

Parius's body trembled. The sinew in his neck strained. His jaw twisted. A halo of light appeared above his head consisting of a thousand sparkling cinders that burst upward through his flesh like droplets of sweat. It was his spirit being drawn from his body. Much more of this, and Parius would cease to exist. All that would remain would be a witless husk.

"Have mercy, my lord," cried the witnesses in chorus. The will of the Calabanesi had shifted. No one wanted to see what would happen next. The murmur rose until it could not be ignored.

Tiberius raised his hand. "Stop!"

The Secutor wrenched the Shadow's iron leash taut. The Shadow did not comply; the latent willpower of the enthralled god was somehow resisting the enchantments on the collar that kept him ensnared. Parius moaned pitifully as countless points of shimmering light danced on the air above his body. The Secutor gave the chain a second yank, and this time the hand receded, leaving a trail of red and blistered flesh on Parius's nose, cheeks, and brow.

The sparkling motes of light cascaded around Parius's body in a shower of sizzling embers. Parius collapsed, his chest heaving in exhaustion. He coughed and sputtered, straining to breathe. Lillian sighed with relief. Parius had passed the test. His soul was still his own to command. What was more, he had won the pity of the audience. The hard part was over.

The Secutor tugged the chain a third time. The Shadow withdrew to the foot of the throne like a faithful dog. The nebulous black form seemed to decrease in size, once again bowing beneath the yoke of its chains.

Tiberius motioned to the Secutor.

Grim-faced, the Secutor stepped over Parius's fetal form, and came to stand before Lillian. He lifted her chin with his knuckle, forcing her eyes to come within inches of the dagger's edge. No reflection shone off of the black steel. It was like looking into a pool of ink. The Sundering Stones set in the fuller glimmered with a pulsating light.

"Do it," hissed Lillian.

He pressed the blade to her flesh and the skin eagerly parted. Muscle and bone were cleaved in two as if they were made of parchment. Lillian experienced an agony she did not know was possible, and she bit her lip until she tasted blood. *Pain is momentary,* she tried to reassure herself. *My life is eternal.*

She suddenly felt lighter. The Secutor was finished. He threw the hacked remains of her feathered wings on the ground. A crimson sphere grew around the stumps, pooling on the rain-washed basalt. The blood stood in stark contrast to the pinions, creating a ghastly collage of red on white.

The Secutor nodded gravely, generally pleased with his work. He stepped aside and straddled Parius's broken form. The Secutor's chiseled face creased into a wicked grin as he proceeded to cut off Parius's wings.

With his task near complete, the Secutor returned to Lillian and kissed her forehead. He then took the Sundering Stones set in the blade's fuller and held them firmly where he had laid his wet lips. Lillian felt her energies wane, like water siphoned from a well. Her visioned narrowed to shades of black and white. Her body quaked uncontrollably, her throat closed until her breathing became a desperate death rattle. The world seemed to slow to a miserable crawl, and then she was suddenly outside of herself, watching the purging from an impossible height.

She had passed through to her true form, and in her mind's eye, thousands and thousands of threads were laid bare, flaming tendrils that connected all life. The world became a glorious web, with interconnected blotches of light that shined as brightly as the burning sun. That is, except at the foot of the throne, there existed a hideous void about which the light warped and bent. The Shadow was the antithesis of life, and everything it touched became twisted and polluted. Lillian gazed unflinching into the nothingness and the malevolent spirit looked back.

Movement near the edge of the precipice drew Lillian's attention away from the Shadow. Caught up in the bliss of transcendence she had almost forgotten about her earthly form. The Secutor was evaluating his work. Lillian's body appeared limp and lifeless. Her eyes stared vacantly from their sockets, and drool dripped from her lower lip. Satisfied that the sundering would prove sufficient, the Secutor cast her body backward, sending her tumbling over the precipice and into the endless fathoms beyond.

With a shudder, Lillian returned to her plummeting body. The sundering was through. The ruse had worked. She reached out, embracing the fall as weightlessness overtook her. The individual threads of the web she had spent a lifetime weaving slowly encroached. One-by-one she plucked them. A thousand notes became a thousand chords, and the world hummed in reply. Lillian smiled blissfully as the dissonance came into sudden harmony.

CHAPTER

I

IMEL KATAN

In a time of plague, men chose war. The irony of it all wasn't lost on Emethius. He sat in his saddle, wishing that the slaughter would stop, knowing that it wouldn't, at least not until the rebels were beaten into submission.

Dead grass shifted about the ankles of his horse, creating a ceaseless rustle that frayed his nerves. The wind tore across the land without end. It came cold and steady, causing Emethius's cheeks to burn as if they were on fire. Despite the chill, his clothes were sodden with sweat. Fear and exhaustion had a way of doing that to a soldier.

Emethius longed to sit beside one of the countless sputtering fires that glowed across the military camp. But that was not his duty. He had been summoned to advise the praetor, and so he patiently waited.

Beside him, Praetor Maxentius was restless in his

saddle, his face a dark grimace. Emethius took this for an ill omen. Battle and death were not far away.

"The sooner we put the rebels to the sword, the better," muttered Emethius under his breath. He had sat astride a horse everyday for nearly two fortnights, and his ass felt like a single giant bruise. He couldn't think of the last time he had disrobed. His undergarments were worn threadbare, and the coarse binding straps of his armor had rubbed the flesh along his shoulders and ribs raw. He had more open sores than he cared to count. He stunk of horse, and iron, and blood. Battle would put an end to these hardships, be it through death or a final victory.

For the hundredth time that evening Praetor Maxentius raised a spyglass to his eye, sighting the ominous tower that appeared only as a dim outline against the night sky. He followed a pair of men walking the parapet with the lens. "Traitors are a step below vermin, Captain Emethius," said Maxentius, repeating a sentiment he had expressed so often it might as well have been the slogan for the campaign. "It's the supreme sin. I feel like I need to bathe that blasted tower in fire. It's the only way I can purge the land of this rebel taint."

"You would not be the first to try to burn Imel Katan to the ground," said Emethius. "Countless others have tried — all have failed. They say the fortress was built by witchcraft. You cannot destroy evil with evil, or so it is said."

Praetor Maxentius flared his brows at the suggestion. He was not accustomed to anyone telling him he was incorrect. "I'll see that it burns when this butcher's work is through," growled the praetor. "Even if I need to use an entire forest as kindling." He smacked the looking glass against Emethius's chest.

Emethius stifled his opinion; sometimes the praetor wanted words, and sometimes he wanted silence. Emethius hastily collected the spyglass from the praetor's outstretched hand and returned the delicate instrument to its container in his saddlebag.

Emethius's horse stomped his feet in response. Manos was the gelding's name. The beast was clearly tired of being idle. The feeling was not unfounded. They had already delayed for three crucial days, giving the enemy ample time to fortify the ruins of Imel Katan. The chime of rebel hammers had been ringing nearly non-stop since they arrived. The longer Praetor Maxentius delayed the assault, the more nervous everyone seemed to get. The gods only knew what traps the rebels had lying in store for them.

"My men are prepared for the advance, praetor," called a rider that approached out of the night. The rider drove his horse between Maxentius and Emethius, edging Emethius's smaller gelding aside. The man was Saterius, Maxentius's son-in-law. He looked like a beast, wearing a wolf skin cloak over his armor. His face was a dark mask, painted black in preparation for the coming battle. Only the whites of his eyes and sneering teeth revealed anything of his countenance. "We've soaked the ladders and battering rams in water. The men's armor has been dulled with mud."

Maxentius nodded curtly.

"A frontal assault is folly, praetor," said Emethius, knowing well Saterius's intent. They had already debated the matter half-a-dozen times in the past few days.

"Wise men know when their advice is needed. Seldom do they speak otherwise," snapped Saterius.

"A wise man, eh?" Emethius scowled at Saterius. "A wise man does not throw the lives of his men away. The praetor has ordered me to his side so that I might advise him." He turned back to Maxentius and repeated his opinion even louder. "The frontal assault is a mistake."

"I heard you the first time," said Maxentius, his

voice a low growl. His eyes never strayed from the tower.

Emethius readjusted his leather cuirass, wishing he could disappear through the neck hole. Saterius smirked like a child who had just bested his sibling.

Saterius was a hammer, the kind of blunt tool every commander needed in their arsenal. *Go there, kill that.* Saterius would never question the order, nor would he disappoint. But this operation required precision. Emethius could only pray that Maxentius would listen to wisdom before it was too late — they had already lost too many men.

The loyalist army had pursued the rebels across the Billowing Flats, engaging them in battle seven times in as many days. When loyalist forces stormed the rebel encampment at the close of the seventh battle, most thought the war was finally won. But Herald Carrick, the rebel commander, had somehow managed to elude capture. He led the tattered remnants of his army to the shores of Lake Libith, taking refuge in the abandoned fortress of Imel Katan.

The fortress was built upon a peninsula that reached out toward the center of the lake. With water on three sides and the loyalist army blocking the peninsula's neck, there was nowhere else for the rebels to go; this would be their final stand.

Emethius stared across the frozen pool with loathing. Lake Libith was a cursed place. During summer the waters were inky black, and sat unwavered by the wind. In winter, when little else in this region froze, the water succumbed to ice. This was how they found it now. Although fall had just begun, a thin layer of ice already spanned from the mainland to the peninsula.

Stretching the length of the treeless peninsula lay the ruined stone mounds of a once grand city. Vine-encrusted walls tilted at disorienting angles, creating canyons in the footprints of crumbling structures. In an age long since past, the Merridian people had set the city to the torch. Most of the city had burned, yet the Tower of Imel Katan would not yield to flames. It remained standing at the head of the peninsula almost mockingly, daring its besiegers to attack.

"The herald is watching," said Saterius with a nod.

For the first time in a dozen generations the tower was occupied. The stone portals of its balconies glowed like the eyes of a giant. A gaunt figure stood silhouetted against the highest portal.

"He appears more frail than I remember," said Emethius.

"War has a way of thinning a man," replied

Praetor Maxentius.

"I imagine he'll be a few pounds lighter when I take off his head." Saterius laughed at his own joke. No one else did.

Herald Carrick, the man leading the rebellion, was once the head of the Tiber Brotherhood, one of the five holy orders. He was a man known for his severe temperament and fiery sermons. Over the years, Emethius heard Herald Carrick preach on many occasions. Nothing the herald ever said would have convinced Emethius he was capable of treason, let alone the blasphemous accusations he leveled against the High Lord of Merridia.

"High Lord Valerius is a false prophet," Herald Carrick had so treasonously proclaimed upon the steps of the Court of Bariil. *"That is why the gods have abandoned the people of Merridia."* Soon thereafter, heretics loyal to the herald stormed the palace and kidnapped High Lord Valerius and Prince Meriatis.

"The fool thinks he can escape the justice of the Throne of Rose," said Saterius with a snarling laugh. "The branches of the Rose grow long. The thorn bites deep. There is no escape."

Praetor Maxentius's deep growling voice pierced the night. "Are you eager for death, General Saterius?," pressed Maxentius. "I will gladly send forward any man who is eager to meet his end."

The young general shrunk beneath the gaze of his superior. "No? Then speak of more sensible things than justice. The world has no justice; simply gods, men who would be gods, and the mortals foolish enough to follow them."

The general scowled bitterly and gestured toward the tower. "Those who live a long life learn to accept any handout fate offers, be it just or not. What do you make of our enemy's position, Captain Emethius? Has fate afforded us any gifts, or is Imel Katan as unyielding as it appears?"

Emethius had been sizing up the fortifications all day, marking weaknesses and strengths — low points in the wall, places were debris provided natural cover, and areas the rebels seemed keen on reinforcing. Emethius was quick with his assessment. "Siege engines will be ineffective, praetor. Ruins stretch the entire length of the peninsula and will prevent maneuvering the towers and catapults into position. A battering ram could potentially penetrate the postern gate, but may the gods protect the men sent on that mission. The rebel archers atop the battlements will see that a dozen men die for every one that enters the inner bailey. Saterius's ladders are long enough to reach the parapets east of the gatehouse, but his men will break against the fortress like flame licking ice.

Most will fall. Few will gain a footing atop the wall."

Emethius directed Maxentius's gaze to the northern tip of the peninsula. "Imel Katan's true weakness is its curtain wall. Herald Carrick retains too few men to properly man the battlements. Out of necessity, he will leave the highest walls ill-guarded. Our attack must be multi-pronged, and quick. A few swords over the north wall could turn the battle in our favor."

"Ha! The north wall is fifty feet tall," said Saterius, scoffing at the proposal. "How do you plan to get over them — sprout a pair of wings?

Emethius ignored the man. "Time will be precious once the assault begins. The slower our assault, the more time Herald Carrick will have to consider his counterstroke. I fear what the rebels will do to the high lord and the prince if defeat seems certain."

Maxentius's head bobbed with approval — he rarely displayed a higher level of praise. "Remember, one plunge of the traitor's sword will make our entire cause in vain," said Maxentius. The weight of his potentially prophetic message quieted even Saterius's bluster.

A high pitched neigh sounded to the west, followed by the thunder of galloping hooves.

"Riders," announced Saterius.

Maxentius nodded. "They are overdue."

A host of cloaked riders rode into view. Each bore a flaming torch, a brazen display of force meant to dismay the rebel sentries. Emethius estimated that the host numbered not a man short of four hundred.

Loyalist soldiers rose from their fires and began to cheer as the warhorses paraded into the encampment. The foremost rider blasted his trumpet triumphantly, and a dozen other riders blared in reply. Emethius spied the flash of silver fangs and snarling lips upon the division's fluttering standard.

"The Fifth Legion," muttered Emethius. That could only mean one thing — at long last, the Dragon Helm had come to battle!

Emethius's feelings of joy and wonder faded fast. The Dragon Helm's arrival could only mean one thing — the machines of war were about to be set in motion. His blood ran cold.

Maxentius raised his hand in greeting. "Hail, Lord Fennir."

"Hail, Praetor Maxentius," came the replying cry.

The whites of Saterius's eyes flashed to darkness beneath the snout of his wolf cloak. His body stiffened as he spurred his horse out of the way, making way for the fast approaching lord.

Lord Fennir rode up alongside Praetor Maxentius, bringing his stallion to a halt. "My mother has sent me to see to my uncle's freedom," announced Lord Fennir loudly, wasting no time for pleasantries.

"I have delayed the assault, just as Lady Miren instructed," said Maxentius, granting the lord a curt bow. "But I fear the delay has been costly. The rebels have had ample time to prepare their defenses."

Fennir smirked. The young lord's olive skin and gray-black hair would lead many to suspect his royal lineage, but it was his eyes that confirmed it. They were neither blue nor green, but both at the same time. His armor was jet black, inlaid with silver tracery. Etched in the center of his breastplate was a blossoming rose, the symbol of House Benisor. His silver crest glittered in the torchlight, giving the impression that he was glowing. Upon his head he wore a black helm fashioned in the likeness of a snarling dragon — this was the dragon helm from which he earned his nickname.

Praetor Maxentius's appearance was less assuming. Though he was of royal lineage, he was first and foremost a Soldier of the Faith. He wore a simple suit of polished steel and bore no markings in honor of his lineage, save the rose pommel of his sword. His face was chiseled with clefts and creases, badges of honor from his long years in the field. Although his age showed plainly on his face, his body was still strong. He sat upon his horse unbowed by the weight of his armor.

Lord Fennir gave Praetor Maxentius a dismissive wave. "Had your leadership been more competent, the delay would not have been necessary. The heresy would have been crushed in its infancy, and my uncle would be free. My only regret is that I did not intervene sooner — much folly might have been avoided."

A cold murmur ran through the host of gathered men. Emethius had never heard someone speak to Praetor Maxentius in such a disrespectful manner. But Lord Fennir was no haughty lord or insolent soldier, Emethius had to remind himself.

Fennir was High Lord Valerius's only nephew, and stood to inherit the high lordship if events turned sour. Emethius guessed at Fennir's true intentions; Fennir assumed that the assault would fail and both High Lord Valerius and Prince Meriatis would die. Fennir wished to be present on the field of battle when his ascension was declared.

"What parley have you gained with the rebels?" asked Fennir.

"As it was the day we arrived," answered Maxentius. "No word has left that damnable tower, and not a man I have sent has been received."

"It is of no matter," said Fennir, his face curling as if he tasted something sour. "Herald Carrick is a fool. I will not negotiate with one so ensnared. We will begin the assault at midnight."

Emethius wanted to spit in the young lord's face. "*One so ensnared is likely to fight to the last man,*" Emethius wanted to yell in reply. "*One so ensnared is likely to kill the high lord.*" He had to swallow his ire. It was not his place to talk.

Maxentius's brow furrowed in consternation, but he did not openly question Lord Fennir's decision. "General Saterius, array your men. Your task is to harry the walls east of the gatehouse with your ladders and draw the defenders to your position. Don't commit unless you see an opening. I will lead the main assault on the gatehouse."

Emethius's eyes flared wide. "Praetor, I would ask you to reconsider. An assault on the gatehouse..."

Maxentius silenced Emethius with a wave of his hand. "The battle will be won or lost at the gatehouse. I ought to be there."

Lord Fennir scowled. "A commander's place on the battlefield is far from danger. I will be the one taking the gatehouse."

Maxentius gave Fennir the slightest of bows. "If it pleases the lord, the glory shall be yours."

"I am honored," said Lord Fennir with a self-confident smirk. He was oblivious to the trap Maxentius had laid at his feet, and into which he had boldly stepped.

A dozen men will die for every one that reaches the inner bailey. The prediction echoed in Emethius's head. He felt tempted to warn Lord Fennir of the danger, but Maxentius's glowering eyes told him to remain silent. Emethius's loyalties lay with his gods, the high lord, and the praetor, in that order. He owed nothing to this brash young lord.

With a wave of his hand, Maxentius dismissed the men to prepare for the forthcoming battle. As the men dispersed, Maxentius gestured to Emethius. "Captain Emethius, please remain a moment longer. There is something we need to discuss." He waited until they were alone before elaborating.

"What unfolds before the gate is yet to be seen, but I will not wait for Fate to decide the future of this realm. Your task is to secure the high lord."

"You want me to take my men over the north

wall."

Maxentius nodded and quickly spelled out the nature of Emethius's mission. When he was finished speaking, Emethius placed his hand over his heart and bowed. "I swear upon my life, I will see the high lord to safety."

"I am certain you will, but there is one more thing. As I am sure you are well aware, there are unsettling rumors concerning Prince Meriatis."

Emethius nodded. He knew the rumors all too well. Disquieting rumors. Rumors that didn't make sense. Rumors that spoke of treason, heresy, and madness. But Emethius didn't believe them; he couldn't believe them.

"If you were to come across the Prince Meriatis while in the tower..."

"My loyalties are with the high lord and the gods."

"Very good," said Maxentius, turning his attention back to the tower. "Until the fates overcome us, captain. I wish you the best of luck."

CHAPTER

II

THE RED COMPANY

The camp erupted. Men rushed from their tents, beating the sleep out of their limbs. Squires hastily tacked the horses of their masters, while knights struggled to put on their armor. Blades thrummed against shields and men whooped and hollered as they tried to steady their nerves for the coming battle. Many purged their stomachs, hacking up the putrid remains of their evening revelry.

Emethius set off at once to marshal his men. He discovered they were already gathered, two score in all, roused from their tents by the arrival of Lord Fennir's riders. Emethius halted beyond the light of the campfire and watched. Brother Seius, the company's chaplain, was leading the men in a quiet prayer.

The bandy-legged brother paraded around the prayer circle, bowing and gesturing as he made his rounds. He touched the heads of some men and flailed his arms toward the heavens when he came to others. It was all very practiced and rote, but the passion in his voice was genuine. "We, who have long paid tribute, pray to you now," called Brother Seius. His freshly shaven head bobbed to an unheard melody. "Protect these men, o' gods of Calaban. We are your servants in this time of treachery. Let our blades smite the black hearts of our enemies. Let these men bask in the glory of your light during their hour of need. Please, gods, hear our prayer!"

"Blessed be the gods!" called the men in chorus. The soldiers began to recite their own personal prayers. Emethius gave the men a moment. Faith had a way of quelling worries and steadying hearts that Emethius's own words simply could not match.

The Red Company was a cavalry unit, a mixture of skilled lancers and archers. His best bowmen could hit a moving target at thirty paces while riding at a full gallop. Every single member hailed from Henna Lu or its surrounding province, and Emethius had known most of these men since childhood. He had gone to school with Sexmund and Berit. Emethius once broke his fist on Big Oswyn's chin during a fight over a girl. Perin's family owned an estate only half-a-league from Emethius's boyhood home. Emethius loved each of these men like a brother, yet he would soon be leading them off on a suicide mission. He choked down the bile that was creeping up his throat.

"May the gods give me the wisdom and strength to bring them all home safely," whispered Emethius. He gestured toward Mount Calaban, which stood somewhere far beyond the horizon, then placed his hand over his heart. He thought the stars might have twinkled in reply. *The gods favor the faithful,* he reassured himself. *They will not ignore our prayers.*

The only soldier standing outside the prayer circle was Lieutenant Malrich, Emethius's second in command. Never had a more godless man taken the oath of a Soldier of the Faith. Emethius could only chuckle at the spectacle. Malrich was smacking himself in the face, struggling to drive the sleep from his body. When that didn't work, he took a long draught from his canteen. That seemed to do the trick.

"Ahhhwoooooo!" bayed Malrich, as he raised his head and howled at the dim sliver of the moon. He gave his entire body a vigorous shake and took another draw from the canteen. When he spotted Emethius giving him a queer look, Malrich held out the canteen in offering. "Fancy a drink, captain?"

"It smells like lantern fuel," said Emethius, wrinkling his nose.

Malrich smirked. "Aye? It's only a tad less poisonous." He hooked the canteen in his belt, and began to issue orders to the men. "Step in line! Is that as fast as you can move, Ewan? You couldn't cut cheese with the edge of that sword, Fyri. Didn't I tell you to sharpen your blade after the last battle? Why is your mail rusty, Nestor? Did you learn to do your warpaint from your mother? You look like a dockside whore." He walked down the line, insulting each soldier in turn. No one seemed to mind — if anything, it cut the tension. Every man was smiling and laughing by the time Malrich completed his review of the troops.

When Malrich was promoted to the rank of lieutenant, many of the soldiers balked at the prospect of serving under a man so estranged from the faith. But then they saw Malrich fight. He was a true bruiser. Put a weapon in Malrich's hand and sic him on an opponent — it never took long for Malrich to prove his worth. Any dueling partner Malrich faced in the practice yard returned to the barracks black and blue, their armor dented and gouged. The foes he faced in battle rarely returned home at all.

Emethius won the men's respect in another manner — he kept them alive. This would be the company's twelfth battle since the start of the war. He had yet to lose a man. Servinus had lost a hand at the Battle of Estri, and Vernin had his lower jaw shattered to ruin by a rebel cudgel, but so far, no one had ended up on the funerary pyre. Emethius could only pray his improbable record would continue.

"At attention!" barked Malrich.

Emethius stepped before his men and clacked his heels together, causing the unit to immediately fall silent. "You may wear leather armor, but every piece of steel stays here in the camp."

"Would you like us to ride into battle naked?" asked Perin, tossing aside his helm.

"We're not riding anywhere." Emethius gestured toward Imel Katan. "We're going over the wall and rescuing the high lord before a rebel puts a knife through his throat."

A disquieting murmur rose amongst the cavalry men.

"I've never been much for walking," said Berit, his face curled in a pout. "And I've definitely never been much for climbing and sneaking about."

"This is good Tremelese steel, captain," protested Big Oswyn. He knocked on his breastplate, as if to prove the point. "If I leave it in the camp, it's likely to be stolen."

"That armor belongs to you no more than it did the corpse you looted it off of last week," said Emethius coolly. "Which would you prefer, to leave it here, or sleep with it at the bottom of Lake Libith for all eternity?" The eyes of every man wandered to the black lake and the thin layer of ice that spanned the distance between the shoreline and peninsula.

"Y-y-you mean for us to go across the ice?" stammered Quintus, a rotund man that had turned more than a few chairs into kindling. "Thin ice and I don't exactly get along, if you catch my drift."

Malrich smacked the back of the Quintus's head. "The captain doesn't mean for you to do anything other than follow orders! Now strip off your armor. Light and quick, that's the Red Company's way."

The rest of the men took off their armor in sullen silence. No one liked the order, but no one was keen on facing Malrich's wrath, especially when he was hot with a belly full of liquor.

"The ice will be thinnest at the middle," said Emethius, giving his men their final instructions before they departed. "Be wary of foot and keep your distance from one another. Stay at least two spans from the nearest man. Listen to the ice and it will speak to you. Remain silent on the approach — hand signals only. Every rebel eye will be focused on the gatehouse. I intend to keep it that way."

A horn blared to the east, followed by the steady tap of drums. The assault began. Lord Fennir and General Saterius led the main host forward. A river of men, blades, and steel raged across the thin sliver of raised earth that connected the mainland to Imel Katan. They met no resistance along the central span of the peninsula, but as they neared the gatehouse, a flaming ball of pitch came catapulting over the fortress walls. It exploded on the group of men bearing the battering ram, causing the men to scatter, their clothes aflame. A trumpet sounded from one of the tower's balconies, and a salvo of flaming arrows poured from the battlements. Explosions erupted up and down the lines of the besieging army. Balls of yellow flames and twirling clouds of black smoke filled the air. Suddenly the entire middle third of the peninsula was engulfed in flames.

"Damn butchers. They're using tar oil," muttered Malrich, as he watched his comrades writhe and dance. Their arms flailed helplessly as flames enshrouded their bodies. The shrieks of dying men drifted across the lake, a stark reminder of what lay in store for the soldiers of the Red Company.

Emethius bit his tongue — what happened at the gatehouse was beyond his control. He nodded to his men; it was now their turn to advance.

"Keep your distance from one another," Emethius advised, as he led the company to the banks of the frozen lake. With boots covered in mud, they crept out onto the ice, leaving a trail that was discernible even at night. Emethius cursed under his breath. *So much for stealth.*

The ice moaned and creaked with every step Emethius took. He splayed out his arms and widened his stance, hoping to disperse his weight enough to survive the transit. The going was painstakingly slow. As they neared the mid-point there was a crack followed by a soft splash. Emethius's fear was realized.

Two men were gone. An inky black hole was all that marked their passage into the chilly fathoms below.

Lieutenant Malrich, who was nearest, slid on his belly to the edge of the hole. He looked back at Emethius and flashed a series of hand signals. *No sign of life.*

"Don't stop. Keep moving," commanded Emethius in a hissing whisper. The men nodded mutely and continued their advance. Most skirted the hole in the ice by a wide margin. Miraculously, the rest of the unit managed to reach the peninsula without further incident. They came ashore only a few hundred paces from the fortress's north wall.

To the south, the battle before the gatehouse raged on. Smoke from burning oil shrouded everything in a glowing haze. Even so, Emethius could vaguely make out the outline of ladders against the fortress wall. The chime of clashing steel indicated that some of General Saterius's men had gained a footing atop the battlements.

Emethius took no time to revel in the good news. He hastily led his men into the ruins that wreathed the fortress's curtain wall. It was a maze of crumbling and moss plastered walls that tilted at ever perceivable angle except vertical. They took refuge with their backs against a wall that was hardly chest high. Its brittle crown was worn to a rounded point. Emethius peeked over the top, evaluating the fortress wall. The battlements were barren, save for a few rebels who were preoccupied with watching the battle unfolding to the south. The Red Company's approach had thus far gone unnoticed.

Emethius sighed with relief.

"It looks taller up close, eh?" said Malrich as he

sidled alongside Emethius.

"I might have underestimated the walls height by a few spans," Emethius admitted. "Who did we lose?"

"Quintus and Perin," reported Malrich matter-of-factly. "The damn fools were walking close enough to hold each other's hand. You warned them."

"That I did," muttered Emethius, although the fact did little to ease his heart. He shook his head. They were good soldiers and deserved better than a watery grave. He ignored the impulse to slow down and be more careful. "We'll mourn another day. Our job has just begun."

Malrich grunted in agreement. He rubbed the stubble on his chin, as he gauged the resistance that awaited them atop the wall. "There are four sentries, by my count. Maybe a few more ducked down below the wall. No telling how many are in the courtyard beyond. The men are armed with spears. I see no signs of bows."

"Lead a dozen men over the wall. Silent and quick," instructed Emethius.

"Silent and quick," repeated Malrich. He bobbed his head, taking no further time to mull the order. He singled out a dozen men to follow, then raced toward the wall spinning a grappling hook.

Emethius smiled with appreciation. Malrich was often slow to act of his own accord, but once given an order he did not hesitate for a second.

In quick fashion Malrich and his men clambered up the wall and over the parapet. From his vantage, Emethius could see little of the ensuing skirmish. The rebel spears swung downward, there was a guttural scream, a single clash of steel and then silence. Malrich's head popped over the battlement. He waved for the rest of the company to make the ascent.

Emethius was the last to scale the wall. He found Malrich leaning over a rebel body, cleaning his blade on the dead man's trousers.

"Quietish," reported Malrich with a droll shrug. Three rebels lay dead atop the battlement. "The fourth made a run for it, but didn't make it very far." He gestured to a still figure lying in the middle of the courtyard that ran adjacent to the wall. A pool of blood was slowly growing around the figure's upper torso. Half an arrow protruded from the middle of his back.

Emethius looked to the battle unfolding before the south wall. Back in the encampment, the screams of anguish and the clash of steel had only been dim sounds carried on the wind. But up here atop the fortress wall, they were deafening to the ears. The fire raging before the gatehouse was now burning so wildly that banners of flames were leaping above the battlements.

"We need to move, captain," said Malrich. "I believe we got all the sentries, but there's no way to be certain. Someone could be sounding the alarm as we speak."

Emethius gestured toward the black walls of Imel Katan. "Find me a way into that tower."

Malrich waved his hand and barked out orders to the men. "Get ready to move!"

As the others moved out, Emethius glanced down at the leather vambrace he wore on his left forearm. There was a single deep gouge that ran the width of the armor. He pulled out his dagger and scored two deep hash marks running parallel to the first. "Quintus and Perin," said Emethius, giving a name to each line. Quintus owned a winery south of Henna Lu. Perin was a young lordling who had just come into manhood. Neither would be returning home.

"Quintus and Perin," Emethius repeated. He would not forget the names of the two men who had died under his charge. He descended the rampart stairs, grimly certain that he would have more lines to add before the day was through.

CHAPTER
III
THE PRINCE

The tower of Imel Katan protruded from the center of the fortress complex like a thorn pointing toward the heavens. Its stone walls were black as soot and seemed to suck all of the color out of the sky. Its exterior was nearly featureless, save for the flying buttresses that sprouted from its sides like the spindly legs of a spider. Legend told that the tower's steeple was once encased in gold. Whatever mineral graced the pinnacle had been stripped away long ago. The top of the edifice now resembled the gaping maw of a dragon roaring at the sky.

Emethius eyed the tower with disquiet. Imprisoned somewhere within the fastness of that tower was High Lord Valerius and Prince Meriatis.

Praetor Maxentius's orders had been simple — sneak into the complex unseen, storm the tower, and secure the high lord and the prince until help arrived.

If help arrived was more like it.

The cries of dying men still rent the air, but the familiar sounds of battle had vanished. There was no ring of clashing steel, no cries from terror-filled men. *Something has gone amiss.*

Thus far, Emethius and his men had managed to sneak through the fortress complex without being spotted, creeping past lichen-covered granaries and empty stables, barren drill yards and derelict barracks. *This fortress could house ten thousand men and still have room to spare,* realized Emethius, as he slunk beneath the shadow of a ruined temple that was twice the size of the Court of Bariil. His men took sanctuary behind one of the temple's collapsed minarets. They could advance no further.

There were two entrance portals on the west face of the tower, but they were both sealed by rusty iron doors. Emethius sent Young Fyri to scout the perimeter of the tower and see if there was another way into the building. Emethius was starting to fear the worst. The lad had already been gone for more than half an hour.

"If we delay here much longer we're going to be seen. Don't doubt it for a second," whispered Malrich, making sure only Emethius could hear his opinion. He thumbed nervously at a patch of stubble on his chin. "It might be best to return to the encampment. If the main host has failed..."

"We wait a minute longer. I'm not abandoning the mission until I'm certain."

As if in reply a small cloaked figure flopped over the crest of the collapsed minaret. Before anyone could put an arrow through the unannounced visitor a small voice quietly rasped out, "It's me, Fyri."

Emethius sighed with relief and rushed to Fyri's side.

"The main gate is broken... consumed by flames," managed Fyri between forced breaths. "It's as you feared... Lord Fennir's host has been turned back. General Saterius's ladders have been reduced to kindling. The rebels are licking their wounds on the far side of the compound. There's an open portal leading into the tower, all right, but there's about a hundred rebels between us and the passage."

That was grim news, indeed.

Malrich's eyes darkened. "What do you want us to do, captain?" Emethius didn't need to ask Malrich for his advice — it was written clearly on his face. *Retreat was the best option.*

"I'm going to rely on the wisdom of our men." Emethius turned to the rest of the company. Fear-filled faces regarded him expectantly. "Does anyone see another way forward?"

Silence resounded.

A few of the men kicked at the earth. One soldier sheathed his sword, as if the issue was already settled and they would soon be retreating back to the encampment.

"A curse shrouds this whole wretched place, but I feel it here the worst," called Berit from the rear of the unit. Ever superstitious, he was fumbling with the interlocking rings of the Weaver's chain he wore around his neck. "If Lord Fennir has retreated, it would be folly for us to press onward. We're outnumber ten to one, and we have no reinforcements."

There came a flurry of "ayes" from amongst the men.

Emethius tried to hide his frown.

"Berit speaks the truth when he says this place is cursed," said Brother Seius, happily feeding into the man's paranoia. He gestured toward the far side of the tower. "The Cul killed King Ordin over yonder. They say his spirit still walks these grounds."

"In truth?" sputtered Berit. "I keep seeing shadows out of the corner of my eye, but when I turn around there's no one there." He turned to

Emethius. "Pardon me for speaking out, captain, you know I'd follow you anywhere. But this tower is haunted. That's why the devil Carrick chose it for his last stand. We can't go in there expecting anything other than death."

Brother Seius put on a grave face and nodded in agreement. "To be honest, captain, this whole mission is beginning to feel a bit like Lunen's Last Charge. That is, minus the horses, of course."

"Lucky for you, I'm not my father," said Emethius, careful to hide his agitation.

"Lucky for me, I'm not *my* father — the gods rest his soul." Brother Seius crossed himself. Several men grumbled their agreement. Emethius scowled.

Many of these men were the second, third, or even fourth generation to serve in the company. More than a few had lost a family member a decade earlier when Emethius's father — Lithius Lunen — led an ill-advised cavalry charge against a host of heretic spearmen. Emethius's father survived, but more than half of the company did not. The Red Company earned its moniker that day. Emethius had spent his entire career making sure such a tragedy never befell the unit again.

"How many Henna Lu boys do you Lunen's intend to send to an early grave?" asked Brother

Seius, not knowing when to stop.

Malrich turned on the irksome brother. "Your death won't be a Lunen's fault if you keep running your insubordinate mouth," growled the lieutenant. He placed his hand on the pommel of his sword.

Malrich was not one for idle threats and everybody knew it. Brother Seius wisely raised his hands and backed away, but it didn't matter, the damage was already done. Every soldier looked at Emethius with wide bewildered eyes. They all wanted to turn back; fear had won. *Maybe it's a sound choice. There can be wisdom in fear*, thought Emethius.

"I'm sorry captain, but the numbers just don't add up." It was Big Oswyn. On an ordinary day, Oswyn would volunteer to lead the charge, but this was no ordinary day. "We are two score minus two, against a number we do not know. What hope do we have?"

"Or we are nearly two score unknown," said Emethius. He set a reassuring hand on Oswyn's back. "There is no turning back, not if we want to keep our oath." He slowly shifted his eyes from one man to the next, meeting each man's gaze in turn. "We are more than just Merridians, we are Soldiers of the Faith. Have you forgotten why you are here? Our mission is to rescue the high lord and

49

his son. None have ever undertaken a more important mission."

The mention of the high lord caused many of the men to drop their heads in shame.

"I will gladly give my life for High Lord Valerius," said Big Oswyn. The majority of the men nodded their head in agreement. Brother Seius glared at Oswyn from the rear of the unit. This seemed only to embolden the big man. "Captain Emethius hasn't failed us in the past. I don't expect that to change today. Tell us where to go, captain."

Lieutenant Malrich clacked his sword against the brick wall causing everyone to jump. "Now, let's try this again. The captain asked if any of you yellow bellied fools saw another route into the tower. Speak up!" Emethius gave his second in command a sly smile; he was grateful to have Malrich at his side.

"There's a murder hole above the portal," called Young Fyri. A dozen pairs of eyes turned expectantly upon the young lad. Fyri noticeably quailed, his neck shrinking into his shoulders. "It's.. er... high, captain."

Emethius looked over his shoulder, spying the portal and its rusty iron door. Fyri was right, there was a black chute in the portal ceiling directly above the door. It was hardly more than a man's girth in width. The sluice was devised to douse intruders with flaming oil and boiling water. Emethius had noticed the trap, but had given it little thought. It was too high — at least fifteen feet of empty air spanned between the opening and the floor.

"Good idea, Fyri," chimed Brother Seius, his voice dripping with sarcasm. "Why don't you sprout a pair of wings and turn yourself into a bat. You'll be up there in no time."

"I can do it," snapped Fyri, finding strength in the chaplain's doubt. "I'll need a boost, but the rest of the climb should be a cinch – I've climbed taller walls before." He was already looping a coil of rope around his shoulder.

Emethius didn't waste another second. He and Fyri hustled across the open bailey; the clack of their heels sounded unusually loud in the empty space.

The marble facade that had once veneered the exterior walls of the tower had fallen away in sheets, leaving a shattered mound of white stone before the base of the tower. Emethius clambered over the mound on his hands and feet, reaching the entrance portal. Grotesque stone creatures guarded either side of the door. They resembled griffins, but instead of eagle heads, each had the face of a bear.

Emethius looked away from the statues and girded himself to receive Fyri.

As deft as a circus acrobat, Fyri leapt from the top of the debris mound, sprung from Emethius's shoulders, bounded off the nearest wall, and propelled himself up and into the murder hole. His hands somehow found finger holds in the seemingly seamless stonework, and he slithered upward into the inky nothingness of the sluice.

Emethius stared up at the murder hole, wishing he could see Fyri's progress. All he detected of the young soldier was the scrape of his fingers and toes as he inched his way higher and higher. Bits of dried tar rained down on Emethius's head. Finally, after what seemed like an eternity, the rope came tumbling out of the hole, drawing taut with a pop.

Good man. Emethius waved for the rest of Red Company to follow. Malrich began to send men across the open expanse of the bailey in pairs.

Emethius made his ascent. The hole was smaller than it appeared from the ground, and he was forced to turn his head sideways to fit through the narrow passage. He blindly groped his way upward; ten feet, twenty, thirty. *This tunnel must go all the way to the fourth or fifth floor of the tower,* realized Emethius. Finally his head struck solid stone; he could go no further. *Am I stuck?*

"There's a bend in the path, captain."

Emethius managed the bend with some care. It was not a friendly squeeze. He collapsed into a nearly pitch black hall. Fryi tried to help Emethius to his feet, but Emethius waved him off.

"Help the others. They're right behind me."

Fyri nodded dutifully. The lad's forehead and cheeks were marred with sticky tar and ash.

Emethius was exhausted, but he didn't take a second to rest. He needed to investigate their surroundings before he drew his entire unit into a trap.

He was standing in a lengthy hall, most likely the same width as the tower. He had not noticed it from below, but there were dozens of embrasures cut into the west face of the wall. Once, archers could have fired arrows down upon a besieging foe from this position, but now the narrow openings were clogged shut with bird nests and droppings. The carcasses of dozens of mummified pigeons littered the floor. Emethius shuffled through the macabre carpet, coming to the room's sole door. It was made of heavy wood, reinforced with rusted bands of iron. It was locked from the inside. This would explain why the rebels had not gained entry. Emethius thanked the Weaver for his good fortune.

The only light in the room filtered through the door's keyhole. He set his eye against the hole and was immediately forced to stifle a gasp.

The tower's great hall lay beyond. The rebels were using the space as an makeshift infirmary. Every single table was occupied by a body, some living, some deceased. Maps, food, and tankards had been scattered across the floor as healers hastily made room for the sudden influx of injured men. Emethius stopped counting after he reached a hundred. "By the gods, if the rebels have this many casualties, how many did we lose in the battle?" he whispered to himself in disbelief.

At the nearest table, a Tiber Brother was trying to remove an arrow from a man's chest. Another pair of brothers were struggling to hold the writhing soldier down. The man screamed as the brother worked at the arrow. Suddenly the man went still. One of the brothers checked for a pulse. He shook his head sadly, and they moved on to the next soldier who needed care.

These are my countrymen, thought Emethius, as he stared into the fixed pupils of the dead man. Merridians killing Merridians. It was pure madness. Emethius had never thought he would see such horrors in his life. Then Herald Carrick's rebellion happened, and since that day Emethius's men had shed enough Merridian blood to water a forest. Emethius had somehow kept his own blade unsullied — it was his men who always did the killing. Even so, he felt the weight of every lost life on his shoulders.

One by one, the men of the Red Company clambered into the hidden room. Big Oswyn pulled up the rear. It took the full strength of a half-dozen men to tug Oswyn through the final bend in the sluice.

Malrich took a knee beside Emethius at the door. "So what's out there, captain?"

"The hacked up remains of Carrick's army," reported Emethius.

"Oh, is that all?" Malrich puffed out his cheeks in mock exasperation and proceeded to drain the rest of the canteen down his throat. "What's the plan?"

"We wait."

"For what?" said Brother Seius, inserting himself into the conversation. "For someone who doesn't have a plan, you sure were in a hurry to get up here."

"War requires flexibility," said Emethius. "Patience will provide us with an opening. I'll let you know when I see it." Emethius turned away from the brother and pressed his eye against the keyhole.

Lieutenant Malrich stayed by Emethius's side, working at a divot in his blade with a whetting stone. Brother Seius busied himself by making rounds amongst the men. He was eager to remind everyone of the grim possibilities that awaited them on the other side of the door, and he granted a blessing of absolution to those who wished to receive it. Emethius rejected the offer. He didn't need a blessing, he needed luck, or the divine intervention of the Fates. *I'm not my father,* he reminded himself. *I'm not leading these men to their death. This is not Lunen's Last Charge.*

"The grand irony in all of this is that Praetor Maxentius probably thinks we're dead," said Malrich, as he worked at his blade. "If by heroic deeds we win the day, there's going to be joy and celebration like you've never seen. But if we falter, and High Lord Valerius remains a prisoner in his own land, no one will even know we made it this far." He checked the edge of his sword against his cheek, shaving off a patch of stubble. He seemed pleased with the result. "Such is the fate of a lowly Soldier of the Faith. Eh?"

"That's why we cannot fail," replied Emethius.

An hour passed, and then another. Over that course of time, a dozen injured rebels succumbed to their wounds. The number of men in the great hall thinned. Healthy soldiers seemed to be steering clear of the great hall; there were never more than a score of able-bodied men present at any given time and most were Tiber Brothers. The brothers would put up no resistance — an oath of pacifism was part of their vows. Emethius's men could take the hall in a heartbeat, and he was half tempted to give the order, but a voice in the back of his head told him to wait.

"Patience," he whispered to himself. He ran his thumb along the gouges in his vambrace, counting them over and over again. "One, two, three. Perin, Quintus, and..."

One by one, the torches in the great hall guttered out, yet the room was actually getting brighter. At first Emethius thought the fire before the gatehouse had spread to the fortress. *Maybe the cursed tower can burn after all.* Emethius almost laughed at the notion.

"It's dawn, captain," said Malrich. He gestured to the embrasures in the wall. They were glowing with dim morning light.

Emethius shook the cobwebs from his head, and pressed his eye back to the keyhole. A smirk creased his lips.

"What do you see, captain?"

"What I've been waiting for all night, Mal. Rouse the men, it's time."

Malrich shuffled the length of the hall, kicking each man awake. He kept a finger pressed to his lips to indicate silence was needed. The only sound Emethius heard from his men was the hiss of steel drawing from sheaths.

Emethius stayed focused on the great hall. A slim bent-backed man was making his rounds amongst the injured rebels. Emethius could not see the man's face, but his purple cape and plumed helm gave him away. *Herald Carrick.*

The rebels would never kill High Lord Valerius without Herald Carrick issuing the order, and here the man stood. All Emethius had to do was neutralize the herald before the order passed his lips.

Emethius's men took up position on either side of the door. A few crossed their hearts and pointed toward the heavens. Malrich spit into each of his palms and clutched the hilt of his greatsword with both hands. Brother Seius paced listlessly at the rear of the pack; he would remain behind and tend to any casualties.

Emethius turned to his brothers in arms. "We are sworn to strike down the disciples of the Shadow. We are virtuous in cause and deed. We are humble in triumph. Our faith is unshaken by defeat. We are the holy army of the gods. We are the Soldiers of the Faith."

Emethius was alone when he started reciting the solemn oath of his martial brotherhood, but by the final line every soldier in the company had joined him in chorus, Brother Seius included. Emethius nodded with approval and whispered his final decree. "It is honorable to die in the service of the high lord. If this is our fate, I will see each of you in the feasting halls of the hereafter."

"Until the fates overcome us," said the men in unison.

"Until the fates overcome us," Emethius agreed.

He turned over the locking bar that held the door shut. It squealed like a dying animal, a clear alarm to any wary rebel in the great hall. Without a moments hesitation, Emethius threw his shoulder into the door, causing it to burst open.

The soldiers of the Red Company poured into the great hall. The eyes of a hundred defeated rebels wandered up to look at Emethius's company. For a few confusion-filled moments there was a general degree of shock amongst all parties. The Tiber Brothers continued to tend to the injured as if nothing was out of the ordinary. A few injured soldiers rolled off their tables in surprise. On the far side of the hall someone vomited, while another man called for water. No one lifted a blade in defense.

"Praetor Maxentius, commander of the second legion and Praetor of the Soldiers of the Faith, demands that you surrender and release High Lord Valerius and Prince Meriatis," barked Emethius, not knowing what else to say.

The mention of the prince's name sent a disquieting murmur through the hall. "Fuck Praetor Maxentius," shouted a rebel. Someone else threw a tankard full of mead. Emethius was able to dodge the projectile, but it struck Big Oswyn square in the face. Oswyn sputtered and cursed, his nose smashed and bleeding. That was all it took to snap the able-bodied rebels into action. Blades rattled from sheaths. Half-a-dozen healthy men sprang forward from amongst the wounded. A few of the injured men tried to stand on legs that did not wish to comply.

"Kill the bastards," shouted someone farther down the hall.

A rebel wearing chainmail charged with his sword aimed on Emethius's gut. Malrich stepped forward and crushed the man's arm with a hewing stroke of his greatsword. The chainmail kept the blade from piercing the rebel's flesh, but it did nothing to stop the blade from grotesquely breaking the rebel's arm. The rebel gawked at his arm, which now had a second elbow. Malrich didn't give the man more than a second to contemplate his injury; he threw the stunned rebel over a table and pointed his sword at an another rebel who was reaching for a dagger. "Don't," snapped Malrich, pressing his blade to the rebel's neck.

On the far end of the hall stood Herald Carrick. His purple cape swirled as he turned to investigate the cause of the tumult. The herald regarded Emethius queerly, his mouth parted with genuine surprise.

Those eyes... I know those eyes.

The herald spun away before Emethius could get a better look at him and retreated up a spiral stairwell at a dead sprint, abandoning his men to fend for themselves.

"He's going to kill the captives!" shouted Malrich, putting words to Emethius's thoughts.

Emethius sprung into action. "Hold the floor, he's mine!" Emethius sprinted the length of the hall, leaping over injured men and shoving aside bewildered Tiber Brothers.

One of the injured soldiers leveled a crossbow on Emethius's head. Emethius ducked just as the quarrel took flight. The feather fletching brush against his ear as the projectile whizzed past. The steel-headed shaft exploded against a support column, sending off shards of stone.

Big Oswyn was on the man before he could set another bolt to string. Oswyn yanked the weapon free of the man's hands, then turned the weapon on its owner, breaking out the man's teeth with the butt end of the crossbow.

Emethius didn't slow for a second. He hit the first step of the spiral stairwell at full speed, heedless of whatever danger lay ahead. Behind him, Malrich was barking out orders in the great hall. "Bar the door! Seize their weapons!" Someone frantically cried for help, trying to warn the other rebels of the attack. Emethius ignored the impulse to turn around — his men would have to deal with matters on their own. The safety of High Lord Valerius and Prince Meriatis were all that mattered now.

Emethius reached the landing of the next floor, expecting to meet resistance. Instead he was met by the noisome odor of death. Row after row of neatly arrayed bodies filled the majority of the hall. Their arms were folded across their chests. Their fixed eyes gazed squarely at the ceiling. The lone living person in the room was a man wearing a green robe and skullcap — another Tiber Brother. He stepped from one body to the next, pricking the forehead of each corpse with a rose thorn.

Emethius kept going, racing higher and higher up the spine of the tower. He could hear Herald Carrick just around every bend, yet somehow the damnable man outpaced him. Emethius could not believe the elderly herald could move with such speed.

He's going to the steeple, Emethius realized.

A sudden gust of wind lashed at Emethius's cheeks, dry and bitterly cold. The stairwell had come to an abrupt end, and Emethius found himself standing atop the pinnacle of Imel Katan. The sudden flare of the morning sun blinded him, and for a moment all he could do was grope at the undulating shapes that surrounded him.

"Herald Carrick, don't do it," roared Emethius, as he desperately tried to blink his eyes into focus and make sense of his environment. He could hear the herald shuffling to his right, and Emethius followed, tumbling over a pile of bricks in the process. His vision began to clear. Forms emerged from the light — old rotten scaffolding, thin sheets of hammered copper, weathered stonework. The shattered remains of the steeple lay all around him. He clambered over the debris, chasing after the herald.

63

Herald Carrick was hunched over on the far side of the pinnacle, shoving a rectangular pine box toward the precipice. The box was little larger than a coffin, and a soft banging came from within.

"Oh, gods!" cried Emethius, finally piecing together what he was seeing. One more push, and the makeshift coffin would plummet hundreds of feet into the courtyard below carrying with it whoever was trapped inside. "Away from the box!" hissed Emethius. He jabbed his sword into the small of Herald Carrick's back just as the herald was about to give the box a final push.

The man paused mid-motion and rose stiffly, his arms raised above his head in surrender. A hiss of laughter passed his lips. "I wondered if Maxentius would send you," said the herald. He pressed his foot against the pine coffin, threatening to send it teetering over the edge.

"I'll do it, betrayer!" Emethius dug the tip of his sword through the fabric of the herald's purple cape, finding the soft flesh underneath.

The herald wheeled about and lashed out with his own sword, which he somehow managed to draw in the flurry of motion. Black steel flashed mere inches from Emethius eyes. Emethius fell back a pace and took up a fighter's stance.

"Betrayer? Is that what you see when you look at

me, Emethius?" The herald's mocking voice was little more than a rasp. "Long have we all been betrayed, a veil pulled over our eyes. You are the one who has been blinded from the truth. See me now, and know that you, too, have been betrayed."

I know those eyes.

Emethius's breath caught in his throat. This man was not Herald Carrick. The familiar face had grown wrinkled and sullen, as if the man had lived ten lives since the last time he and Emethius had met. But the eyes Emethius recognized, the eyes he could never mistake. They were old and weary, yellowed somehow, and full of fear. But they were the same eyes Emethius had known since he was a child. Before him stood Prince Meriatis Benisor, son of High Lord Valerius, and rightful heir to the Throne of Roses.

"The rumors were true," Emethius muttered, mostly to himself. This was not a war between a heretic herald and the high lord. This was a war between father and son. Between young and old. Between the past and the future. Emethius's stomach churned and he felt like he was going to vomit.

"Betrayer," muttered Emethius again, only this time he did not know who it was directed toward. For how could the prince betray his own father?

"Lay down your blade, Emethius, I haven't the heart to kill you." Prince Meriatis lowered the tip of his own sword to show he intended Emethius no harm. "You're confused, as all men are. You don't understand what you've stepped into. Praetor Maxentius has done such a splendid job weaving his lie that you never realized *you* are the rebel."

Emethius's mind wandered back to the first confusion-filled day of the rebellion. The palace was burning. High Lord Valerius was reported killed. Then there were rumors that the high lord was safe at his estate south of the capital. Finally, word leaked that High Lord Valerius and Prince Meriatis had been taken captive in a failed coup. Through it all, Praetor Maxentius had been in command. He placed the capital under martial law. He personally saw to the interrogation of captured rebels. He was the one who announced that Herald Carrick was the leader of the rebellion. *Maxentius knew all along.*

"The truth can be troubling, Emethius. Do you feel those twinges of doubt clawing at your brain? I don't fault a single man for rallying to Maxentius's banner." Meriatis gestured outward toward the loyalist encampment. "Every one of you thought you were doing your duty to the throne. But now is the time to be sensible. Please, lower your blade."

Emethius raised his sword instead. "Who is in the coffin, Meriatis?"

Meriatis smirked and looked sidelong at the box. "A man who has lost his way. A man who would lead us all into the clutches of the Shadow. One push and we save Merridia from this madness. If you lift one side, I'll lift the other. We can end this together."

Meriatis once again moved toward the box, causing Emethius to jump between the prince and the coffin. There came a soft knocking from within, followed by a pitiful moan.

Meriatis threw back his head and laughed, revealing a deep cut in the side of neck that had been raggedly sutured shut. An inch to the right and it would have been a death blow. Apparently, Emethius was not the first person to face Prince Meriatis in combat today.

"Don't make me finish the job," said Emethius, jabbing toward the neck wound. "Tell me, who is in the coffin?" He already knew the answer, yet he needed to hear it from Meriatis's own tongue; Emethius would do anything to stave off the inevitable for a moment longer.

Meriatis ignored the question. "Maxentius wasted a fine host of men against my walls." His voice choked with genuine grief, and his eyes glistened with tears. "Maxentius should not have come. He should not have challenged my will!" He pawed at his face. "They forced my hand, Emethius. I did not want war."

"Yet war found you," said Emethius. He was still reeling from shock. Had this been Herald Carrick, Emethius would have already put a blade through the man's gut. But this was Meriatis, the prince Emethius had sworn to protect, the prince Emethius had once loved like a brother. Emethius struggled to force his prejudices from his mind. *I am a Soldier of the Faith,* he reminded himself. *My high lord is depending on me.*

"Is High Lord Valerius in the coffin?" demanded Emethius.

Meriatis's face contorted as if the very demon of his nightmares had been mentioned. "My father is no longer of significance. Or at least he shouldn't be. Lies, he always told lies. He and his whole corrupt court. *The Calabanesi are saviors!*" he croaked, mimicking his father's voice. "*Pay homage! Give thanks! Bow your head in servitude to the demons of Calaban!*" He gazed at Emethius with wild eyes. He was in a mercurial state, and his mood seemed to shift between elation and grief with every word he spoke.

Meriatis grinned devilishly. "They can die,

Emethius, the gods can die like all of us. And I have the tool." He gestured toward Emethius with his sword. It was like no blade Emethius had ever seen before. The blade was nearly black, the steel rippled. Dull gemstones ran the fuller that looked not so dissimilar to moonstones.

"Blasphemy!" cried Emethius. "Blasphemy, all of it! You dare challenge the gods? If they heard such words, you would be consumed in fire."

"Would I?" roared Meriatis. He raised his sword skyward, more as a challenge to the gods than to Emethius. "Strike me down, oh gods all knowing! Do you hear my call?" His voice blared from the pinnacle of Imel Katan, but no divine response came. Meriatis's face fell into shadows. "Omniscient divine fools, if they are even gods at all. I have my doubts."

"What madness has seeped into your heart?"

"Is it a madness?" asked Meriatis. "That is what they told me of course. My father. Maxentius. The Gray Prophet. No one would heed my warning." Meriatis chuckled, cocked his head to the side, and opened his arms wide, gesturing to himself. As he did, the wound reopened in his throat, and a steady stream of blood began to spill down his chest. "I implore you, Emethius, do I look like a madman?"

Looking at him now, Emethius knew that

Meriatis was mad, or at least very sick. Either way, Meriatis was now the enemy and he had to be stopped.

"Will you not come in peace?" Emethius begged, knowing there was little hope in that.

"Would you?" asked Meriatis. His face hardened, gripped by a sudden sobriety. "I challenged the gods and failed. There will be dreadful recourse."

"You will have to face me," said Emethius, growing stern and immovable. "I am more skilled with a sword than you."

"Perhaps in the practice yard," said Meriatis. "But the specter of death makes it different." With that said, Meriatis approached with his sword at the ready. Emethius stepped forward and presented his own blade. Their deadly dance began.

Emethius had never killed a man in combat, but that did not mean he didn't know how to handle his sword. He was viciously good with a blade, and throughout his years of schooling he had won titles and renown for his mastery of fencing. Despite Emethius's martial skill, Meriatis did not fear him. The prince attacked like a madman, swinging his sword in wild hewing arcs. Sparks filled the air as Emethius deflected each of Meriatis's strokes with expert precision.

Across the pinnacle of Imel Katan they fought, striking high and low, gaining advantage and disadvantage with each deft motion. No refuge could be found anywhere, save behind the remains of the old rotten scaffolding, which was quickly hacked to tinders and kicked aside. Twice during the duel, Emethius could have plunged his blade into Meriatis's chest, but each time he refrained. *You cannot kill the prince,* nagged a voice in the back of his head, *such is an act of treason.* Instead, Emethius attempted to disarm Meriatis. Emethius's reward for his noble efforts — a deep wound to his thigh and a lacerated shoulder.

Growing weary, the two locked blades. The violent clang rang from the pinnacle like a bell. Emethius and Meriatis drew near to one another.

"I'm warning you for the last time," said Emethius. "End this now. I will not stay my blade a third time."

"You need not," growled Meriatis through clenched teeth. "For we are finished!"

Meriatis thrust out his sword, pushing Emethius back on his heels. Then in one quick motion, Meriatis freed a dagger from his belt, swung his arm around Emethius's back, and sunk the blade to its hilt just below Emethius's rib-line. For a moment the two remained standing, eyes locked, breaths intermingling.

"You cheat," whispered Emethius as his body went chill.

Meriatis opened his mouth to respond. Blood came out instead of words.

During the prince's final act of treachery, Emethius had struck with lightning speed, thrusting his sword through Meriatis's gut.

For a moment, the two stood in silence, glaring at one another through fast-dimming eyes. Their knees gave out simultaneously, and together they slouched to the ground, still locked in a deadly embrace. A shadowy haze slowly drifted between them, until Emethius's vision glazed over and he saw no more.

CHAPTER
IV
THINGS PAST

Emethius was unsure of his surroundings. Glaring light cascaded through the translucent leaves overhead, giving everything an otherworldly green hue. His head ached and he tasted blood. He tongued his teeth, checking to see if they were all still there.

Several boys garbed in off-white tunics pranced around him, chanting as they circled. "Silly fool, hurt himself, tried to fight, went to night!"

"You had enough?" challenged a voice. "Honestly, for a moment I was worried I killed you."

"Hardly," said Emethius. His jaw was sore and his ears were ringing. He spit a mouthful of blood at his challenger's feet. "We Lunens are resilient."

"You're going to be a resilient corpse if you don't stop getting back up," said the larger boy, who had already knocked Emethius down twice. A titter of laughter sounded from the ring of onlookers. "That goose egg on the back of your head looks ready to burst."

Emethius gingerly ran his fingers through his thick blond hair and discovered a large welt forming on the back of his head. His fingers came back sticky and red.

"I'd say you've learned your lesson," said the boy. "Just stay down this time — ain't no one going to think less of you."

Emethius didn't listen, couldn't listen. He still had something to prove. He staggered back to his feet, shook the cobwebs from his brain, and balled his tiny fists. Most of the onlookers laughed, but Emethius gave their ridicule no mind.

Emethius was slim for his age of ten years, and he was well aware that this opponent was beyond his skill and size. But that didn't matter. This wasn't about winning — it was about setting the tone for the rest of the school year. His father had advised him to pick out the biggest bully and punch him in the face. Unfortunately for Emethius, the biggest bully also happened to be of royal blood. Now, Emethius dreamed of only one thing — to land a single punch to the face of this hazel-eyed fool, this Prince Meriatis, this son of the high lord.

"I'm not done," said Emethius, as much a

reassurance to himself as it was a challenge to the prince.

Meriatis shrugged, clearly indifferent. He came in with a right hook faster than Emethius could react. In the blink of an eye, Emethius found himself once again lying face down on the ground, this time with a mouthful of dirt.

Emethius groped at the loose earth, and rose shakily to his hands and knees.

"Come now," scoffed Meriatis. "Only a witless fool would get back up. Stay where you are — there's no shame in knowing your place in the world."

"He's a worm eater, that's what he is!" yelled one of the boys in the crowd.

The prince cocked his arm back, and lunged forward for another strike, but this time Emethius was ready. He threw a fistful of dirt into Meriatis's face. Meriatis cried out, suddenly blinded, and punched at the air. Emethius dodged Meriatis's flailing fist and swung in with a punch of his own, striking Meriatis hard in his right eye. There was a satisfying *pop* and Meriatis floundered backward, falling in a heap.

Emethius leapt atop Meriatis's chest and cocked his arm back.

For a moment, the crowd went silent. Then

someone yelled, "Hit him again!"

"Yeah, do it!" agreed someone else.

Emethius complied, punching Meriatis in his other eye.

Emethius expected Meriatis to cry out, or to try to shove Emethius off of him. Instead, Meriatis did something completely unexpected. He began to chuckle, softly at first, but it soon grew into full-blown sidesplitting laugher. The onlookers shuffled uncomfortably, not certain what to make of the prince's odd behavior.

Meriatis squinted at Emethius beneath his fast-swelling eyebrows. "Oh, please, hit the prince one more time," said Meriatis, mimicking the onlookers who were goading Emethius on.

Emethius was tempted to fulfill Meriatis's wish, but his hand was throbbing. During the span of his short life, Emethius had learned a few things about hitting from his father. Unfortunately, the drunkard never had the courtesy to teach Emethius the proper way to throw a punch. Emethius gave his hand a few sharp shakes, silently wondering if he had broken something.

"The Headmaster's coming!" screamed one of the onlookers.

The children scattered like mice caught in the kitchen by a knife-wielding chef.

Emethius considered fleeing with the others, but one look at the giggling prince wallowing on the ground revealed there was no point. He had given the Prince of Merridia a matching pair of black eyes. He wasn't getting away with this one. Emethius flopped down next to Meriatis and awaited the inevitable.

•   •   •

"Your father would not be proud," chided Brother Cenna, as he wagged his plump finger in Meriatis's face. "Not proud at all. Fighting other students. I'd expect better behavior from a street urchin." The yellow and green banded skullcap he wore tilted this way and that with every disapproving shake of his head. It was drawing dangerously close to falling off, and Meriatis couldn't look away from the shifting cap. Brother Cenna snapped his fingers in front of the nose of the young prince. "Pay attention!"

A droll look overcame Meriatis's face and he nodded dumbly. "Of course, headmaster. My apologies. You were saying?"

"I was saying you should have more sense than that." Brother Cenna had Emethius and Meriatis seated in front of his desk. Brother Cenna was perched upon the lip of the desktop. He reached forward and lifted Meriatis's chin, checking beneath the boy's two swollen eyelids. "I'm pleased to report that you'll have these marks for awhile. Whenever you look in a mirror these bruises will remind you of the consequences of behaving like a bully."

Meriatis gave the headmaster a foolish toothy grin. "I will wear them as a sign of my remorse." He attempted to wink at the headmaster, but his swollen face wouldn't accommodate such deft motions.

Brother Cenna shook his head in exasperation. He readjusted his cap for the dozenth time, and turned his wrath to his next victim. "And you, Emethius. I know your father personally. He is a very stern man. If he knew that I let you get into a fight on your first day of school, and with the prince, of all people..." He held his head, as if the whole idea was simply too much.

"You didn't let me do anything," Emethius muttered sullenly under his breath.

"That's true," said Brother Cenna. "It would seem you made this foolish decision all on your own. But we adults bear the burdensome responsibility of trying to keep you safe." He examined Emethius's split lip and the welt on the back of his head which was the size of an egg. He sighed. "Somehow you came out the better of this fight."

I beat the prince! Emethius struggled to hide his brimming pride beneath a scowl.

The headmaster saw right through his false veneer. "Only a fool takes joy in hurting others," said Brother Cenna, placing a firm hand on Emethius's shoulder. A blinding pain flared through Emethius's left shoulder, and try as he might, he couldn't avoid flinching.

Brother Cenna's eyes narrowed. He yanked back Emethius's shirt collar, revealing the grotesque bulge in Emethius's left collarbone. "The Weaver help me, what did you do to this boy, Meriatis?"

A cold panic seized Emethius. "He, didn't, ah..., I..."

"I kicked him while he was on the ground, headmaster," said Meriatis, quick to interject. He looked sheepishly at his feet. "I got carried away. I didn't mean to break anything."

That was a lie. Meriatis had not kicked Emethius while he was on the ground. In truth, Meriatis fought with a great deal more honor than Emethius did. But that wasn't going to stop the headmaster from directing the blame where it didn't belong.

"I'm fine, headmaster, really." Emethius pinwheeled his left arm to support his claim.

For a second it looked as if Brother Cenna was going to slap Meriatis across the face. But in the end, he muttered something to himself about "pampered royals." His hands fell to his sides and he exhaled slowly. "This child has been here for one day, and now I have to write his father to tell him he has a broken collarbone? Lord Lunen is not going to like this, not one bit." He shook his head in disbelief as he began to rummage through his desk for parchment and pen. There was a low rap at the door just as he dipped his pen in an ink well. "One moment," said Brother Cenna, walking off to answer the door. "Keep your hands to yourselves and wait right here. I'll be back." He pointed for emphasis, and then stepped outside to speak with whoever was at the door.

As soon as the headmaster's huffing breaths had traveled from earshot, Meriatis spun in his chair and smiled at Emethius. "You performed brilliantly," said Meriatis. "I was especially impressed by your trick."

Emethius did not know how to respond. "Trick? What trick?"

"When you threw sand in my eyes," said Meriatis. "It was a clever move."

"It was cheating at best," said Emethius rather glumly. He was starting to feel ashamed he had resorted to a foul trick to win the fight.

"You couldn't beat me, and you were not going to accept defeat," countered Meriatis. "What's more, you were fighting with one arm tied behind your back." He nodded toward Emethius's misshapen collarbone. Meriatis gently guided Emethius's shirt collar back over his shoulder. "You did what you had to do to win. My father would commend you as a tactician. Guile is not a sin, and there are certainly no rules in war."

"Not even in the schoolyard?"

"No," said Meriatis, shaking his head. "Not even there. That's your first Royal Academy lesson — it's something the teachers won't tell you." He tried to wink again, this time having even less success than before. He looked liked a squint-eyed raccoon. Emethius had to stifle a laugh.

"Now, where were we?" interrupted the headmaster. They both fell silent as the Headmaster shuffled back to his perch atop his desk. "Ah, punishment! That is what you both need. Five lashes a piece!"

Emethius gasped in horror.

Meriatis didn't flinch. "But I am the Prince of Merridia," he whined.

"That you are," answered the Headmaster matter-of-factly.

Meriatis turned about in his chair and lifted his shirt over his head, exposing his bare back. "A lash could leave a scar. Are you truly so bold as to mar my beautiful and perfect royal flesh?" challenged the prince.

At this the Headmaster wavered. "You are right, my little lord. But you're not getting away unpunished. Kitchen duty for a fortnight."

"A week."

"This isn't a negotiation. Ten days."

Meriatis grinned triumphantly and settled back in his chair.

The thought of this spoiled brat avoiding a lashing while he took the brunt of the punishment filled Emethius with a sudden rage. He built up his courage to interject, but never got the chance.

"But...," continued Meriatis. "You cannot leave me un-marked and strike the boy who is far less responsible for the fight. I threw the first punch, after all." Emethius gawked at Meriatis, shocked that he would lie to protect him. "If you're not willing to lash me, it would be unjust for you to lash..." He paused. "What was your name again?"

"Emethius."

Meriatis nodded. "You cannot lay a hand on Emethius."

The headmaster scowled. "Your father would be

impressed by your sense of fairness, Prince Meriatis." He did nothing to hide the sarcasm in his voice. "Now get out of here, both of you. If I find you fighting again your sweet tongue will do nothing to fend off my lash." He pointed toward the door.

Meriatis jumped to his feet and performed a low bow. "Good day, headmaster." He grabbed Emethius's good hand and pulled him from the room.

As they bounded around the corner, Brother Cenna's voice called after them. "Emethius, see Brother Morgant about that broken bone, then return to your dormitories and tend to your studies. You're both grounded for the night."

They did not do as they were told.

Meriatis led Emethius outside, laughing with relief as he bounded down the stairs.

"Why did you lie about my shoulder?" pressed Emethius, as soon as they were alone.

"A good prince is supposed to protect the defenseless." His back stiffened and he stood at attention. He gave Emethius a mock salute.

"I'm not defenseless."

"You are against whoever did that." Meriatis nodded toward Emethius's collarbone.

"It was an accident."

"Uh huh." Meriatis shrugged with indifference. "If that's the story that works for you, so be it. Who am I to judge?" He tugged on Emethius's hand. "Come on. I want to show you something."

Emethius was suspicious, but he let himself be led onward. The academy was located within the walls of the palace. It was a sprawling complex full of temples, legal courts, meeting halls, libraries, residences, dormitories, barracks, and religious and scholarly academies. It was easy for a child to disappear in the mass of people that walked its grounds. They circled around the academy building, skirting the packed courtyard that was still full of students and instructors, and then ducked behind a manicured hedge that grew parallel to the rear wall of the royal residence.

"Where are you taking me?" asked Emethius. He was not sure if he should trust someone who had been pummeling him a few minutes earlier.

"Be patient," replied Meriatis. He peered left and right through the tangle of brush, guaranteeing the coast was clear, then darted to a small metal grate covering a dark ventilation shaft set in the side of the building. Outwardly, the grate appeared to be held down by four heavy iron bolts, but when Meriatis gave the grate a gentle tug, it popped free. He motioned for Emethius to follow, then slid down the ventilation shaft.

Without time to second guess his actions, Emethius charged after Meriatis, diving head first into the shaft. The shaft ran at a much sharper angle then Emethius had guessed, and he slid on his belly the entire way down. Suddenly the shaft opened into a large room, and he fell the last few feet, landing with a thud. A shooting pain tore through his shoulder and neck, and tears involuntarily came to his eyes. Thankfully, the dark interior hid his pain.

"Oh yeah. There's a bit of a drop at the end. Sorry," called Meriatis from the gloom. "Come on. This way."

Rubbing his tender shoulder, Emethius chased after the prince. He could stand upright, but an adult would have to hunch over to move around in the space — the ceiling was quite low. His eyes slowly adjusted to the dim interior. The floor was natural rock, and the space was humid and cold. Dozens of stone columns sprung from floor to ceiling. The smell of mold was too strong to ignore. Crates and casks were stacked everywhere.

"This is the kitchen cellar," said Meriatis. Overhead, the wooden floorboards creaked as the kitchen staff went about their daily tasks. "You didn't get lunch yet, did you?"

"No. Actually, I'm starving," said Emethius, realizing that his stomach felt hollow.

Meriatis reached into a box and pulled out a green apple. He tossed it to Emethius and grinned. "I think lunch can be seen to."

Emethius took a bite and followed the young prince deeper into the cellar. Meriatis gestured to the far corner, where a collection of items had been assembled to emulate a high-backed chair. "My Throne of Roses," said Meriatis proudly.

Emethius had never seen the actual Throne of Roses, but he imagined it looked nothing like the makeshift chair before him. The base was made from a small barrel, the armrests were wooden pallets, and the back was an upturned crate.

"A lord is always gracious in defeat, and today you have earned the high seat," said Meriatis with a grand sweep of his hand. He lowered his head and dropped to one knee in mock obeisance.

Emethius smiled wryly and hopped atop the throne, for a moment supplanting his prince.

The two sat and gorged themselves on fresh watermelon, smoked pork belly, and cheese. Meriatis even produced a bottle of wine from the Estero Vale to quench their thirst. They laughed and joked. Meriatis told Emethius about the current intrigues of the court, while Emethius shared stories about his home in the southlands, a region the prince had yet to visit. It was the most fun Emethius had experienced in months. Had anyone happened across this scene they would have never guessed that an hour earlier the two boys were fighting in the yard. But that was the way it was with Meriatis, or so Emethius would soon learn; Meriatis was quick to forgive, quick to feel sympathy, and quick to love. When the feast was through, Emethius was stuffed. Meriatis wallowed on the floor, painfully pleased with himself.

"I like you," said the prince, quite out of the blue.

"Oh, you do?" challenged Emethius. He sat sideways with his legs dangling over the side of the throne. "If I remember correctly, you were trying to knock my head off a bit earlier." He pinched the goose egg on the back of his head to emphasize his point.

"That happens," said Meriatis. "But of all the boys I've ever fought, you are actually the only one to hit me back."

Emethius laughed. "They just let you smack them around?"

"Yes, they often do. Or they run, or they cry out for help. But they never try to hit me! I often hear them whisper when I pass, *there goes the son of High*

Lord Valerius, there goes the heir to the throne," he croaked in a mocking voice. "They are all my friends in the end, because who wouldn't be. I'll be the High Lord of Merridia one day." Meriatis rolled his eyes at this. "But you're different, Emethius. It's like you don't know your station in life. You hit me, I like that about you. It makes me feel like we're equals."

Emethius smiled at the thought. He knew his father would gnash his teeth at such a foolish claim. *You will never be equals with the Prince of Merridia,* he could hear his father saying. *Men of such high birth look down their noses at men such as us.* But his father was far away, and for the first time in ages Emethius felt free to speak his own mind. "Equals, huh, you and I?"

Meriatis nodded and held out his hand. "Equals it is!"

Emethius grasped Meriatis's hand firmly and gave it a hearty shake. The duo spent the rest of the afternoon working their way through every crate in the cellar, neither of them having a care in the world save what they would eat next.

• • •

"Meriatis..., is he alive?" groaned Emethius through blood-caked lips. It took all of his strength to speak, yet no one seemed to hear. His voice was barely a whisper.

A hand was pressed firmly against the small of Emethius's back, putting pressure on the stab wound Meriatis had inflicted. Emethius was lying face down on a stretcher. The coarse fabric scratched at his face, and for some reason that irritant seemed more pressing then the severe wound in his back. Everything felt oddly distant. The world passed by as if he was floating. "No. I'm being carried," he corrected himself. Soldiers of the Faith sprinted past, heading in the opposite direction. "Someone needs to rescue the high lord," he heard himself murmur. "Coffin... he's in the coffin."

On the periphery of his vision he detected an amber glow. There was a fire, great and severe. Belching columns of smoke blotted out the sun. Emethius would have laughed if he had any strength left in his body. Praetor Maxentius got his wish — Imel Katan was burning.

The stretcher bearers set Emethius down in an open-sided pavilion. Groans and wails of dying men filled the air. In the distance he thought he heard Praetor Maxentius barking out wild orders. Nearby a Tiber Brother was giving someone their last rights. Anointing water splashed across

Emethius's forehead. He opened his eyes, realizing that he was the one receiving the final sacrament.

"Fly spirit, and be free of all pain," said the Tiber Brother.

Emethius tried to shove the Tiber Brother away, but his hands felt like lead weights.

"This is the one who stabbed the prince," whispered a soldier into the Tiber Brother's ear. "It would be best for Merridia if he died. Take pressure off the wound. Let him bleed."

The Tiber Brother nodded knowingly and pierced Emethius's forehead with a rose thorn. "Blessed be the gods of Calaban."

I'm not dead, Emethius tried to reply, but his words were unintelligible.

A mailed hand clasped across Emethius's nose and mouth. It took Emethius a second to realize the man was trying to suffocate him. He bit at his attacker's mailed fingers, getting a mouthful of steel.

"Hey, what are you doing to him?"

His attacker suddenly howled in pain and stumbled backward, grabbing at the side of his head. Blood gushed between his mailed fingers.

"If I ever see you again, I'll take your other ear, you halfwit bastard!" It was Malrich. He threw the man's bloody ear off into the distance and then rolled Emethius onto his side, pressing a rag against the wound. "Hang in there, mate."

"Mal...," managed Emethius through parched lips. He felt cold.

There was a scuffle nearby. Emethius heard other familiar voices and the hiss of blades drawing from sheaths. The Red Company had arrived.

"Brother Seius, get your ass over here and help the captain!" barked Malrich.

Then all fell silent. The painful cries, the undulating voices, the Tiber Brothers granting last rights; everyone drew quiet for a moment that seemed to last forever. It was as if some dark revelation had simultaneously been made by all. Finally, a lamenting cry broke the silence.

Emethius realized why.

Meriatis was carried by on a stretcher, but in Emethius's hazy mind he appeared to be floating on a sea of crimson flames. A woman in white walked beside the stretcher, her arms red to the elbows as she frantically tried to save Meriatis's life. His olive skin had turned the color of ash. The prince's gaze shifted to Emethius as he went past, or so he first thought. *There is no life in those hazel eyes*, Emethius realized. Meriatis was still, lifeless. Dead.

CHAPTER

V

THINGS PRESENT

Emethius awoke to the ringing of a bell.
Gong, gong, gong.

He was lying on his back in a bed. His shirt was missing, and oddly enough, an older woman was standing at his bedside with both of her hands resting on his bare chest. She was talking softly to herself with her eyes closed.

"Don't move," she muttered out of the side of her mouth.

"Huh?"

"Are you keen on having your left lung on the outside of your body?"

"No."

"Then don't move. Don't even talk. Try not to breathe if you can help it."

Emethius still wasn't sure what was going on, but he decided that following the woman's advice was the best course of action. He took slow shallow breaths.

Gong, tolled the bell in the distance.

"I'm performing a transfusion," said the woman after a few moments. Her eyes were still closed, her face strained with concentration. "My vitality can be a bit fickle at times. It's best not to complicate matters by squirming about. This is your seventh transfusion. It took two treatments to patch up your lung and ribs. Another three to get your intestines to stop leaking. The infection was pretty bad. We had to bring in a master healer for that. These final two treatments have been to heal your muscles and flesh."

I'm lucky to be alive, realized Emethius. There were very few healers who possessed the ability to perform a transfusion. Transfusers almost exclusively provided their services to the rich and powerful. He felt a dull tingling in the small of his back, and the muscles in the region began to spasm. That was likely the woman working her craft.

Gong. Gong. Gong.

"It's hard to concentrate with all that racket." The woman finally opened her eyes and lifted her hands from Emethius's chest. She removed a piece of cotton from each of her ears. "That damn bell has been ringing all morning, once for every soul lost in Prince Meriatis's war of treason. It will probably still be ringing come dusk."

Emethius decided it was all right to move a little bit, and he peered out his bedside window. In the distance he could spy the pink dome of the Court of Bariil looming over the surrounding rooftops. The bell atop its dome swung back and forth like a pendulum. He was in Mayal, the capital of Merridia, although he had no memory of how he had gotten here. The last thing he remembered was bleeding to death in a field hospital outside of Imel Katan.

"Lean forward," instructed the woman, as she pulled him into a seated position. Emethius's back screamed in protest, but the woman didn't give him much option to resist. "I'm Sister Beli," said the woman as she removed the bandage covering the wound in his back. Sister Beli was a squat woman, nearly as round as she was tall. Her hair was tied back in a tight bun. The wrinkles on her face implied she frowned more often than not.

"By the time you arrived the wound in your back had already festered. Your whole body was on fire and I thought you were destined for the hereafter. But the gods are good. Vacia has watched over you." Sister Beli held the bloodstained bandage up to her nose and gave it a strong sniff. She seemed satisfied with the results.

"That was your last transfusion. The wound is closed, and should stay that way as long as you don't move around too much. In a few days I'll have you on your feet and walking circuits about the grounds. You're one of the lucky ones. It's rare for a Soldier of the Faith to receive a transfusion. You must know someone important."

I once did, thought Emethius glumly. Outside his window, the bell continued its solemn count, a stark reminder that the gods had failed to protect so many others. "What of Prince Meriatis? Did he survive?"

Sister Beli ignored his question, instead granting him a smile that was full of pity and perhaps even a bit of sadness. "You should try to rest," said the sister, as she helped him lie back down. "You will need your strength in the coming days."

She brought him a bowl of brown gruel. Emethius shoveled a few spoonfuls into his mouth before he slid the bland paste aside. He listened to the mournful knell of the dirge bell, thinking about what each toll represented.

Gong. Perin. *Gong.* Quintus. *Gong.* Meriatis.

He wondered how many Merridians died during the failed assault on the gate. Or worse still, how many members of the Red Company fell after he abandoned them to chase after the prince.

Too many, answered the bell with its incessant gong. The bell chimed on and on, until it became numbing to the senses and ceased to do the fallen any honor.

There was a low cough at the door.

Emethius smiled when he saw his unexpected visitor. "Malrich!" exclaimed Emethius. It was good to see anyone who wasn't going to poke and prod him, but even better to see a true friend.

"How do you fare?" asked Malrich as he entered the room and moved a bench alongside Emethius's bed.

"Well enough," replied Emethius. "I'm alive, and that may be better than I deserve."

"So it would seem," said Malrich. "Some at Imel Katan wanted to let you die after they saw what you did. The prince was loved by many." Malrich's breath stunk of hard liquor, and his eyelids bore a telltale droop. Even Malrich, friend that he was, needed a few drinks to build up the courage to visit the man responsible for killing the prince.

"I loved Prince Meriatis as much as anyone," said Emethius, feeling he had to defend himself. "I guessed Meriatis's fate, but you are the first to confirm it. He is dead."

Malrich nodded. "The prince was unconscious when I found you two atop the pinnacle of Imel

Katan. At first I couldn't comprehend what had happened. Then I heard a knock coming from inside that coffin. I pried off the lid and out crawled High Lord Valerius. Damn near gave me a heart attack."

Emethius had almost forgotten about High Lord Valerius. The high lord's safety was what truly mattered. "I did my duty," said Emethius, more as a reassurance to himself than anything else. "I didn't mean to kill Meriatis, but what other option did I have?"

Malrich gave an indifferent shrug. "No man can draw a sword against another without recourse. I don't judge your deeds foul, but be aware, in the days to come others will."

Gong, tolled the bell.

Emethius turned aside the thought. "What happened to the main host that attacked the gate?"

"From what I heard it was a corpse-riddled disaster," said Malrich as he retrieved a flask from his breast pocket. He took a swig before sharing the tale. "Lord Fennir and his men broke through the gate with a battering ram, and they killed a great many rebels in the process. But the enemy rebounded just as they were gaining a footing. And wouldn't you know it, there was Prince Meriatis leading the charge. Of course that completely baffled the men, seeing as the prince of Merridia was supposed to be a prisoner, not fighting alongside the rebels."

Malrich snorted. "Lord Fennir challenged the prince to single combat. I heard Lord Fennir had the upper hand, and even managed to stab Meriatis in the throat. But when the rebels saw Prince Meriatis stagger from the blow, they made a pincushion out of Lord Fennir with crossbow bolts. No honor in that, but such is war."

Malrich took another draw from his flask, then offered Emethius a drink. Emethius waved him off. "Naturally, the men panicked," continued Malrich, placing the stopper back in the flask. "Some fool sounded the horn to retreat. The causeway was choked with fire, so a lot of the men attempted to flee across the ice. Last I heard they were still plucking corpses from Lake Libith."

That was far worse news than Emethius had predicted. "I believe Praetor Maxentius knew Meriatis was the true leader of the rebellion," said Emethius. "Meriatis said so at least."

Malrich tapped at his head. "I dare not assume to understand the minds of lords, but I think Preator Maxentius sent you in there with a purpose. Given your history with the prince, Maxentius probably hoped you would convince Meriatis to surrender."

"Perhaps, but why hide the truth?" said Emethius. "Why didn't he tell us that Meriatis was the leader of the rebellion?"

"Is that question so hard to answer? How many more would have joined sides with the prince? Would you? Would I? Praetor Maxentius worked awfully hard to keep the truth hidden, but now the truth is out, and all matters are being thrown into question."

"What do you mean?"

"The Blackheart, Emethius. Meriatis rebelled because of the Blackheart."

Emethius had heard rumors during the first few days of the war that this was the cause of the rebellion, but he had never given the idea much credence. The Blackheart was a disease for which there was no cure. There wasn't a family in Merridia untouched by the evil affliction. But it made no sense for the Blackheart to be the cause of the rebellion. *How do you rebel against a disease?*

"Why can't people just accept that Meriatis was trying to steal the throne from his father?" asked Emethius.

"Does that sound like the Meriatis you knew?"

Emethius had to admit it did not. He remembered Meriatis muttering something about killing the gods just before their duel atop the pinnacle of Imel Katan, but that made even less sense.

Malrich leaned forward, and his voice dropped to a whisper. "Just before the outbreak of the rebellion, pamphlets started showing up all over Mayal — nailed to temple doors, left on tavern tables, abandoned in piles in the middle of markets. I saw one once. The pamphlet claimed the gods were withholding a cure for the Blackheart."

"You need to watch what you say, Mal. Such inflammatory claims could get a man in a lot of trouble." He looked to the doorway and into the hallway beyond, making sure no one was eavesdropping on their conversation. "War has a way of perverting the truth. You're too smart to be giving this nonsense much credence."

"You're likely right," said Malrich. "But something *is* going on. People are being asked to sign loyalty oaths. "The war might be over, but the ideas of the rebellion are alive and well. I fear the real butcher's work is about to begin. There will likely be a purge."

Emethius waved off the thought. It did him no good to question the decisions of his high lord or his gods. "Can we turn aside from such treacherous speech?" said Emethius. "I am tired and need to rest."

"That he does," said Sister Beli as she stepped into the room. Emethius had not heard her returning down the hallway, and could only pray that she hadn't overheard any of the conversation. She crossed her arms and scowled at Malrich. "I think you've provided Master Emethius with more than enough excitement for one day."

Malrich hastily tucked his flask into his breast pocket and grinned. "The high lord has declared tomorrow a day of mourning. There's going to be a ceremony to commemorate the dead. Praetor Maxentius has ordered all of his officers be in attendance."

"I'll have the final say on that matter," said Sister Beli as she showed Malrich out the door.

As Malrich departed, he leaned a long thin object wrapped in cloth against the wall. "For when you have found your strength," said Malrich, patting the bundle.

Sister Beli escorted Malrich down the hall, scolding him along the way for bringing liquor into her house of healing. Malrich responded by downing the rest of his flask right in front of her.

Emethius chuckled softly to himself and turned his attention to the bundle Malrich had deposited beside the door, staring at it until he finally succumbed to an uneasy slumber.

In his dreams he was back atop Imel Katan. His hands were dripping with blood. Meriatis lay dead at his feet, pierced through the heart. Emethius tried not to look at the body. *The high lord is all that matters now,* he tried to reassure himself, as he pried off the lid of the coffin with the tip of his sword. To his great surprise, High Lord Valerius was not trapped within. Instead it was a shadow, inky black and reeking of brimstone. It came boiling out of the coffin, rising higher and higher, until finally it coalesced and took form. It had hoofed feet, wings like the sails of a ship, and the body and head of a bear. It trod over Meriatis's corpse and pressed Emethius to the lip of the tower.

"I wish to make mortals out of the gods," hissed the Shadow. *"I wish to make the Calabanesi pay for their sins."* Glowing cinders poured from the demon's mouth as it swallowed Emethius whole.

CHAPTER
VI
THE HIGH LORD

Emethius awoke with a start and involuntarily rose upright in bed. A shooting pain screamed up his spine. It felt as if every muscle in his back was spasming. His clothes were sodden with sweat. He raised his palm to his brow, finding it cool and clammy.

He had slept so long it was almost sunrise. Everything outside his window was a shade of gray, even the Court of Bariil's pink dome. In the distance a bird was singing to welcome the dawn. Sometime in the middle of the night the bell had stopped its incessant toll. Emethius wondered what the finally tally was.

He scooted to the edge of his bed. The pain was nearly blinding, but he grit his teeth and stood. His duties would not wait until he was fully mended. He collected the bundle Malrich had left beside the door.

He unfolded the cloth cover and held his sword aloft. For the first time in his life, Emethius's weapon bore the scars of battle. He ran his finger over the leather grip and found it stiff from dried blood; Meriatis's blood. Unable to look at the blade any longer, he hid it back within its sheath. It felt unusually heavy in his hands.

I'm half a skeleton, realized Emethius as he undressed and stood in front of a mirror. His elbows and knees stood out prominently, his ribs looked like the grooves of a washboard. His jawline was gaunt. The only thing that truly resembled his old self were his eyes. Still brown, still piercing.

Someone had left his uniform in a footlocker at the end of his bed. The slacks and jacket were gray save for the red rose embroidered upon the chest. He gingerly put on each article of clothing, cringing with every bend and turn. The uniform no longer fit him — it was much too large — and he felt like a child trying on his father's clothes. Emethius had to cinch his belt several holes tighter to keep the tip of his scabbard from dragging on the ground.

We Lunen are resilient, he reminded himself as he took his first wobbly steps toward the door.

He set out into the city just as the sun was cresting the horizon. The streets were already packed.

Mayal was not only the capital of Merridia, it was considered by many to be the center of the world. The city consisted of a series of islands situated in the Bay of Lares, a brackish body of water that formed where the Estmer River emptied into the Sea of Ro. Trading galleys from all over the world made call to Mayal's ports. No matter where one went in the city, it was always possible to spy the masts of ships.

Every major religious order had its headquarters in Mayal, and sworn brothers and sisters were everywhere. Emethius walked by half a dozen street preachers on the way to his destination, each one extolling a different brand of doom and gloom. "The gods of Calaban despise you," cried one, from atop a raised platform. "The Shadow's creep is ever expanding," expounded another. "Look not to Calaban for salvation!"

One preacher Emethius passed was burning the entrails of a freshly killed pig. The man's face was curled in a sour grimace as he prodded the smoldering entrails with a stick; he appeared unhappy with whatever he saw.

The streets became congested as Emethius neared the center of the city. A surging throng was moving westward along the narrow cobblestone lanes and stone bridges that spanned the canals. All were headed toward the Grand Plaza, the location for the ceremony in remembrance of the dead. Emethius followed the flow of traffic until he neared the plaza. Then he turned aside and entered a columned walkway that led to the walled palace compound.

The royal palace was closed to the public and the front gate was under heavy guard. Soldiers of the Faith were redirecting everyone toward the plaza. Emethius dodged the searching eyes of the watchmen and ducked behind a fountain. He pulled aside a metallic grate set into the fountain's base and squeezed through a narrow service shaft. He descended a rickety ladder and found himself in the palace catacombs.

The palace compound was built upon a slab of limestone that rose out of the sea like a balled fist. Over the eons, natural springs had hollowed out tunnels in the limestone isle, much like a termite mound.

The tunnel Emethius entered was as black as night, the air rank from mildew and stagnant water. Emethius ignored his senses and relied on muscle memory to navigate the labyrinthine network of tunnels. As children, he and Meriatis used to traipse around in the tunnels without the slightest care in the world, playing hide and seek or King versus

Cul. He found it funny how a child could be fearless while an adult was daunted by the simplest unknowns. *Perhaps that's because I now know what lurks in the shadows.*

After a few minutes of walking blindly, he was greeted by the sun's rays. He slid aside an unlocked portcullis and found himself standing within the inner bailey of the palace complex. The courtyard was empty.

Before him rose the marble facade of the Court of Bariil, the holiest temple in all of Merridia. It was a massive edifice, built ages ago when Mayal was new and the gods wished for it to prosper. He passed through the entrance portal and entered the temple.

The main hall was a cavernous and dark space. There were hardly any windows in the ancient building, and those that existed were narrow and opaque. The base of the temple was fashioned in a hexagon, studded on each side by a deep alcove. One alcove housed the temple's main entrance; within each of the others was a shrine dedicated to one of the five god-saints.

As Emethius crossed the chamber and drew near the dais upon which stood the Throne of Roses, a veil of shadow filled the hall. It was as if the sun had fallen behind a cloud. Everything dimmed, and a booming voice called from the gloom. "Who are you to boldly enter this holy temple unbidden?"

"It is I, Emethius Lunen, Soldier of the Faith." He dropped to one knee and bowed, knowing what was expected of him. "I am on an errand to see the high lord."

"And who is he to enter the Court of Bariil, he who has killed the heir?" answered the voice. "Go now, and seek no audience. The high lord holds you in contempt. You are unwelcome."

"I seek the high lord's ear, and I will not stop short of my purpose," said Emethius, raising his voice in challenge. "It is true — I did kill the high lord's son. And now High Lord Valerius has a father's right to pass judgment. I have come to lay my life in his hands."

The shadow suddenly lifted as rays of sunlight poured down through the rotunda windows and illuminated the dais. There stood a grand throne crafted from a single piece of hammered copper. A fissure ran through the center of the throne, and it looked half-finished, pockmarked with dents and gouges from the seemingly careless hammer strokes of the artisan who sculpted it. The throne was one of a matching pair. Its twin was the Throne of Tiberius, which was situated far away high upon the pinnacle of Calaban. The twin thrones served as a conduit, through which the high lord could directly commune with the king of the gods. It was said that only the most pious and powerful minds could survive the touch of the perilous Throne of Roses.

At the base of the dais, perched upon a simple wooden stool was an ancient figure robed in crimson. He sat bow-backed, as if weighed down by a lifetime of toil and grief. Upon his head of short cropped hair he wore a circlet of gold. The crown was set with gemstones of jade, opal, amethyst, ruby, and onyx. Each precious stone represented one of the five holy orders over which the High Lord of Merridia reigned supreme.

Emethius approached High Lord Valerius and unsheathed his sword. He fell to his knees and set his face against the stone, presenting his blade to the high lord. "I have come before you seeking judgment," said Emethius. "If you ask me to, I will lay this blade to my own flesh, for it is noble to do as one's lord commands. Is this the justice you seek?"

"Judgment has already been passed," said High Lord Valerius. He placed his trembling hand under Emethius's chin and lifted him upright. "What you did was not a sin. You may rise and sheath your sword. So the High Lord of Merridia has declared."

Emethius stood. "Your judgment is just, high lord," began Emethius. "But for a moment, I ask you to set aside your lordship. Please, face me as a father of a lost son."

"Is that truly what you seek?"

"Yes," said Emethius, blinking back the tears welling in his eyes.

Valerius rose with a sudden fury and unsheathed his own sword, a three-foot blade of rippling black steel. Moving with a speed that was stunning for a man of his age, Valerius pressed the tip of his sword into Emethius's throat. "As a father of a lost son I would avenge Meriatis's death," roared Valerius. His hazel eyes raged with fire, and for a second Emethius was certain the high lord was going to ram the blade through his taut neck; Valerius's posture slackened, and his voice fell to a whisper. "But sorrow and loss should not undo the love that binds us, and I love you, too, Emethius."

Emethius wasn't sure how to respond to such compassion. Shouldn't there be a consequence for killing the prince? Shouldn't he be punished? "I can only beg for your forgiveness," said Emethius finally.

"I will pray day and night that the gods grant me the grace to give you what you want," said Valerius.

He sheathed his blade and motioned for Emethius to follow. "Walk with me, Emethius. My eyes are not as strong as they once were, and I wish to see things that have grown dim to me over the years."

Emethius offered the high lord his arm, and the two walked to the central colonnade that ran in a circle beneath the base of the dome. The spiral columns reached into the gloom, each one depicting a different era of Merridian history. Emethius ran his finger along the carvings that were etched into the face of the nearest stone pillar. The scene depicted King Ordin, who led his people across the sea only to die at the hands of the Cul.

Emethius thought it odd, how the passage of time had a tendency to compress a person's entire life into a moment. Few alive could say a single word about what King Ordin believed, or who he loved, or how he lived. Yet the people of Merridia worshiped him as a martyr all the same.

Emethius wondered how he would be remembered, if he was remembered at all. The slayer of Prince Meriatis, perhaps. The man who ended the line of Benisor. *No,* thought Emethius, *I will not be forgotten.* But what was remembered would not be who he truly was. He felt cursed that this would be his legacy.

High Lord Valerius patted Emethius's hand,

perhaps seeing the turmoil in his eyes. "Whenever I saw you as a child you made me smile," said the high lord. "Do you know why? It's because you made Meriatis smile. He enjoyed life when you were around and loved you dearly. You were the brother he always wanted."

An overpowering sense of shame gnawed at Emethius's heart. By the end, he had grown to hate Meriatis as much as he loved him.

"I treated Meriatis poorly more often than not," said Emethius.

Valerius shook his head. "No, you treated him better than he deserved. He was a dark boy, yet you made him bright at times. I never had great hope in the child. His heart was blackened long before his time. But after he met you things changed, at least for a while. It was not until these last few years that it returned, darker than before, and more maddening." Emethius noted a tremor in the high lord's hand. "You cannot blame a man for his actions once the Blackheart has ravaged his mind."

Emethius raised an eyebrow at this. Was this how the high lord tried to save face? Meriatis's actions were almost excusable if one believed he was afflicted by the Blackheart. But Emethius had his doubts. Uncontrollable violence, mania, a seething hatred — these were the symptoms of the afflicted. Meriatis was troubled, maybe even delusional, but he still seemed to have his faculties about him in the end.

"From what I saw, I would not have concluded Meriatis was afflicted by the Blackheart," said Emethius.

"You only saw the last guttering spasm of the flame. I saw the madness when it was a raging fire." Valerius shook his head bitterly. "No, Emethius, the man you killed was not my son. Meriatis died years ago. What you killed was a husk." He walked Emethius toward the exit.

"When I was a young prince, not much older than you are now, I was approached by a soothsayer as I walked the streets of Mayal. She warned me that I would be the last of my line to rule Merridia. At the time, I took her for a madwoman, but if I were to meet her again, I would ask her what other prophesies she has. Every true heir to the Throne of Roses has fallen before their time. Meriatis and my nephew Fennir both died at Imel Katan. My brother, Isir, passed on years ago. I am the last, and when I die my line shall fail." Valerius's eyes were filled with sadness, and Emethius found himself pitying the high lord. He was no longer the powerful high lord Emethius had looked up to as a child, but a broken old man whose life's work had gone to ruin.

"We should mourn for both Meriatis and Fennir," said Emethius. "But we cannot fall into despair. Hope is not yet lost. There is still one who can maintain the Benisor line."

Valerius took no solace in this remark. Emethius was referring to Leta, Valerius's daughter. Only two years Emethius's senior, she was still of childbearing age. There should have been considerable hope that Leta would produce an heir, but her life had been cursed by tragedy. Her husband was killed in a heretic uprising shortly after they wed. From their union she bore a son, but he fell ill and died while only a young child.

"My daughter has long been a widow in mourning," said Valerius. "She spends her days in service to the goddess Vacia and will not take another husband; her grief is too great."

They reached the twin copper doors that led out to the courtyard. "Merridia has always been surrounded by shadow, but the total dark has been kept at bay," said the aged lord. "Have you the slightest clue why, Emethius?"

Emethius remained silent, realizing that Valerius had not meant for him to answer the question.

"It is because we have relied on our faith to guide us," explained Valerius. "I rule by the grace of the gods and in compliance to their will. Throughout history it has always been so. That is why the high lord has never taken on the title of king. A king is accountable only to himself and his desires, but I am accountable to the gods."

Valerius sighted. "I will die soon. Who will rule then? There are men of faith who would prove wise rulers, but they are not rightful heirs. And there are rightful heirs, but they would serve more as a king than a high lord. It is an unsettling choice, and one I will soon have to make." He opened the temple door. "I have a ceremony to lead, and it is your time to depart."

"Of course," said Emethius. He placed his hand on the pommel of his sword. "May I escort you to the ceremony? The rebellion may be crushed, but that does not mean there are not still men roaming the streets that would like to do you harm."

Valerius shook his head. "I will not be guarded in my own city, even if the times have grown truly vile. After what has transpired, the people of Mayal need me to appear steadfast." He looked to Emethius with sincere eyes. "You are wise, Emethius, and such is a virtue. Go now and prosper, until the Fates overcome us."

"Until the Fates overcome us," repeated Emethius. He bowed low and parted from the presence of his lord.

. . .

Emethius left the palace complex the same way he had entered. Once outside the palace walls, he joined the confluence of people heading toward the Grand Plaza. By the time he arrived, the plaza was nearly full. A temporary platform had been raised near the western edge of the plaza, and the delta of the Estmer River served as a shimmering backdrop.

As Emethius worked his way toward the front of the crowd, a drummer tolled a few solemn taps to announce the arrival of the high lord's procession. Soldiers of the Faith led the way, parting the crowd with lengthy spears. High Lord Valerius came next. Emethius could see him easily. The high lord was a head taller than most of the common folk, and he passed down the narrow lane with his chin uplifted and his gaze set straight ahead. The sight of the high lord enlivened the crowd, and people rushed forward, hoping to run their hands along his crimson robe. Others fell prostrate, and pawed at the high lord's feet as he passed.

Next came a great many people of high birth, lords and ladies who had remained loyal to the throne throughout the rebellion. Praetor Maxentius was there, as was his son-in-law, General Saterius. Saterius still wore his wolf skin cloak, but he had traded in his armor for a fine silk uniform. Ferrus Leair, Lord Admiral of the Elyim Fleet, came next. It was his ships that sailed up the Estmer River and broke the rebel siege of Burrowick.

Behind the admiral walked Lady Miren, Lordess of Chansel. She was the high lord's sister-in-law and wife of the late Lord Isir. From head to foot she wore black. She was still mourning the death of her only son, Fennir, who was killed while trying to take the gatehouse of Imel Katan. In her arms she carried the Dragon Helm, a token of her son's valor.

Beside Lady Miren walked the Priestess of Vacia. Emethius smiled upon spying her; it had been many months since he had the pleasure of seeing Leta Benisor, the daughter of the high lord.

There were heavy wrinkles around Leta's eyes and cheeks, sure marks of the many hardships she had endured losing a husband, a son, and now her brother. The wrinkles did not mar her beauty. In fact, they made her seem more distinguished and serene. Her eyes were hazel, as it was for all of the descendants of Benisor. They shined like polished opal when they caught the light of the morning sun. Her hair was as black as obsidian; braids ran over her shoulders and down her back. Since the death of her mother, which was now over a decade past, Leta had served as the matriarch of House Benisor. She certainly looked the part, dressed in a regal gown made of silver cloth and white lace, over which she wore a spotted ermine cloak.

Seeing Leta now, Emethius couldn't help but remember his childhood. During his youth, Emethius spent most of his summers with Meriatis and Leta at the royal estate in the foothills of Mount Calaban. Back then, Leta had loved to laugh, sometimes at Emethius, sometimes with him; he never really cared which it was, he simply enjoyed seeing her happy. Emethius spent countless summer nights trying to steal a kiss from the girl. It was an ignorant infatuation that ignored the caste into which each of them was born. But such was the way of a child's innocent mind. As an adult, Emethius still adored Leta, although it was not as it was before. He now understood his limitations. Still, he wondered what her laughter sounded like now.

Herald Cenna, the newly appointed master of the Tiber Order, commenced the ceremony with an oration about the nature of sin and redemption. The soft weeping of Lady Miren could be heard over the droning voice of the herald. Leta reached out and gripped her aunt's hand warmly. In doing so, she revealed the pale white skin of her left hand. From fingertips to forearm, the skin of her left arm was covered in porcelain scars that resembled bolts of lightning. In public she almost always kept the pale flesh hidden beneath an elbow length glove, but today she brazenly displayed the scar to the crowd. Throughout the audience, people were nudging one another and gesturing toward Leta.

This was Leta's subtle way of reminding the people of Mayal that her father wasn't the only person in the family to be touched by the gods. She received the scars as a child when she accidentally touched the Throne of Roses. Many saw them as a sign that the gods deemed her worthy. Emethius grinned. High Lord Valerius might not see Leta as a possible heir, but Leta clearly had different intentions — why else display the scars for all to see?

Herald Cenna shuffled back to his chair, having finished his sermon. A murmur hummed through the crowd. Most in attendance had come to the plaza hoping to hear the high lord speak, but no one was certain whether he would do so.

To everyone's delight, High Lord Valerius rose from his chair and walked to the edge of the platform. He held out his hands with his palms facing toward the crowd and blessed the gathering in a slow sweeping arc. The audience fell silent.

"We are a society of sinners," began Valerius, his sonorous voice rising until it filled the entire plaza. "We have ignored the teachings of our gods, and so, we have found ourselves plighted by plague. Throughout Merridia mothers kneel at night. Not for food, water, or a plentiful harvest. They pray that their children are not plucked from their breast and driven to madness by the ravages of the Blackheart. All too often these prayers go unanswered. The Blackheart creeps as it ever has, and those that we love fall to torment.

"Repent!" cried dozens of people within the crowd. Countless others fell to their knees and began to perform the ritualistic gestures of the faithful, crossing their hands across their necks and faces.

Valerius nodded with approval and continued his sermon. "To those of you who have not yet felt the wrath of Calaban, do not assume you go unseen. There is no hiding your true nature — the gods see all. They will embrace the remorseful sinner with one hand, while drowning the arrogant saint with the other. Salvation is guaranteed to no one.

"There are some amongst us who have sought

an easy path to salvation. They believe that the words I preach are a deception and that the gods of Calaban are false." He squinted into the crowd, singling out individuals with his eyes. "I say to thee, beware, ye who looks to Calaban with disdain, for Calaban is unblinking, and sees your inner light!" His face twisted with sorrow and he looked down at his own feet. "My warning has come too late for many. My own son could not withstand the temptation, and thus he succumbed to the allure of the Shadow."

A noticeable gasp hummed through the crowd. Prince Meriatis's betrayal was a common topic within people's private homes, but no one dared to discuss the matter in public; to do so was a treacherous offense. A few began to openly weep upon hearing this news, others nodded in stark agreement. High Lord Valerius's face hardened as he looked back over the crowd.

"So how do we as a people move forward?" asked Valerius. "Each of us must play our part. We must not seek vengeance against the sword bearer of the rebel cause, nor wish doom upon their kin, for those too are sins, and thus our fall will only be greater. We cannot ignore the widow or the child of those who betrayed us, for they are first amongst us, knowing best the true consequences of our collective failings. We cannot forswear those afflicted with the Blackheart, for they are but agents of Calaban's divine plan, sent amongst us to expose our darkest sins. Now, go forth and become the embodiment of our faith. With a strong heart, accept the fate that the gods have bestowed upon you. Be grateful for this day of peace, and for everyday hereafter with which we are blessed." He held his hands out toward the crowd. "Until the fates overcome us, and we depart from this land!"

"Until the fates overcome us!" called the gathering in unison.

Valerius then turned and fell to one knee. He kissed the ground, bowing toward the invisible monolith of Calaban that stood far beyond the horizon in the west. All across the Grand Plaza, the faithful citizens of Merridia copied their high lord. But even as they did, a disquieting murmur rose from the crowd. Here and there amongst the audience, a few refused to bow.

At first, Emethius mistook them for the elderly, slow to take on the posture of the pious. *No, these men are young and hale*, Emethius realized. He couldn't help but gasp in shock — this was a purposeful act of protest.

All told, a few hundred remained standing in defiance. They held one hand across their mouths and another across their eyes. Collectively, they turned their back on the monolith of Calaban.

This sent the crowd into an uproar. Soldiers of the Faith, overzealous and not willing to see their gods dishonored, rose to their feet, and rushed toward the protesters. Herald Cenna's tiny voice called for calm from atop the dais. This had the opposite effect. Soon, all of the gathering had risen. Everyone seemed to be pointing an accusative finger at someone else. Neighbors called each other out. Husbands and wives looked at one another in disbelief. Soldiers shoved their way forward, trying to seize the protesters before they disappeared into the crowd. Given the ensuing chaos, Emethius would have been surprised if a single protester was arrested.

Apparently the ideals of the rebellion *were* alive and well. Emethius shook his head as he waded his way through the unruly mass of people. Malrich was right — the true butcher's work was only beginning.

CHAPTER
VII
PRIESTESS OF VACIA

The chattering voices drew to a halt when Leta entered the Vacian Monastery. Although she always conducted herself with absolute grace, the sisters of the Vacian Order were convinced it was an act. They were unable to comprehend how someone cursed by such an unfair life could press forward. Mother of a dead child, widow of a dead husband, mourner of a dead brother. The Vacian Sisters always looked at Leta with pity in their eyes.

They should pity the afflicted instead, thought Leta.

The monastery was part of the greater palace complex. Designated as a house of healing, the sisterhood had long battled the Blackheart within these walls. The interior was purposefully austere, designed to soothe the minds and spirits of the sick. The walls were painted white, and the floor was cream-colored marble. The outside world was hidden by nearly opaque windows that glowed dimly with morning light. The only ostentatious object within the entire hall was a fountain capped by a porcelain statue of Vacia, the patron goddess of caregivers and the sick.

Leta walked across the empty expanse, the heels of her sandals clacking against the polished stone. The monastery had been designed to house scores of sick, but in recent years, the number of patients had dwindled. The Blackheart seemed to be progressing quicker than anyone could remember. Many patients were degrading to full psychosis within a year of first showing symptoms. By the time most families brought their afflicted kin to the monastery, they were already gripped by madness. If the patient was deemed a danger to others, the court quickly condemned them to death. In truth, there was very little actual healing going on in the monastery; it had become little more than a way-station to the afterlife.

Twelve sisters were waiting for Leta near a windowless wall. Each sister stood beside the bed of one of the condemned. The poor afflicted wretches shifted listlessly against their leather bindings. All sense of reality had left their dilated eyes, and they stared about themselves in unblinking wonder.

The babble of the fountain's cascading water

echoed in the hall. Sadly, it was not enough to drown out the long slick stroke of a whetstone being drawn against a blade. Sir Rupert awaited in the adjacent courtyard, and he would soon use his ax to send these afflicted bodies into oblivion.

Leta peeked through a window that overlooked the monastery's central courtyard to check on Sir Rupert's preparations. The chopping block was already in place, as were the burial shrouds in which the deceased would be transported. She could vaguely make out Sir Rupert's stocky silhouette as he took a few practice swings with his ax. Sir Rupert was a dwarf, a characteristic that was of particular importance in this matter.

It was considered a supreme sin for one talsani to kill another. In the case of the Blackheart victims, the Court of Bariil utilized dwarven executioners to work around this commandment. Leta felt awful putting such a burden on Sir Rupert's shoulders, but someone had to do it. In centuries past, a mass execution such as this would only occur once or twice a year. But now the Blackheart was so prevalent that executions were occurring nearly every week.

Leta scowled at the thought of her own role in the process. Granting the afflicted their final sacrament used to be the job of the high lord, but her father refused to perform the sacrament since Meriatis's passing. Leta had grudgingly accepted the task, knowing that if she ever hoped to sit upon the Throne of Roses, she would have to demonstrate her ability to fulfill the duties of the high lordship.

Sister Beli, her lady-in-waiting, circulated the room like a mother hen. The folds of her white dress spun this way and that as she sped from cot to cot checking restraints and evaluating patients. One sister was sent running from the room to collect fresh holy water, while another was commanded to pluck the petals of a living rose.

Sister Beli finally turned to Leta and curtsied. "All is secure and arranged to your liking, priestess."

Leta collected a basin of chilled water from one of the sisters. The water was infused with crushed rose petals, and took on a pink hue. When she was young, the smell of rosewater reminded her of summer, laughter, and joy. Lately, the cloying scent caused her stomach to turn; she was forced to swallow down her bile.

She cupped her hand, collecting some of the fragrant water, and spilled it across the brow of the first patient. The man's body should have been strong and robust, as he was in the prime of his life. Instead, he was bone-thin and covered with open sores, most of them self-inflicted. He licked his chapped lips as his eyes shifted lustfully over her body. Leta ignored the obscene leer and pricked his forehead with a thorn. Blood pooled in droplets.

"Fly spirit, and be free of all pain." She waited the allotted time, then pressed a rose petal to the wound with the palm of her pale left hand. The patient stirred, resisting the restraints that held him in place. "Blessed be the gods of Calaban," said Leta.

"Until the fates overcome us," said the man, reciting the obligatory reply. Somewhere, deep within the recesses of his tormented mind a memory of the past remained. *This is good*, thought Leta. *His soul might still be saved.*

She shifted to the next patient, a young man who had yet to lose all his vigor to the ravages of the Blackheart.

"He's been condemned by the court," reported Sister Beli as she looked over her ledger. "He stabbed his father-in-law and the constable who came to arrest him."

Leta nodded, accepting the information without question. Sadly, it was not an unusual tale. In any given week, over half the patients she saw were condemned by the court. She pricked the man's forehead, and for a moment starred into the man's lively eyes.

"Please, I have done nothing wrong." The man implored her with a sweet voice that hid the evil residing within his soul. "They call me a rebel, but all I've done is speak the truth. Why is the Throne of Roses so afraid of words? You cannot condemn me to death. This is murder!"

"Tsk-tsk," chided Beli, placing her hand over the man's mouth. "Silence your serpent tongue."

Leta had learned long ago that it was best not to speak with the afflicted. She fought off the sensation of pity and laid her palm against the man's forehead. "Blessed be the gods of Calaban." The man's body began to tremble as the baleful spirit trapped within came to terms with its fate. She walked to the next patient and began the sacrament anew.

If only this hand could truly heal, though Leta, as she pressed the pale flesh of her palm against the sweltering brow of a young mother.

"Blessed be the gods of Calaban."

The woman said nothing.

"She has eaten her tongue, my lady," said Beli.

Leta sighed and moved on.

The Hand of God is what the people called her. She knew such words were foolish and misguided, but her father insisted it was true. She had touched the Throne of Roses and survived. The throne broke most who touched it, yet Leta had passed the test relatively unscathed. Her left hand had turned ghostly pale, cobwebbed with white streaks, but she was otherwise without physical mark.

"Blessed be the gods of Calaban."

"Until the fates overcome us," said the next patient, a gnarled old woman many times Leta's age.

What few knew, not even her father, was that she was not the only one who touched the Throne of Roses on that fateful day. Meriatis had perched himself atop the throne, arrogantly believing himself ready to face the gods. There he sat still as a statue, lost to the world, until Leta pulled him off. In the brief time in which she was in contact with the throne she had seen something terrible, that even today, she did not fully comprehend. But Meriatis had sat upon the throne for several minutes before she grew brave enough to yank him free. An unprepared mind was not meant to commune with the gods, yet Meriatis had. Looking back now, Leta had little doubt that this was the moment Meriatis turned against the gods.

"Blessed be the gods of Calaban," said Leta, as she pressed a rose petal to the forehead of an elderly man who had skin like folded leather.

The afflicted patient responded by emitting a shiver-inducing cackle. "He is not your maker, but your master all the same," said the man in a venomous voice that echoed from the vaulted ceilings. "You will face him in time, and all will be brought to shame. He will smother the land with brimstone and spoil, and all who remain will bend their backs in toil." He lurched forward, pulling against his restraints with an unnatural strength. The leather bindings groaned, threatening to break. The Vacian Sister responsible for tending to the man rushed forward and looped a chain about the man's neck, yanking his head back against the table.

Leta cursed under her breath. She knew the rest of the afflicted patients would recite the exact same cryptic passage from the *Requiem of Cataclysms*. It was always this way. One would quote the book, then the others would follow suit. It was as if they were all of the same mind. Leta was finished.

She ordered Sister Beli to grant last rights to the remaining condemned. Sister Beli stuffed a cotton ball in each ear and dutifully went about the task without complaint. She passed from patient to patient, humming quietly to herself as she splashed rosewater and pricked foreheads, paying no mind to the tirade of curses that now filled the hall.

The only patient who didn't join in on the chant

was the man who had claimed his innocence. Tugging at his restraints, he looked about himself in absolute horror. Leta pitied them all, but there was nothing else she could do.

Leta bathed her hand in scalding water. Although her fingers throbbed from the heat, she held them submerged. Herald Cenna assured her that heat was the only way to cleanse oneself of the affliction's taint. Finally, when she couldn't bear it any longer she relented to her instincts, and dried her hands on her dress. She slipped a flesh colored glove over her left hand, concealing the scar the Throne of Roses had given her. Leta waited until Sister Beli was finished before departing from the monastery to report to Herald Cenna.

She found the herald in an adjacent courtyard. A dozen school children were gathered around the elderly man, using the courtyard steps as a makeshift amphitheater. They were listening with feigned interest as Herald Cenna droned on about the three branches of the Sundered Soul.

The students were all dressed alike in white togas that were carefully starched to hold their flat, rigid shape. Leta remembered wearing the exact same attire when she was a child; the togas felt like sandpaper against bare skin. She almost had to laugh at their unenviable position, seated as they were in the sweltering sun in a scratchy toga while Herald Cenna prattled on about nothing of interest.

When Leta was a child there were over five hundred students enrolled at the Royal Academy. Noble houses from all over the realm sent their children to the academy. Now, there were only a few dozen students in attendance. There was anecdotal evidence that families were simply having fewer children, but Leta believed the Blackheart was the true cause of the dwindling enrollment. So many children were dying from the disease that parents were afraid to send their children off to school. It made Leta sad to think that these children would not share the same experiences she had while a child. *I was raised in a time of hope, while these children live in a time of fear.* She shook her head. The gods seemed to understand nothing of fairness.

Leta leaned against a support column that was part of the covered walkway that ran the interior perimeter of the palace compound. The stone was cool against her back, a relief after spending the morning in the stifling hot monastery. On the far side of the open plaza she could the Sea of Ro spanning forever into the horizon. Waves were beating against the breakwater, and farther in the distance whitecaps foamed. A storm was rising in the east, great blooming clouds that rose above the gray water like anvils. She welcomed the breeze, certain that it would soon turn to rain. *Rain is purifying,* she thought. *This whole damned city could use a good bath.*

"You are all brittle twigs, dancing in the breeze," said Herald Cenna, lecturing to the group of bored students. "But as you age you will become as hard as oak or as wispy as the willow. Your souls will become resilient, and in time, you might even have branches of your own." His eyes were half-closed as he talked, and he looked likely to fall asleep at any moment. "Such is the nature of the Sundered Soul, it divides and expands, and it converges and collapses — an eternal cycle of death and rebirth. But it has not always been this way. Once, there was only a single soul, the One Soul as it were called. But it was broken asunder into its three essential parts — light, shadow, and fate." Herald Cenna splayed his fingers for effect, forming three branches sprouting from his palm. He wiggled his thumb. "The people of Merridia are children of the light."

One of the pupils eagerly waved his hand over his head and blurted out a question. "If we are all just branches of the same One Soul, what does that make the Cul?" asked the child, a blue-eyed boy with hair the color of sand. "Surely we are not related to those devils."

"I wish I could say you are right, but it is widely accepted that the Cul are the demon spawn of the Shadow," said Cenna, wiggling another finger. "All life exists somewhere along the web, the Cul included."

A little girl seated in the front row gasped and stuck out her tongue as if she had eaten something sour.

The blue-eyed boy snickered at the notion. "We're all related, eh?" He ribbed the student seated next to him with his elbow, a young girl with a sullen face. "You're great-grandsire might have been a Cul, Ionni. That would explain why your father is such an untrustworthy sot."

The victim of the accusation stood up and balled her fists. "If you don't stop running your mouth, I'll put my fist through it."

The boy began to cackle in the girl's face, which was a poor emulation of a Cul's call. The girl cocked back her arm and was about to punch the boy when Herald Cenna intervened. "That's quite enough, Ionni," said Herald Cenna, as he waded in amongst the children and separated the two. "Master Petrius, you can stand next to me for the remainder of the class. No complaining - you've earned this one."

Leta recognized the boy. He was Orso Petrius, the son of General Saterius Petrius. She couldn't help but think that the child had inherited his father's ugly face.

"To elaborate on Master Petrius's rude outburst, we are no more related to the Cul than we are the sharks in the sea and the birds in the sky," said Herald Cenna, keen on making this a teachable moment.

Leta had known Herald Cenna since she was a child, only back then he was Brother Cenna and the headmaster of the Royal Academy. She had once sat in the exact spot these children were in now and listened to Cenna lecture. At a later point in life, Cenna was the one who held her hand as they lowered her husband's body into a sarcophagus. Cenna was at her bedside when she gave birth to her son, and he stood beside her when her sweet child succumbed to the Blackheart. Cenna was a kind man with a gentle soul, yet with age came a brooding, and while he used to talk only of forgiveness and love, a breath of doom had now seeped into all of his sermons.

Dark words for dark times.

A moan wafted from beyond the wall that separated the monastery from the central plaza.

Leta grimaced. The Blackheart victims were being taken to Sir Rupert. The children began to tilt their heads this way and that as they tried to home in on the disquieting noise. A wet smack floated from beyond the wall, like an ax hewing green wood.

"Harrumph." Leta coughed loudly into her hand. "Herald Cenna, if I may interrupt." She nodded in the direction of the monastery.

"Hmm, ah yes! Of course, Priestess Leta. We need to talk don't we?" He waved at the collection of students, dismissing them with a flick of his wrist. "Go, have lunch. Report back at noon. I'm not done with my lecture on the One soul."

The students ran off as if they had just been released from prison. Leta kept an eye on the departing children to guarantee that Orso and the bullied girl went in separate directions.

When she looked back to Herald Cenna, she found that one child had remained behind, an older boy in his mid-teens. He hobbled forward on a pair of crutches and positioned himself obediently at Herald Cenna's side. The red sash he wore across his chest indicated he was a leech boy, a first year initiate in the Tiber Order. He was tasked with serving as Herald Cenna's assistant in the oftentimes unsettling task of transfusion.

"How many patients were there today?" asked

Herald Cenna, once the children were out of earshot.

"Twelve," answered Leta.

There was a second chop from beyond the wall, which caused Cenna to flinch.

"Twelve. Hmm, that's odd," said Cenna, thumbing at his chin. He was a member of the council that decided the fate of the afflicted. "I thought we sent you eleven. Jot that down, Treves."

Cenna's assistant rummaged through his pockets until he found parchment and a charcoal pencil. He struggled to balance on his crutches and write at the same time.

Herald Cenna sighed. "I'll have to check my notes when I get back to my study. If I remember correctly, there were a few nasty ones mixed in with this lot, victims with souls as black as night. I hope the blessing and final sacrament went smoothly."

Leta smiled sheepishly. She didn't wish to bother the old herald with her problems, but she had noticed an unsettling pattern. This was the fifth time the Blackheart victims had begun to recite that dreadful passage from the Requiem of Cataclysm since she took over sacrament duties from her father.

She was about to tell Herald Cenna as much

when she noted Treves was writing furiously. *He's recording a summary of our meeting*, Leta realized. She wasn't keen on having an account of her own inadequacies recorded on paper; Cenna she could trust, but there was no telling who else might get their hands on those papers. She sighed, deciding it was best to keep the information to herself for the time being. "All went well, herald," she lied.

"Good, very good. You're doing the work of the gods, you know. You are granting them a chance to rejoin the Sundered Soul cleansed of their sins, and more importantly cleansed of the Blackheart's taint."

"Do you believe that, herald?"

He appeared genuinely offended. "Am I not Herald of the Tiber Order? I would be a poor representative of the gods if I didn't stand behind the testaments of my faith."

"Then you believe that Meriatis is damned. A broken branch of the Sundered Soul, forever doomed to torment because he did not receive his final sacrament." In her mind's eye she envisioned the Sundered Soul as she had been taught. A core of light, brighter than the sun, from which sprung a million upon a million branches. Each tendril of light was a soul, an essence of life. Then she envisioned some of the tendrils of light growing dim and shedding from the core of light like cankered limbs dropping from a tree.

Cenna's lips pursed, and his skin creased along wrinkles he had earned from a long life of frowning. "I didn't say that."

"But you believe it," said Leta. The scratch of Treves's charcoal pencil grated on her nerves, and she had to fight the impulse to rip the parchment out of his hand. "You're a fatalist. You're resigned to the fact that not everyone can be saved."

"There are things we cannot change, and your brother's fate is one of them. We can remember him, both the good and the bad, and learn from his mistakes. It is our task to live a good life, graced by the fair gifts of our gods and tempered by the edicts laid out in the holy scriptures. We must check our desires, our wants, and our greed. Your brother failed in that regard, and thus his soul must pay an eternal price. So say we who have the faith."

"Until the fates overcome us," said Leta, under her breath.

"Until the fates overcome us," echoed Treves, as he continued to jot down notes.

"Until the fates overcome us," said Herald Cenna, nodding with satisfaction.

The first crack of thunder tolled overhead and large droplets of rain began to spatter against the cobblestone. Leta took this as her cue to leave. She curtsied and smiled, outwardly accepting Cenna's judgment of her brother. But in truth, she felt awful inside, like there was a cancer eating at her soul.

The problem was, she understood her brother's scorn for the Calabanesi. How could she love the gods while they let the Blackheart run rampant? How could she love the gods after they allowed her mother, husband, and son to die? It was in this thought that she came to a dark certainty about her faith.

I don't love the gods, realized Leta. *I fear them.*

Perhaps that was precisely what the gods wanted.

CHAPTER
VIII
LETTERS IN THE DARK

Winter upon the Sea of Ro came heavy that year. Snow drifts piled to the second floor windows of buildings, and for the first time in living memory many of the canals froze solid. Word from the west was even worse. Ice dams had formed on the Osspherus River, threatening to give way and flood the towns and villages downstream. The people of Etro reported that Mount Calaban had been hidden behind storm clouds since the start of the season. The flow of traders out of Emonia slowed to a pitiful crawl. Food prices soared.

Emethius hoped the harsh weather would cause people to hole up in their homes beside a warm fire and thus bring a sort of forced tranquility upon the city. That didn't prove to be the case.

Although the war was officially over, peace did not return to Mayal. Repercussions of the rebellion could be felt everywhere. Public trials were held for several of Prince Meriatis's co-conspirators. Most were executed, their hanging bodies left on display in the city's central plaza for over a month. Angry loyalists, seeing it as a demonstration of their faith to weed out the godless rebel sympathizers, picked up where the tribunal left off. Homes gutted by the fires of lynch mobs sat derelict and unattended, and on more than one occasion, the people of Mayal woke up to discover a tarred and feathered body swinging from what people were now calling the Hangman's Bridge.

The truth was, people were using the rebellion as an excuse to go after personal foes. Emethius imagined nine out of ten accusations were false. Foreigners and the destitute got it the worst. Entire families of runaway serfs were expelled from the city, accused of distributing rebel pamphlets. Their guilt couldn't be proven, but no one came forward to attest to their innocence either. Emethius was disgusted that the Court of Bariil did nothing to stop the madness, but the word on the street was that High Lord Valerius was doing everything he could just to keep his throne.

For his own part, Emethius decided to keep his head down. By killing Meriatis, he had made more enemies than he could count. Rebel sympathizers blamed him for the failure of their movement, while loyalists didn't trust him because he was once Meriatis's best friend. He doubted anyone had the gall to accuse him of being a rebel, but that didn't mean a lynch mob wouldn't descend on his house in the dead of night to enact the people's justice. Emethius made sure to always sleep with his sword close at hand.

Praetor Maxentius had suggested Emethius return to his family estate outside of Henna Lu until calm returned to the city. Emethius saw the wisdom in Maxentius's advice, but each time he prepared to leave Mayal, he delayed, lying to himself that he would only stay for a few more days. A few days turned into a week. A week turned into a fortnight. Then the snows came, and that settled matters. He wasn't going anywhere until spring.

"I should have left when I had the chance," grunted Emethius to himself on one especially cold winter night. The chill air had awakened the wound in his back, causing spasms to gallop up and down his spine whenever he tried to lay flat. Sleep wasn't an option, not with pain like this, so he spent the better part of the night stooped over in an old rocking chair nursing a glass of wine.

"Wouldn't be this damn cold in Henna Lu," he

muttered as he downed the last of the wine. Of course, if he went home there would be other unpleasantries to deal with.

He stared at the frost-covered window and contemplated whether or not he should open a second bottle, when there came a noise from the street. It was a soft scratching, like a shovel clearing a lane through the snow. Were it not the middle of the night, Emethius wouldn't have given it a second thought. He exchanged the empty wine glass for his sword.

The scraping sounded again, this time just beyond his front window.

No one should be creeping beneath my windowpane, especially not at this time of night. Emethius silently drew his sword from its sheath. The wood in the hearth had reduced to glowing embers; if someone peeked through the window, Emethius would go unseen, and if an intruder came through the door, they would likely head for Emethius's bed, thus exposing the would-be attacker's back to Emethius's blade. Such assurance did little to ease his nerves.

Emethius gathered his blanket about himself and stared long and hard at the door, waiting for the noise to return. *Screech.* It sounded like the claws of a cat grating against the doorjamb. His eyes focused like a hawk on the handle. The locking bar was in place, but he knew a swift kick was all it would take to break down the door. A flash of shadow suddenly darkened the crack beneath his door.

That was simply too much. Emethius was a trained soldier. He wasn't about to wait for someone to come barging through his door.

Emethius jumped from his chair, and rushed to the door. He was certain he would catch the culprit in the act, and he poised his sword ready to thrust. But when he threw open the door, he was greeted by swirling snow and an empty street.

Row houses formed an urban canyon for more than a hundred paces in either direction; Emethius doubted anyone could have fled with enough speed to slip from view. *Curious,* thought Emethius. He stepped out onto his landing to make sure he wasn't missing anything and immediately caught his toe. There was a hollow thud, and he fell sideways into the snowbank that had grown beside his stoop.

Discontent, freezing, and now covered in snow, Emethius rose and brushed himself off. He eyed the object that had tripped him. A small rosewood box had been deposited upon his top step. A piece of parchment was nailed to the lid. It read:

"*The Wayward Prince weeps for your sins. I watch you*

in his stead."

Emethius mouthed the words, and as he did a crippling anxiety washed over him. *The Wayward Prince.* His hairs bristled from gooseflesh, and he was suddenly seized by the unshakable sensation he was being watched.

As he retreated back into his home an even more unsettling realization came to mind. The snow in the street was smooth and un-trodden. Whoever had brought him this message had not left a single track.

. . .

At first light, Emethius ventured out into the snow-covered streets and made for Malrich's house. The lieutenant of the Red Company lived with his family in a small two room house near the waterfront.

Emethius gave the door a single hard knock and waited. He knew it would take Malrich several minutes to respond. Malrich was a proud man, and Emethius had little doubt that he would want to get his household in order before answering the door for an unannounced visitor.

On the far side of the door, bottles clanged and a broom swooshed. When Malrich finally opened the door there was sweat on his brow. "Emethius, what an honor!" he exclaimed. Malrich's eyes were black-rimmed, and his breath smelled of drink. Emethius noted several empty bottles near a toppled brazier. Malrich gestured for Emethius to enter. "What's possessed you to visit my home on such a gloomy cold morning?"

"Breakfast, of course," said Emethius with a smile. He held up a sack filled with rolls and cheese. "I've brought a treat."

Malrich accepted the food graciously, and gestured for Emethius to take a seat. It was a simple home, about as much as a man of Malrich's paygrade could afford. There was an open parlor in the front and a private bedroom in the back. Malrich began to busy himself, pouring drinks, setting out plates, and throwing a fresh log on the smoldering remains of a fire. Lively flames soon rose within the hearth.

Emethius dared a glance into the back room. The door was slightly ajar. Through the crack Emethius spied a women huddled under a fur blanket sitting in a wicker rocking chair. Her skin was stretched taut over the ridges of her cheekbones and the sunken hollows of her eyes. Her face was covered in scabs, and she was nearly bald save for a few patches near the base of her crown. She fidgeted endlessly with a scorched leather sandal, turning it over again and again in her hands. Her fingers were rubbed raw from the repetition. An elderly woman sat beside her, slowly feeding her drops of water from a sponge.

"How is she, Mal?" asked Emethius, looking away from the tragic sight. Malrich's wife had shown the first symptoms of the Blackheart three years earlier. Her deterioration had been slow but steady.

"She's worse than she's ever been, and better than she will ever be." He sighed wearily. "Ali's mind is fading, but despite outward appearances she is still physically strong. We can't risk leaving her alone — she might hurt herself. But don't worry about that right now, my mother-in-law knows what she's doing." He motioned to the elderly woman currently tending to Ali. Malrich smiled, acting as if this were all perfectly normal, and placed a stool in front of the table. "Please, have a seat."

"It's good to hear that Ali still has the strength to fight the affliction," said Emethius, not knowing what else to say. He plopped down on the stool and laid the rosewood box upon the table.

"What's this?" asked Malrich, eyeing the box shrewdly. The sigil of the Tiber Brotherhood was inlaid in the rosewood cover.

Emethius opened the lid, revealing a bound collection of parchments encased by a leather cover.

Malrich read the first page and his eyes flared wide. "This is Herald Carrick's journal. How did you come upon this?"

Emethius explained all that had transpired the night before. Malrich was flabbergasted.

"Why would someone want you to have this?"

"I'm not entirely certain," said Emethius with a shrug. "I couldn't sleep after my late night visit, so I spent the waning hours of darkness reading through the journal. Much of it is rambling concerning the Blackheart. There is a list of possible cures: worm stomach, dragon marrow, elk tears, immersion in freezing water, or better yet, fire." He couldn't help but laugh at the absurdity of the remedies. "They seem more likely to kill you than to help." Malrich didn't seem to find it nearly as funny.

Emethius awkwardly cleared his throat. "But look here, this is what really caught my attention." From the center of the book, Emethius produced a piece of folded parchment. He laid it out upon the table, revealing a hand-drawn map of Eremel. The crag of Mount Calaban was drawn at its center, from which radiated a series of circles. Calculations and underlined numbers were scribbled next to the names of major cities and towns. A hundred and five next to Etro. Fifty-seven beside Burrowick. Two hundred and twenty-three next to Caore. Emethius detected no pattern in the numbers save that they seemed somewhat proportional to each location's population. There were a few lines of poetry written beside Mount Calaban in a wavering hand.

> *Deep in the mountain*
> *In hollow roots underground*
> *In the fastness of Calaban*
> *The Shadow is bound*

"What do you make of all this?" asked Emethius, after allowing Malrich a moment to look over everything.

"This is a bunch of rebel doctrine," said Malrich, thumbing through the pages. "Maybe it's a trap. Someone probably took this off of Herald Carrick's corpse at Imel Katan. My guess — someone gave you this journal with the intent of ratting you out. Next thing you know, a pack of soldiers will show up at your door, accusing you of serving the rebel cause. This is all the evidence it would take for a tribunal to find you guilty."

At first, Emethius had come to the same

conclusion. He had almost thrown the wooden box, contents and all, into the fire once he discovered it belonged to Herald Carrick. But the message nailed to the top of the box read like a riddle. *The Wayward Prince weeps for your sins.* Emethius picked his words carefully. "Do you know the Legend of the Wayward Prince?"

"I was never one to pay much attention in school," said Malrich. He rummaged through the bag of food, producing rolls and a wedge of cheese.

"The Legend of the Wayward Prince is an old and sad tale," explained Emethius. "But the fact that this letter carries its name causes me to wonder. The legend concerns the eldest son of High Lord Leair. Prince Kein was the lad's name. He foolishly chased a Cul raiding party into the Great Northern Ador. Kein's host was ambushed, and he became separated from his men. Although his body was never found, most assumed the prince was killed. High Lord Leair even erected a great mausoleum in his honor."

"I've seen the mausoleum," said Malrich, handing Emethius a roll stuffed with cheese. He began to prepare one for himself. "It's down there near the east harbor. Covered in carvings of roses and the Calabanesi. It's empty, huh?"

"Not exactly," said Emethius. "A hundred

seasons came and went. On the eve of the fall harvest a haggard beggar suddenly appeared in the fields of Sirote, a small village located on the south shore of Lake Virta. The town folk tended to the beggar as best they could, but try as they might, they couldn't fully heal the man. It was as if there was a poison in his blood.

"In his few moments of lucidity, the beggar recounted a terrible tale. He claimed to be Prince Kein, and that he was held captive in the Great Northern Ador by a group of warriors that called themselves the Pirem Lu. The gods ordered the Perim Lu in all matters, and in exchange for their obedience, the Perim Lu were granted unnatural and godlike powers. The Perim Lu claimed dominion over the Northern Ador, and none who saw them ever escaped, save Prince Kein, who managed to gain his freedom by throwing himself into a river during a flood. The tale was one of the last sensible things the man ever said. Within a matter of days Kein grew wretched, and his mind was lost."

"The Blackheart?" Malrich raised his eyebrow dubiously.

"Perhaps," said Emethius, with a shrug. "Herald Carrick made such a claim in his journal." Emethius opened a dogeared page in the journal and pointed out a line of beautifully written script. "Carrick believed that Prince Kein, or whoever it was that emerged from the forest, was the first person to ever be afflicted by the Blackheart. His sources seem solid. The Tiber Brother responsible for providing care for the beggar took very meticulous notes. The man's symptoms were nearly identical to the Blackheart. The disease seemed to progress less quickly back then, and the beggar lived for many years under the care of this Tiber Brother. The townspeople of Sirote came to refer to the beggar as the Wayward Prince."

"Was the beggar actually Prince Kein?" asked Malrich

Emethius shrugged. "When word finally reached High Lord Leair that his son might still be alive, he sent a court steward to Sirote to investigate. The steward was convinced the beggar actually was Prince Kein, and even tried to bring him home to Mayal so that High Lord Leair could make the final judgment. Unfortunately, the beggar died on the journey. By the time they reached the Court of Bariil the body was beyond recognition. Even so, High Lord Leair took the steward at his word, and entombed the beggar's body in Prince Kein's mausoleum."

"So, Meriatis and Kein are alike?" asked Malrich.

"Each of them was doomed to madness by the gods."

"I don't know." Emethius threw his arms up in exasperation. "I would have never made the connection between Meriatis and Kein had I not received this message. I want to know who placed this package on my doorstep, and I want to know their purpose. I have a feeling that whoever is behind this, they're not done sneaking around my stoop."

"What would you have me do?" asked Malrich, clearly reading Emethius's intent.

"I would never ask you to abandon Ali..."

"You would never ask me to abandon Ali," Malrich agreed. "But you need a second set of eyes." He glanced into the back bedroom. Malrich's mother-in-law was feeding Ali a few grains of rice at a time. "Come night, Ali's old mum is a better caregiver than I am anyway. I won't be missed." Malrich rapped an empty wine bottle with his knuckle. "When do we begin?"

• • •

Emethius and Malrich approached the first few nights of their stakeout with stern military professionalism, each taking two hour shifts until dawn. The few false alarms they encountered resulted in the discovery of a small mouse and a startled drunk. When the fourth night came, Malrich brought two bottles of rum to liven things up. He offered one to Emethius.

"I haven't the stomach for the hard stuff anymore," said Emethius, gesturing to his now healed wound.

"Fair enough," replied Malrich, taking a swig straight from the bottle. "I guess my stomach will just have to do the work of two this evening." He earnestly went about the task of drinking both bottles, and probably would have finished the job had he not passed out toward the end of his second watch.

Emethius let Malrich sleep — as drunk as he was, Malrich wasn't really a viable watchman anyway. Besides, it would soon be dawn. Emethius's heart fell a little. He was so certain the culprit would return. His eyes began to feel heavy, and he found himself counting quietly to himself. There was a rhythm to it, a quiet tapping. *Tap, tap, tippy, tap.* His eyes snapped open, his mind roused to sudden wakefulness.

The tapping was coming from outside.

He held his breath and listened.

There it was again. That telltale *tap, tap, tapping.* He suddenly remembered now, he had heard it the night before. It sounded like a dog's nails grating against a stone floor. But the streets were lined in snow. No one walking the streets would make such a sound. It was almost as if...

He shoved Malrich so hard that the drunk oaf fell over in his chair and landed on the floor. He rose with a huff. "What do you think you're doing? No need to rough up a lad just because he fell asleep on the job."

Emethius placed a finger to his lips and pointed toward the rafters. Malrich's eyes grew wide. Someone, or something, was on the roof.

The tapping continued, stopping from time to time, as if the culprit had a moment of caution, before moving again. They followed the noise as it went from ceiling to wall, and then began to draw eerily near Emethius's front door.

Emethius slowly set his hand over the door latch. He mouthed the words, "*Three. Two. One.*"

He hurled open the door, and for a moment his eyes were locked only inches apart from two silvery spheres. There was a hiss, and then a flurry of movement as the culprit scrambled back up the wall. If Emethius had time to make sense of what he was seeing, he would have likely let the culprit escape, but he was acting on impulse, and he reached out and grabbed a hold of whatever he could. His fingers latched around cold scaly flesh. With his revulsion overpowered by curiosity, he thrust his weight around, like a man throwing a hammer in competition, and hurled the intruder into the far corner of the room.

Malrich slammed the door shut and barred the exit with his body. "What in the name of everything holy is that thing?" he blurted, recoiling in a mixture of shock and horror.

The intruder lay against the far wall in a tangled heap of tattered cloth. It kicked and flailed, righting itself, and spun around, flashing a row of jagged pearly teeth.

Emethius's first instinct was to run for the door, his hackles rising from the prospect of being locked in a room with whatever this creature was. Malrich, on the other hand, moved toward the beast with the type of fearless swagger one only possessed when drunk beyond reason.

"It's a giant fucking chicken!" yelled Malrich with a mixture of surprise and glee as he grabbed for the creature's neck. The beast hissed in response, and ran full speed toward Malrich, ramming its snout into the hapless drunk's chest. Malrich fell on his rump and the creature leapt over him. It scratched frantically at the locked door, turning over the knob with its tiny clawed hands.

Still lying on the floor, Malrich lunged after the beast and managed to grab the creature's foot. The beast spun around and chomped down on Malrich's wrist, drawing blood. "Knock the bastard out," yelled Malrich, as the creature sprang across the room, making for the window.

Emethius darted after the beast, but he was half-a-second too slow. Desperate to escape, the creature jumped headfirst into the window. The glass shattered, but the creature didn't quite make it through the window frame. Its legs floundered miserably in the air, the creature's torso hanging half in and half out of the apartment.

Using all his strength, Emethius grabbed the creature's tail, and with a twist of his body threw the beast across the room. It struck the wall snout first. The creature regained its feet and managed a few wobbly steps before Malrich brought Herald Carrick's journal crashing down on its head.

For a moment the two stood bent over in exhaustion trying to regain their breath.

"You didn't kill it, did you?" asked Emethius.

Malrich shrugged. "I don't even know if you can kill that thing."

The two cautiously approached the downed beast. Emethius used his foot to pull aside the tattered piece of fabric the creature wore knotted around its neck like a cape. Malrich was right; the creature actually did resemble a large bird, albeit a plucked one. Small tufts of feather-like scales hung awry all over its body, pulled loose in the scuffle. From the tip of its tail to the point of its beaked snout, the creature was almost as long as Emethius was tall. It didn't weigh much — not more than a couple stones. In truth, the creature was not much more than taut scaly skin stretched over a scrawny frame of muscle, sinew, and bone.

"Biggest damn bird I've ever seen," concluded Malrich. He rubbed at his wrist where the creature had bitten him. A matching pair of teethmarks ran on the front and backside of his arm.

"It's not a bird, you daft twit," answered Emethius. "It's a female dragon whelp. We have captured a dragon."

Malrich gave the creature a puzzled look as he sucked at the wound on his wrist. "Nope. That can't be right. Dragons are extinct."

"I'd say the history books are wrong on that one. Help me tie her up."

They bound the dragon as best they could, tying her legs like they would a hog. Malrich took off his belt and cinched it about her snout.

"What about her wings?"

They were disproportionately small when

compared to the rest of her body; Emethius doubted she could actually take flight. Just in case, he wrapped her upper torso in a blanket. Satisfied the dragon no longer posed any serious threat, Malrich and Emethius leaned back in their chairs and waited. This time, when Malrich offered Emethius a drink, he did not decline.

"What does a dragon whelp have to do with Meriatis and the rebellion?" wondered Malrich aloud.

"I plan on asking her that when she wakes up."

The dragon regained consciousness shortly before dawn. The beast remained as still as a statue — its shifting eyes were the only thing that revealed it was awake. The twin slits flickered between Emethius and Malrich, burning with hatred.

"Do you think we've treated you unfairly?" challenged Emethius. "You've come sneaking to my door like a stalker in the night. You're fortunate to still have your life."

The dragon's eyes settled on Emethius. It was like looking into an inkwell. Some base instinct in Emethius's head told him he needed to look away, to stare at the floor, and show submission to the beast. Emethius resisted the urge, and held the creatures baleful gaze. This seemed to please the dragon, and the corner of her mouth upturned in the slightest of smiles.

A dragon only smiles at its prey, Emethius reminded himself as he carefully removed Malrich's belt from around the dragon's snout. "Can you speak?" asked Emethius as he quickly moved out of striking distance of her jaw.

"I can speak in a thousand dead languages you would not comprehend," hissed the dragon in the old tongue.

Emethius struggled to keep his surprise from showing on his face. "Let's stick to the common tongue. That, and an explanation of why you are here."

The dragon flashed her teeth in a toothy grin. "I have come as a messenger of the Sage and Sorceress," said the dragon switching to the common tongue. She spoke with a heavy accent that bore twinges of the Tremelese dialect, but there was something else there as well. Something foreign. Something far more ancient. "I meant you no harm, although my treatment causes me to believe your intent is otherwise."

"You got better than you deserved," said Malrich. He raised his bloody wrist. If you try to bite me again, I'll be plucking those teeth right out of your skull."

Emethius ignored his friend's bluster and took

on a diplomatic tone. "If you are a messenger, do your job. Deliver your message."

The dragon's lips curled in a toothy grin. "In your hasty assault my letter was lost, although if you check near the door..."

Malrich was already on his feet. He held up a piece of parchment, and for a moment glanced over the text.

"What does it say?" asked Emethius, not taking his eyes off the dragon.

Malrich opened his mouth, but the dragoness spoke first. "The Wayward Prince awaits you. Find me at the Abbey of Atto Ifoire at midnight on the next new moon."

"That's in eight days," said Malrich.

"Indeed," said the dragoness. "Our paths have met too soon."

"But met they have," said Emethius. "Why reference the Wayward Prince? Does this have something to do with Prince Meriatis? And why did you leave Herald Carrick's journal on my doorstep." He held up the journal which now had a slight bend in the spine from Malrich using it as a cudgel.

The dragon clacked her teeth. "You will have answers to these questions when you meet me at the abbey."

Emethius frowned. "Why not tell me now?"

"It's not something I can tell," said the dragoness resolutely. "Its something that must be seen. The Sage and Sorceress would have it no other way."

"Well, perhaps we will just keep you here until your masters change their minds," said Malrich.

Emethius shook his head. "Other than sneaking across my roof and leaving cryptic messages at my door, you've done nothing that shows you have ill intent. I will meet you at the abby in eight nights." He undid her bindings. "If you have truly come as a friend, share with me your name and those of your masters. It's only fair that I know who I'm dealing with."

The dragon arched her back like a cat, stretching her lanky torso and limbs. She gave her wings a few test flaps. "In your tongue I go by the name Ftoril Bato Mason. If and when you prove your worth, you will learn the names of the Sage and Sorceress."

Then quite unexpectedly, the dragoness leapt the entire expanse of the room and darted through the broken front window.

Malrich watched the dragon disappear into the gloom. His disapproval was written plainly on his face. "We should have..."

"Don't say a thing," said Emethius, cutting him short. *We should have kept the dragon captive. We should have marched the beast to the Court of Bariil and turned her over to the high lord.* But something told Emethius that he needed to find out what the dragon was hiding. Her cryptic message had him intrigued. "Are you with me on this, Mal?"

"Aye, captain. I'm with you," said Malrich. He gave Emethius a lazy salute, settled back into his chair, and took a lengthy draw from his bottle of rum.

•   •   •

The great hall of the Abbey of Atto Ifoire loomed at the top of the bluff. The building lay in ruins. Its lone standing wall teetered on the edge of the cliff, pockmarked and defaced. Emethius imagined the slightest breeze could send it toppling over, yet the wind howled strong and steady and still the wall remained.

"It seems only fitting that this is where the little devil wished to meet us," said Malrich. He hitched his cloak up about his cheeks to stave off a sudden gust of wind. The chill bit to the bone, and Malrich's teeth gave a sharp chatter. "I can feel it. There's something wicked in the air."

Emethius had to agree; this truly was an evil

place, and his nerves were fraying with each passing minute. Midnight had come and gone, and Ftoril had yet to show her snarling face. Emethius compulsively rubbed at the vambrace that protected his left forearm. There were four deep lines gouged into the face of the hard leather, where there had once been three. *Meriatis,* mouthed Emethius, giving the new line a name.

The abbey was originally a monastery for the Vacian Order. Supposedly, the goddess Vacia led the Merridian pilgrims to the bluff upon which the abbey was built, and from that vantage, revealed the cluster of islands that would eventually become Mayal. Standing now atop the sheer stone bluff, Emethius could spy the dim city lights shimmering half a league in the distance.

In an age long since past, pilgrims from the farthest reaches of Eremel ventured to the abbey, hoping to bathe in the blessed waters of its bathhouse or feel the healing hands of the sisters who called the abbey home. But over the years, as the number of Blackheart victims grew, the abbey took on a more dire purpose. The Vacian Sisterhood was tasked with finding a cure for the blighted affliction. The sisters tried every possible concoction to cleanse the soul of the affliction's taint. Nothing worked, and countless patients died tormented deaths within the abbey's walls. It became a forsaken place, and its upkeep was ignored. Eventually the abbey began to crumble, much like the cursed souls it housed. The structure had been abandoned for more than a century. Its doors were left unbarred, and wild things moved in, replacing the patients.

"The Shadow creeps as it ever does, but I feel it here within these ruins most of all," said Emethius. "I'm getting tired of waiting. Let's go search the abbey. Maybe we're missing something."

He led the way into the abbey's waste. Its southern walls had collapsed, and its domed ceiling lay in heaps across its once grand hall. The abbey's bell tower still stood, but it tilted at an angle. Standing in the central courtyard was a lone statue. It was sculpted in the likeness of the Calabanesi, but its stone wings were sheared from its back, and most of the god's face had been chipped away by a vandal.

Emethius had only walked a few steps into the courtyard when a low hiss sounded to their rear. Both he and Malrich spun, seeking daggers they had concealed within their cloaks.

"Follow quickly," called the voice. The foreign accent left little doubt; it was Ftoril. A shadowed figure galloped across the court and clambered up a forested hill.

"Ftoril?" called Malrich into the night.

There was no answer, save the sound of clawed toes raking against stones.

"Let's go." Emethius hustled after the sound of pattering feet which was already growing distant.

The night was dark, without even a sliver of moon to help illuminate the way. Emethius slipped on loose rocks and caught his toes on hidden tree roots. Only a soft rustle in the brush signaled that Ftoril was still ahead of him. Finally, Emethius found himself atop a hill overlooking the abbey's ruined great hall.

"We are here as you requested, Ftoril," called Emethius. "It's time for you to hold up your end of the bargain — why are we here?"

"In time, in time." The small dragon bounded from the shadows and leapt into a tree, taking refuge in its boughs. "Merridian, ever wise, should know it is best not to rush things. Wait and be patient. You will see when it is time."

"And when will that be?" grumbled Malrich as he joined them atop the hill.

Ftoril did not respond.

Malrich plopped down on a rotten stump and and began to fuss with the lid of his canteen. Emethius repositioned his dagger so it could be quickly drawn and joined Malrich on the stump. The darkness was so absolute Malrich was little more than a shadow sitting beside him. Ftoril remained perched in the tree; the dim glow of her eyes was the only thing that revealed her position. Emethius let his hand slowly wander to the hilt of his dagger — just in case.

Emethius turned an ear toward the abbey. A muffled moan sounded on the wind. Or perhaps it truly was the wind. He didn't think much of it until the sound repeated itself, this time with more strength. Emethius jumped to his feet. The abbey was not as vacant as it appeared. No one spoke. All ears homed in on the sound. It grew louder with each passing minute — first a murmur, then a wail, and finally a loud braying cry.

Malrich couldn't take it any more. "Is this why you brought us here, to listen to a banshee howling in the night? The damn place is haunted. We'd be fools to linger. We need to go."

Emethius did not respond. A light flickered on the periphery of his vision, drawing his attention inland, away from the abbey and the sea. "They're coming."

A procession of torchbearers were walking along a path that ran directly beneath the hill upon which they were waiting. After spending so long in the dark, the torches seemed to shine as brightly as a beacon fire. Emethius felt inclined to shield his eyes, lest he lose his night vision.

"Quickly now," whispered Ftoril, leaping from her perch. She slithered along the ground like a serpent. Emethius and Malrich followed, staying low and quiet. She led them to a rock overhang that jutted above the path. They arrived just as the first torchbearers were passing by below.

There were a dozen in all. Each wore a black cloak that concealed everything but their face. A soft clank resounded with every step. The men wore mail beneath their cloaks, Emethius surmised, and if the bulge on their right hip was any indication, they carried swords as well. This was a formidable host of fighting men, but who were they off to fight, or what were they meant to defend?

Emethius got his answer when the middle of the procession passed beneath the overhang. There, flanked on either side by a guard, walked a bow-backed figure with a halting step. There, concealed in the darkest of night, walked Valerius Benisor, High Lord of Merridia.

The progression disappeared around a bend. The steady rattle of shifting steel faded into the ether, replaced once more by the pitiful wail drifting from the abbey.

Ftoril spoke in a hissing whisper. "Now you have heard the cry of a familiar voice and seen the light in the father's eyes."

"I-I saw him die," stammered Malrich. "The prince was as pale as a statue. He was set right through the middle by Emethius's blade. No, this cannot be true!"

"But it is," hissed Ftoril.

"Prince Meriatis lives," whispered Emethius. "I would not have believed one without the other, but I know that voice, and I would not mistake the face of my own high lord."

"This is witchcraft," challenged Malrich. "Some trick by the dragoness. We are being played, Emethius." His hand shifted to the hilt of his dagger, as if to remind Emethius that killing the dragon was still an option.

"The day I doubt my eyes is the day I lose my sanity," said Emethius. "We mistook death for something quite like it." He guided Malrich's hand away from the hilt of his dagger.

"So you did," said Ftoril. "For the Wayward Prince lives. He has been healed of all mortal wounds. But in the absence of light a gnawing madness has taken hold. The Blackheart runs rampant, and he has been all but consumed by the

Shadow."

The dragon is using you, reminded a voice in the back of Emethius head. *But how?* He tried to read Ftoril's face, hoping to catch any hint of a lie. "Why have you brought me here, if not to tell me that Meriatis can be saved and that my sins may be undone?"

Ftoril's white teeth shone against the dark of the night. "A cure, you mean? Yes, that is what I offer."

"Why?" asked Emethius. "Who are you to care about Meriatis's madness?"

"My masters care, so I care. It is as simple as that," explained Ftoril. She shrugged with indifference. "Surely this is something a Soldier of the Faith can understand. How many times have you killed because your master told you to do so?"

Apparently not once, realized Emethius. His hand involuntarily shifted to the fourth line he had scored into the leather face of his vambrace. He thumbed at the deep groove that represented Meriatis, wondering if he could rub it out.

Malrich tapped his foot with impatience. "This Sage and Sorceress, your masters, were they behind Meriatis's rebellion?"

"No," said the dragon. "Never anything so foul. The madness of the Blackheart drove him to rebel.

We tried to stop him, but once the war began there was nothing we could do." If Ftoril meant for her face to show anything other than indifference she failed miserably.

"Your story has more holes than a sea sponge has asses," said Malrich, jabbing Ftoril in the chest. "I see a darker cause in your heart than what you admit."

"As do I," said Emethius, certain the dragon was revealing as little as possible. He felt inclined to voice his opinion. "I do not trust you, Ftoril. Your toothy grin hides more lies than I can count, but as you well know, you have me at a disadvantage. My love for Meriatis is undying. I will do whatever is necessary to get Meriatis the cure, but if you betray me or the ones I love, I vow to hunt you until one of us is dead."

"With such an oath, you reveal yourself as the man worthy of this undertaking," said Ftoril. She bowed, sweeping out her stunted wings in a graceful arc. "I have told you the prize, but now you must agree to the price. As we speak a master healer is traveling from Chansel along the Silverway Road. He's supposed to arrive next week. Much ill can befall a lone traveler along the barren stretch that lies south of Estri. The poor soul will run afoul of bandits, I fear."

"Murdered?"

"Delayed," said Ftoril. "Fortunately for the afflicted prince, I stand before the master healer's replacement."

"Me?" wondered Emethius.

Ftoril nodded. "I need someone to sneak into the abbey and speak with the prince."

"To what end?" asked Emethius.

Ftoril hoped atop a rock so that she and Emethius were standing at the same height. "Before the madness took him, Meriatis had in his possession a trinket that my master holds dear. You need to find out what happened to it."

"What kind of trinket?" said Emethius.

"A sword, peculiar in design, with a blade as black as night and a fuller set with gemstones."

Emethius kept his face from showing any recognition, but he knew precisely the sword Ftoril sought. Meriatis had wielded that exact weapon when he battled Emethius atop the pinnacle of Imel Katan.

"Does the weapon have a name?" wondered Malrich.

Ftoril smirked. "It has had different names in different ages, but all roughly translate to the same thing. The blade that drives away the Shadow."

"Shadowbane," said Emethius, conjuring up the

title Ftoril would not say. "Shadowbane, the fabled blade that can make a mortal out of a god."

CHAPTER
IX
LADY MIREN

The Court of Bariil's interior was dark. During the day, its opaque windows seemed to suck all of the light out of the world, but at night it was as black as coal. The only light in the entire temple was from Leta's oil lamp. The seemingly endless expanse consumed the dim light. The ceiling high above was not to be seen. She tried to coax the lantern flame to grow, but it was only getting weaker. The growing knot in her stomach confirmed what she had already suspected — they shouldn't have come here.

"We need to do something," said Emethius. His voice was oddly calm as he paced a circuit around the central colonnade that wreathed the dais. He disappeared behind a column and reemerged on the other side, sometimes a boy, sometimes a man. He held a bloody sword in his hand, beset with gemstones that glowed with an unnatural light.

"Meriatis wasn't ready. I told him he wasn't ready. The throne is not a toy."

Leta nodded dumbly and followed Emethius's gaze to the Throne of Roses. For what seemed like an eternity, Meriatis had been perched atop the throne with his short childish fingers locked around the copper armrests. His eyelids fluttered in their sockets, and drool was beginning to dribble from his lower lip. There was an electricity to the air, and the hairs atop his head rose in defiance of gravity.

Don't touch the Throne of Roses. It was a simple rule, known for generations. The throne put a man in commune with the gods and would break the mind of the unworthy. But poor Meriatis, foolish child that he was, could not resist the temptation.

They had sneaked through the maze of tunnels beneath the palace complex in the middle of the night and broken into the temple through a ventilation shaft. Emethius had playfully challenged Meriatis to touch the throne. Not one to back down from a dare, Meriatis had plopped himself down upon the throne and declared himself the High Lord of Merridia. The smile on his face vanished the moment his bare flesh came in contact with the throne, replaced by a palsied mask of terror.

This was another one of Meriatis's cruel jokes,

Leta was certain. The boys took devilish glee in harassing her. It was just a myth that the Throne of Roses could break a man's mind. Her father sat atop the rough hammered copper every day, and didn't so much as bat an eyelash. Leta edged as close to the throne as she would dare and clapped her hand in front of Meriatis's face. Meriatis didn't even flinch.

"He's running out of time." Emethius pointed at Meriatis with the sword, redirecting Leta's attention.

Meriatis's pant leg had turned a shade darker. Urine began to pool in the seat.

"Blessed gods," she gasped. This was no jest — the stakes were truly life or death. Without hesitation she clasped Meriatis's wrists and yanked backward with all her might. Meriatis rolled forward from his seat like a sack of sand. But in that desperate life saving motion, the little finger of Leta's left hand came in contact with the throne's armrest. It was only for a split second, but the ensuing moment seemed to last an eternity.

A searing pain tore through her body. Every muscle seized at once. Then there was light, a blinding radiance hemmed by a sea of abyssal black. Leta swore she saw inky shapes squirming in the darkness, like the tentacles of a sea serpent trying to strangle its prey. But there was something else hiding in the gloom; something that forced the world on bended knee, something that broke the gods. It was grinning at her like a wolf. And when its lips parted the scent of sulfur filled her nostrils and polluted the air in her lungs.

The vision shifted, and Leta was suddenly outside the temple in the Grand Plaza. Standing opposite her was a plain looking man. Dark skin, a soft round chin, brown hair and eyes. One of the sea folk from Elyim perhaps. "I have only spoken the truth," said the man, softly, as if it were a statement not intended for Leta's ears. His eyes fell earthward, his face filled with resignation. Leta found herself overwhelmed by a sensation of pity.

The plaza was packed with onlookers — all of Mayal had come to see the spectacle. The man turned his back on the crowd, his face proud and certain.

Leta saw herself seated atop the dais beside her aunt. Lady Miren's mouth hung open, startled that this man would turn his back during the sacrament. She was horrified, in fact; she pointed at the man with her finger quivering in rage. "Seize him!"

The masses were spurred into action, and they began to beat the man with flailing fists. And still the man stood, impassive amidst a storm of rage.

Slowly he turned, or perhaps it was the world that was revolving around him. He met Leta's eyes and reached out to her, grabbing her left hand. The silk glove she always wore wicked away in a bath of glowing cinders, and his fingers locked around the white pallid flesh of her wrist. His grasp was like ice. His hand was dead, rotten, crawling with worms. Maggots spilled out of his eyes, and when he opened his mouth it was as black as a grave. "I have only spoken the truth," repeated the man. "Why is the Throne of Roses so afraid of words?"

• • •

Leta awoke gasping for breath. Her silk nightgown was soaked through with sweat, yet she was freezing. Her left hand pulsed painfully. Her arm had fallen asleep, tucked awkwardly beneath her pillow. She gave her hand a fitful shake, driving blood back into her fingertips.

"What an unusual dream," muttered Leta, as she rolled over and cast her arm across her husband's side of the bed, hoping to find comfort in his embrace. Her hand came to rest upon his cold pillow.

She grunted with annoyance, more at herself than anything else. A sane person would have gotten rid of the extra pillow long ago. She encountered enough reminders of her loss over the course of any given day — why she continued to torment herself at night, she could not say. Knowing she would find no more comfort beneath the sheets of her bed, she rose and prepared to face the day.

Leta's first order of business was not something she looked forward to. She was scheduled to join her aunt, Lady Miren Benisor, for breakfast. Leta took her time getting ready and purposefully arrived late, hoping to make the encounter as brief as possible.

She was not surprised to find Sir Rupert, House Benisor's master-at-arms, standing guard before the entrance to the royal dining hall.

"Running a bit off schedule, priestess?" asked Sir Rupert as Leta approached. He gave her a lazy salute.

"I found reasons to be delayed," said Leta.

Sir Rupert laughed. "I don't fault you one bit. Your aunt is a miserable sot. She's already three degrees off kilter and it's not even noon."

It was nice to know Leta wasn't the only person fed up with her aunt. She gave Sir Rupert a knowing smile. "People mourn in their own way. She's taken the death of her son especially hard."

"We all lost somebody in the rebellion," said Sir

Rupert with a shrug. "There's not much use in sulking about until the end of days, especially when you have a duty to do."

"Speaking of which, thank you for your help at the monastery," said Leta. "What I ask of you is especially awful. If it ever gets to be too much..."

"We Knights of Niselus are soldiers of Calaban," said Sir Rupert, cutting Leta short. "What I do in the name of my gods bears no weight on my conscience."

"I wish we could both be so strong in our convictions," said Leta, patting Sir Rupert's shoulder.

Sir Rupert smiled. "Enjoy your breakfast, priestess." He opened the door to the dining hall and bowed.

Lady Miren and her guests were already seated. They occupied one end of the grand table that ran the length of the dining hall. The whole table was set, enough chairs and plates to accommodate an entire company of soldiers, yet only five seats were taken.

Herald Cenna was there, his hands templed over his large belly. His leech boy, who never seemed to be far, was leaning against the wall scratching down notes on a piece of parchment. General Saterius was also present. His wolf cloak was folded over an adjacent empty chair. Across from him sat his wife, Lady Gwenn, and their son, Orso.

Gwenn was the only child of Praetor Maxentius. Although Leta and Gwenn were distant cousins, they hardly knew each other. As a child, Leta had always found the girl odd. On the rare occasions Gwenn accompanied her father to Mayal, she seldom came out to play with the other children, choosing instead to spend most of her time closeted in her room having one-sided conversations with her imaginary friends.

Gwenn was still young, hardly a woman at all. She had boyish features, slender hips, and short-cropped hair. The poor girl had terrible acne scars, which she tried to hide by wearing far too much makeup. Her eyes were like pools of black ink, the pupils overlarge, with hardly any iris to note. They gave her an otherworldly appearance. Still there was an elegance about her, an elegance that all of the decedents of House Benisor seemed to possess, no matter how far removed they were from the ruling family.

As it was with most marriages amongst the highborn, Gwenn's was an act of political maneuvering. Gwenn was Praetor Maxentius's only heir, and stood to inherit vast land holdings outside of Henna Lu. By uniting their two houses, General

Saterius and Lady Gwenn might one day be the wealthiest family in Merridia. This was not lost on Lady Miren, who doted over the pair's son as if he was her grandchild.

"Let the lad have his fill," said Lady Miren, sliding a serving tray brimming with biscuits and scones in front of little Orso.

Orso was gleefully kicking the bottom of the table as Gwenn tried to clean strawberry jam off of his face. "When is the next course?" Orso screamed. "I want more. Why do we have to wait for that sour old priestess?" General Saterius sat across from his son, but did nothing to intervene. Gwenn looked hopelessly out of sorts as she tried to rein in the squirming brat.

A child raising a child, thought Leta as she approached the table. She wondered if a smack from the sour old priestess might set the lad straight.

"Um-hum." Saterius cleared his throat loudly, notifying the others at the table of Leta's presence in the hall. His back was turned to Leta, yet somehow he knew she was there.

He misses nothing.

Leta lifted her lips into her best false smile as everyone turned to greet her. "How pleasant it is to see you all," lied Leta. "I'm sorry I'm late. I got caught dealing with matters at the monastery."

Lady Gwenn tucked away the handkerchief she was using to clean her son's face and stood, giving Leta the slightest of curtsies. *It will probably be the other way around in another decade*, thought Leta gloomily. With Meriatis's death, the line of Benisor seemed doomed. The way things were going, Gwenn's pig-nosed son might well be the next high lord of Merridia. *And I will be the old bitter crone that presides over the Vacian Sisterhood.* There was no dishonor in such a fate, but it was certainly not the life Leta had envisioned for herself.

Saterius kissed the back of Leta's hand. "You grace us with your presence, priestess."

"The honor is mine, general."

Lady Miren stayed in her seat — she was not one to inconvenience herself with courtesies. She was still wearing all black, even though the normal alloted time for mourning had long since passed.

"I'm glad you could make it," said Cenna, as he pulled back Leta's chair, seating her beside Lady Miren.

"I am always grateful for the invitation," said Leta as she eased into the chair. Her aunt lived in Chansel, the seat of her late husband's diocese, and had only recently ventured to Mayal to oversee her son's funeral. Leta assumed Lady Miren would return north as soon as she got her son's affairs in order. Yet fall had turned to winter, and spring was not far off, and here she remained. Leta was starting to wonder if Lady Miren was sticking around just to torture her.

Servants materialized from behind wooden screens, bearing silver trays brimming with food: boiled eggs set upon golden pedestals, a finely braised ham hock tenderized and stuffed with truffles, fruit tarts of all varieties, grilled trout covered with lemon slices. There were even apricot preserves mixed with goat cheese, a Chanselese delicacy. The chef had doubtlessly prepared the dish in honor of Lady Miren.

A trio of serving girls were standing behind Lady Miren, and seemed to only be there to serve Miren's needs. She vaguely remembered seeing two of the girls in Herald Cenna's class, but the third she wouldn't forget; it was Ionni, the girl Orso had almost gotten into a fight with. As if reading the wonder on Leta's face, Lady Miren gestured toward the girls. "Lovely things, aren't they. A Tosh, a Caird and a Tribold. I can hardly tell them apart — they all look so much alike."

The girls looked nothing alike, but no one bothered to inform Lady Miren of this fact.

"Girls, introduce yourselves."

Each girl performed a short curtsy.

"Awen Tosh," said the first, a girl with rosy cheeks and a cherub's face. She couldn't have been older than five or six.

"Bree Tribold," said the second. She was closer to Orso's age, although a great deal more mature it seemed.

"Ionni Caird," said the third. This girl was much older than the other two, a teenager on the brink of womanhood. She walked with a bit of a limp. Leta wondered if the girl ended up fighting Orso after all.

Miren chastised each of them for their form. "Stiffen your back when you curtsy, Bree. Cross your feet more, Awen. Make sure to bend at your knee, not your hip. Ionni, hold your shoulders level and straighten up that gimp leg of yours — a lady keeps her knees together."

Leta had to fight not to roll her eyes. Her aunt was such a mean old bitch.

"We'll have to work on their manners a bit," said Miren, turning back to the table. "It has been a joy having children in my house again. They keep my wine glass full and my heart merry. Isn't that right girls?"

"Yes, my lady," said Bree, seemingly eager to please.

Lady Miren had the girls very well-trained, it would seem. *Tosh, Caird and Tribold*; Leta mulled over the surnames. Each was the name of a minor household from the Estero River Valley. *The girls are hostages*, Leta realized with some disgust. Their families must have been too cozy with the rebel cause.

Miren smiled and patted Bree on the head. "Pleasant lasses, all of them, but they do have a twinge of the traitor's blood. That can't be helped. I fault them no more than I fault you." Miren placed her hand atop Leta's in a patronizing manner. "We can't be blamed for the actions of our loved ones."

Leta hid her ire behind a false smile. "I say let's eat."

Cenna fell asleep before a single bit of food passed his lips. Miren began to go through the wine as if she was dying of thirst. Saterius stared broodingly at his egg. Gwenn ate mouse sized portions of everything and never stopped talking.

Apparently a bundle of silk had arrived from Earnway, which Gwenn thought was of the utmost importance. "It is quite possibly the finest fabric I have ever seen," she insisted. "I will make sure to send a length to your seamstress." Leta did her best to seem grateful.

Almost as important was a Tremelese jeweler Praetor Maxentius had commissioned to make Gwenn a brooch to house a large amethyst. She balled her fist to show Leta how large the gemstone actually was.

Leta lowered her nose into her plate and shoveled food into her mouth every time Gwenn looked at her for input, grateful that it was considered impolite to speak with a full mouth.

"I am glad you joined us this morning," said Gwenn, patting her son's head. "Herald Cenna mentioned the other day that Orso was overdue for his evaluation."

"The test? I'm sure I'll get a perfect score," said Orso, bouncing up and down in his seat.

Gwenn slid a half eaten apple back in front of her son. "Please finish your food, darling, and let the adults talk." Orso responded by throwing the apple the length of the great hall. It splattered against the far wall sending pulp everywhere.

Lady Miren raised her eyebrows with disapproval. "*The* test? Orso is old enough for *the* test?"

"He turns seven next month," said Gwenn.

"I wouldn't have guessed," said Lady Miren. She smiled at Orso, revealing lipstick stained teeth.

Orso frowned in reply.

"I usually administer the evaluation around a subject's seventh birthday," added Leta. "They're old enough to understand what's happening, yet their emotions are still raw enough to rouse a spontaneous reaction. If they possess the Weaver's Blessing, it should manifest."

Lady Miren swirled her drink. "It's such a cruel little exam, but I'm sure Orso will perform admirably." She turned and looked at her trio of girls. "Have any of you been evaluated?"

Each girl shook their head.

"Why don't you include these three? You can test multiple children at once, can't you?"

"Yes," replied Leta. "But there are certain dangers."

"Don't be silly," said Miren with a dismissive wave of her hand. "Every adult at this table took the test, and we all survived."

"That's because we all failed the test," said Leta. "That is, except for Herald Cenna."

Cenna blinked awake at the mention of his name. "The test? Oh, yes, the test! I still bear a scar. Some in my order call it the Weaver's love bite. It's quite the badge of honor." He pointed to a spot on his neck. If there was a scar hidden within all of the crisscrossing wrinkles and folds, Leta could not see it.

"These girls are my wards, thus it is my decision," said Lady Miren. "I would be derelict in my duties if I did not have them tested. One of them might bear the Weaver's Blessing and we wouldn't even know it. Wouldn't that be a waste?"

"It is highly unlikely any of them bear the gift," argued Leta. "They haven't the bloodline for it." The Weaver's Blessing was hereditary, and seldom manifested outside of certain households.

"I would like them tested all the same. I would feel awful if I returned north with these girls and they hadn't been tested by the best proctor in the land."

Leta rolled her eyes. She administered the test no differently than anyone else.

"When will you be returning to Chansel?" asked Saterius.

"Soon," said Miren. "My business in Mayal is almost complete. I plan to be in Chansel for the spring equinox."

"What business would that be?" asked Gwenn innocently enough. "I thought the affairs concerning Lord Fenir's estate were settled. Is there some other business you are attending to while in Mayal?"

"I am making sure my son receives justice," answered Miren with a bitter laugh.

The air seemed to be sucked out of the room, and everyone eyed Miren with disquiet. Miren never spoke of her son, not since the funeral, and now she was talking about justice. *What kind of justice?* Leta wondered.

Herald Cenna began to busy himself with his place setting. "Yes indeed, justice for everyone. Hmm... well... this is a fine breakfast. Pass the the ham, would you?"

"What do you mean by justice?" asked Leta.

"The tribunals are growing fewer and farther between," said Lady Miren, as if it were common knowledge. "General Saterius has done a wonderful job tracking down the leaders of the heresy. The last few who remain free have gone into hiding. Still, I think we will have them all locked in fetters within the next few months. The tribunals will finish up shortly thereafter."

Saterius was stone-faced, and showed no indication that he knew what Lady Miren was talking about. He kept staring at the untouched food on his plate.

Leta felt dizzy. "You're holding tribunals? For whom?"

"For that little rebellion your brother perpetrated," snapped Miren venomously. "We are a land of laws; laws that were passed on to us from the gods of Calaban, laws that are necessary for a civilized society. Your brother and his heretic comrades violated those principles. Or have you already forgotten?"

Leta had not forgotten. She wanted to punch the smug look off of her aunt's face. "The war is over," said Leta, using the calmest tone she could manage. "Those responsible have already been brought to justice."

"Are you sure of that, dear? We are getting close. We've held three..., no four dozen trials now. Each name seems to lead to another."

"Why haven't I heard of this?" said Leta, growing sick to her stomach.

"You don't wander through the forest shouting at the top of your lungs when you're hunting vermin. You set traps, and you bide your time. So I have set many traps, and I wait and I watch, and when an ignorant little rat wanders into my snare..." She clapped her hands together, causing everyone to jump in their seats.

Gwenn clamped her hands over Orso's ears. The boy looked thrilled by the prospect of hunting rebels. "Lady Miren, if you would please refrain from such talk in the presence of my son."

Lady Miren did not refrain. She raised her hands above the table like a puppeteer controlling a marionette, splashing her wine all over the table in the process. "Once I catch a rebel, I set a leash about their tiny rebel neck and I let them wander around for a while. I see what other holes they go sniffling about and what rebel friends they go visit. And when the time is ripe the leash becomes a noose." She downed the remainder of her wine, and raised her hand for a refill. The Tosh girl's hands were shaking as she refilled Lady Miren's cup. This seemed to please Lady Miren. She pointed at Leta. "You and I are alike, Leta. We have both lost husbands. We have both lost sons. You, too, would seek revenge if you had the chance."

We are nothing alike, Leta wanted to scream in reply. Miren was spiteful and mean and nasty. Miren sought comfort through the pain of others. Then again, maybe she was right, maybe Leta would seek revenge if it were actually a possibility. But who could she seek revenge against? The gods? Leta looked down at her plate, finding herself more frustrated with each passing moment. "We shouldn't be hunting people now that the rebellion is over, I'm sure of that."

"What if we miss just one rebel? Hmm? Ideas are like cancer, we cut it out, or it grows and takes on a new life, corrupting everyone around it." She motioned to Saterius. "Tell her. Tell her what you found the other day."

Saterius bit his lip, clearly unhappy that he had been called upon to contribute. "We found a whole apartment filled with pamphlets. An old blind women owned the place. She said her nephew would come and go with other men. She had no idea what they were up to. We got her nephew, but his companions slipped our trap."

"You're hunting after people because they are making pamphlets?"

"We're hunting after people because sedition is dangerous, priestess." Saterius's voice was calm, but his eyes were glowering, revealing a part of him Leta had not seen before. Leta had heard rumors that Praetor Maxentius used Saterius like a meat cleaver when needs arose. Some men were all bluster, and some men were silent until they acted. Her father had taught her to fear the latter.

"Maybe the rebellion was a test from the gods," said Leta, turning back to Lady Miren. "Perhaps the Calabanesi wanted to see if we would do the right thing. We are supposed to forgive and move on."

Herald Cenna nodded. "What did your father say during the service in the Grand Plaza? Seek not vengeance against the sword bearer of the rebel cause, nor wish doom upon their kin, for those too are sins, and thus our fall will only be greater."

"How can we move on while the perpetrators of the rebellion, the men who killed my son, are still out there conspiring about our downfall?" demanded Lady Miren

Leta wanted to remind Lady Miren that half-a-dozen faceless men wielding crossbows killed her son, not some specific rebel who had so far eluded her snare; Leta decided such words would be unwise.

"If you want to see what sedition can do," continued Lady Miren, "go north to Estri. See the empty farmland. See what remains of the city. The girls can attest to it." Miren waved for her wards to step forward. "Go ahead, tell Priestess Leta what happened to your homeland."

Ionni Caird was the only one who could manage to get a word out — the other two girls looked like they were on the verge of tears. "All that remains of Estri is the Temple of Tiber and the city keep. The rest is gone. We could see it burning from five leagues away. We stood out on the terrace of my father's estate and watched the fire all night. When morning came, it was like there was a second sun." Ionni's voice was calm and level, but the hatred simmering in the her eyes was undeniable.

"Is that not proof enough of why every last

rebel must be brought to justice?" said Lady Miren.

Leta sneered. "Need I remind you, Estri was a rebel stronghold, not a loyalist bastion. I've heard from reputable sources that the city was set on fire by Soldiers of the Faith long after the rebels were driven out of town."

Lady Gwenn gasped. "This is seditious talk. How can you say such vile things about our fair soldiers? They have taken vows before the gods."

Herald Cenna nodded in agreement. "It's true, priestess. You must watch what you say. Too much wine. Sometimes it loosens our lips and we say things we do not mean." He reached across the table and collected Leta's glass.

Leta scowled. Not a single drop of wine had passed her lips. She stood up, having heard enough.

"I am the Priestess of Vacia," snarled Leta. "My father is the High Lord of Merridia. My line has sat upon the Throne of Roses for a dozen generations. I am the state. Or have you forgotten this? One cannot commit sedition against themselves."

This brought all conversation to a close. Gwenn glanced down at her feet. Orso began to drum his little hands against the table, looking from one adult to another, clearly hoping the fun would continue. For once Herald Cenna looked thoroughly awake. His leech boy was writing furiously on his piece of parchment. Lady Miren seemed more than pleased with the outcome of the breakfast, and she motioned for her wards to fetch her more wine. Only Saterius smiled.

The general leaned back in his chair and eyed Leta as if he was just now seeing her for the first time. It was a cold, creeping stare that cut to her core. "Your brother was also the state, Priestess Leta, until he was not," said Saterius bluntly. "You'd be wise to remember this fact."

• • •

Leta was still furious when she went to bed that night. She tossed and turned, and when she finally did slumber, the nightmares were back, this time more vivid than before. Meriatis sitting atop his copper throne quaking as urine ran down his leg. Lady Miren pointing an accusative finger in Leta's face. The man from the memorial service standing with his back turned in opposition of the gods.

"I have only spoken the truth," said the man, staring Leta dead in the eye.

Leta awoke. The sun was just beginning to peek above the horizon, and a cold hard certainty came with the new day. The man in her dreams — she now remembered why she knew his face. She had seen him in her monastery strapped to a table. He claimed innocence even as Leta granted him his last rights. She cringed as she envisioned the wet chop of Sir Rupert's ax.

He was a clean soul, realized Leta.

But if the man was not afflicted with the Blackheart, how did he end up in Leta's monastery? The horrible truth thundered through her like a poison.

"Oh, precious Vacia, what have I done?"

Lady Miren's tribunal was the answer. She was funneling her convicts through Leta's monastery, using the Blackheart to hide the purge.

"How many?" she gasped. Her patron god was silent in reply, yet Leta knew the truth. Dozens and dozens, that was the tally Lady Marin gave. Leta had performed the last sacrament on dozens of clean souls. Unable to bear the thought, Leta leaned over the edge of her bed and vomited.

CHAPTER

X

THE MADNESS OF THE WAYWARD PRINCE

Emethius couldn't tell where the ocean ended and the sky began; they melded together in the blackness of night. The stars were concealed behind a low curtain of clouds. The waxing moon was vacant from the sky.

Dressed in a gray wool cloak, Emethius was nearly invisible. The sea rolled black around him, lapping against the hull of his skiff and spraying him with near freezing water. His hands were numb before he finished navigating through the maze of half frozen canals that coursed through Mayal. By the time he reached the open waters of the bay his clothes were completely soaked.

I'll be of little use to anyone if I freeze to death, thought Emethius as he turned the skiff's prow into an oncoming wave. The sea was rough, and the undercurrent created by the surge of water flowing from the mouth of the Estmer River threatened to pull him out to sea. It took all of his strength to keep the mainland in sight. His destination, the abbey of Atto Ifoire, was located on the far side of the bay. As the bird flies, it was only half-a-league away, but with the current behaving as it was, it might as well have been a hundred miles.

I'm losing a yard for every two I gain. Emethius doggedly pressed onward and soon was sweating despite the chill.

The dragon whelp Ftoril wove a treacherous web with her intriguing tale. He believed the dragoness when she said Meriatis was alive. What's more, he had seen the fabled blade Shadowbane with his own eyes, so he knew she wasn't lying about that. It was the risk that bothered him. If Emethius's actions weren't treason, they were very close. Conveniently for Ftoril, she had convinced Emethius to assume all the risk. He would be the one tortured for information if things went ill. He would be the one dangling from the hangman's gallows. *But I am also the one responsible for thrusting a blade through Meriatis's gut.* The guilt was unshakable.

Emethius grit his teeth with resolve and pressed onward. After what seemed like an eternity, the far shore finally came into view.

Ftoril was waiting for Emethius on the beach.

"The healer is expected soon," said the dragoness. "Come quickly." She led him to an outcrop of rock that offered concealment and began to hand him objects for his disguise — a hooded fur cloak, a sheer headscarf, a few religious totems, and a collection of thimble size bottles filled with elixirs.

Emethius looked at the objects queerly. "How did you come by these things?"

"They're all authentic, I assure you." She flipped a large medallion inscribed with wards in the air, catching it between her claws. "Old superstitious tools of an old superstitious trade. You couldn't cure a cold with these relics, let alone the Blackheart."

Emethius took off his drenched cloak and was about to put on the cloak Ftoril had offered when he recoiled with shock. Ftoril had handed him a cloak constructed from dozens of fox tails sewn end to end. "This is the cloak of a master healer!"

"I overtook the healer a few miles north of Mayal," said Ftoril, as if the truth should have been obvious. "These are his personal effects."

"You said the healer would be delayed, not killed!" Emethius dropped the cloak in disgust, suddenly feeling faint.

Ftoril swooped forward, catching the cloak

before it fell on the ground. "Careful. Don't be rash." She brushed wet sand off of the hem. "I have bound the healer in a cave. He has a fire to keep him warm and bread and water to keep him nourished. I intend to set him free before the night is through. I thought you understood the stakes."

Emethius glared at Ftoril. "Which stakes: that Meriatis be cured, or that the precious blade you seek be returned to your master? My priority and yours are not the same."

Ftoril waved her clawed finger dismissively. "They are one and the same, you are just blind to the web that has been so carefully woven." Ftoril draped the cloak over Emethius's shoulders, then stepped back and gave his disguise a critical eye. "You look the part, but now you must act the part. Can I trust you?"

Emethius sighed. "Yes, you can trust me." He filled his pockets with the healer's possessions. *I need to set all doubts aside. I have one job — get the information and get out with my head still attached to my body.*

"They will expect the healer to arrive on a horse. The beast is tied to a tree. Ride into the ruins of the abbey's great hall. They will see you before you see them. The ruins are guarded by the high lord's most loyal, hard men who would sooner stick you with a blade than take you alive. If your disguise fails, you will likely die. Keep that in mind." Ftoril explained what Emethius had to do once he was taken to the prince. When she was finished with her directions, she handed Emethius a small glass vial containing a milky white fluid.

"Make Meriatis drink this. It's not a cure, but it will provide him with a few minutes of lucidity."

Emethius popped open the cork topper and gave it a sniff. It smelled like burnt hair. "What is it made from?

"Dragon horn," said Ftoril, tapping a stub of a horn on her head. Emethius hadn't noticed it before, but the missing horn gave Ftoril's head a rather lopsided look.

Emethius placed the vial in his breast pocket. "Dragon bone was one of the remedies Herald Carrick mentioned in his diary. How much more would I need for a cure?"

"For that, you'd need to boil the flesh off my bones, grind my skeleton to dust, and produce a gelatin from my marrow."

Emethius raised an eyebrow. "That's not an impossibility."

"Why don't you give it a try," said Ftoril, baring her teeth.

"Perhaps another time," said Emethius, taking

the healer's horse by its lead. He mounted the horse and began toward the abbey. The horse was a fair breed and well-trained. It calmly plodded along the path as if it already knew the way. Snow began to fall, great big flakes that floated lazily toward the earth. He pulled the hood of the stolen cloak over his head. The fox tail cloak was shockingly warm, almost to the point of being hot.

Such a cloak cost a small fortune, Emethius knew, and was well beyond the means of a Tiber Brother. Members of the brotherhood swore an oath of poverty when they became acolytes, forswearing any claims to inheritance or family fortune. Healers were awarded these cloaks when they attained the title of master. There were only a few dozen master healers in Merridia, and they all took orders directly from the herald of the Tiber Brotherhood. That could only mean one thing; the healer was sent at the behest of Herald Cenna.

It was the first time Emethius considered who else knew Prince Meriatis was alive. High Lord Valerius only had a handful of trusted allies, and amongst them, probably only a select few knew of Meriatis's fate. If the great patron families of Merridia ever found out, they would demand the prince's head. If High Lord Valerius refused, there would likely be a new rebellion, this time with a more assured result.

The abbey's court appeared much like it had the week before, vacant and silent. The damaged statue stared down upon him like a sentinel. Emethius's heart quickened. Wherever the guards were stationed he could not see them.

A voice called out, the words echoing through the ruins.

"*Lep dis re?*"

"*Pasio di fet, vipapi op pajlr,*" responded Emethius in the ancient tongue, reciting precisely what Ftoril had told him to say.

There was no response, only silence. Ten seconds, thirty seconds, a minute passed. A cold shiver worked through Emethius's frame. His hand crept toward the dagger he had concealed in his cloak. If this was a trap, he wasn't going down without a fight.

Quite unexpectedly, a fissure broke in the eastern face of the abbey's lone standing wall. Light poured through the crevice, revealing a tunnel that snaked down into the earth. Resisting the fear now screaming in the back of his mind, Emethius dismounted his horse and squeezed through the entrance.

The second he broke the threshold, a pair of strong hands grabbed him from behind and threw him face first into the earthen wall of the grotto. He was groped from head to foot; every pocket was checked, every trinket critically examined.

"He's armed," said the man, holding up Emethius's dagger.

"Would you ride the North Road without a weapon at hand?" said Emethius, managing to speak despite the rock wall against his face. "The war may be over, but the countryside is still crawling with rebels."

"Heretics," corrected the guard. "Call them what they are. The title rebel gives them an air of righteousness they do not deserve."

"Let's have a look at him," ordered a gruff voice.

Emethius was spun around to face his captors. There were three in all. The man holding him against the wall had a crooked nose and a slanting jaw. The man to his left had bright hazel eyes the color of the sea. *This one is highborn,* thought Emethius, although he did not recognize the man. The third had a twinge of a western drawl, and had a glob of engroot stuck in his cheek. They were all dressed in the clothes of commoners, woolen trousers, plain tunics. Slant Jaw wore a leather jacket, the other two wore fur cloaks. Each had a short sword hanging on their hip.

"Where is Master Fayec?" demanded Slant Jaw. His hand was clenched like a vise on Emethius's shoulder. Emethius was going nowhere until he provided a satisfactory answer.

"Master Fayec fell from his horse and broke his leg," Emethius lied.

"That shouldn't be a problem for a healer," snorted the man sucking on engroot. He spit yellow saliva at Emethius's feet.

"It is for one as inept as Master Fayec." Emethius gave the men his best toothy grin. "I'm his replacement. Here is a letter from Master Fayec. You will see that it bears the brotherhood's seal." Emethius handed the guard the sealed note, which Ftoril had wisely forced the healer to write. "Now please, gentlemen, do not foolishly delay me any longer. The hour is late, and I've traveled a weary road. Let me complete my task and be gone."

Slant Jaw passed the letter over his shoulder to the man with hazel eyes. *He is their leader*, Emethius surmised. The man read over the passage and made a queer expression at the end. He was obviously not satisfied. His tone grew harsh. "Then who are you?" he growled.

"Master Finian," answered Emethius, hoping that was what it said in the letter. "I serve the diocese of Vel Katan."

"My cousin has a butcher shop in Vel Katan," said the westerner. "The name's Agnan Fangir. You know him?"

"Perhaps I know him, perhaps I don't," said Emethius, growing bold. "Remember, gentlemen, this is all hush hush business we're dealing with. I'm not actually here, and if I had to guess, neither are any of you." He shrugged off Slant Jaw's hands and pushed past the guards. "Enough with the inquisition. Where is my patient?"

The hazel-eyed man smacked Emethius in the chest with the letter. "Tell Herald Cenna he's a fool for not telling us there was a change of plans. You're lucky to leave here with your life."

"Tell him yourself," said Emethius as he collected the letter and slipped it into his coat's inner pocket. "Herald Cenna plans to join the high lord the next time he pays his son a visit."

"Visiting the abbey would be ill-advised," said Hazel Eyes. "But who am I to tell the herald what to do? This way, please."

"The patient's condition has worsened since the last healer's visit," explained Hazel Eyes as they made their way deeper into the earth. The tunnel was narrow and the ceiling low. Emethius had to stoop to avoid hitting his head. There were numerous tunnels that branched off from the main path. Most were half flooded with stagnant water. He spotted sleeping quarters, a barely serviceable kitchen, and passages sealed off by rusty iron bars. In more than one alcove he spotted the dull glint of rusted shackles hanging from the wall. One room contained the weathered skeleton of a torture rack. Emethius grimaced as he imagined what the Vacian Sisters did down here when the monastery was still in use.

"He won't eat more than a few nibbles of food — he's growing frailer by the day," said Slant jaw. Nobody referenced Prince Meriatis by name. "It's no use trying to reason with him, the madness has run too far along its course. He's thrown his shit pail at me more times than I can count. And the things he mutters when he's looking at you with those cold dead eyes..." He gave his body a hard shake. "It just gives me the shivers."

They stopped before a heavy wooden door — the only door Emethius had seen in the entire tunnel complex. "We had to chain him up," explained Hazel Eyes, as he turned over the lock. "We won no favors from the high lord, but we didn't have a choice. The patient is growing more violent. I advise you keep your distance."

Emethius gestured for the door to be opened and breathed deep, preparing for the worst. He wasn't ready for the smell. He recoiled as the nauseating stench of refuse struck his nose. Raising the cuff of his cloak to his face, Emethius stepped inside the room and investigated the space.

A lone candle lit the room and it took Emethius a moment to adapt to the darkness. He made out the dim outlines of three figures, two near the door, and a third shackled to the far wall. The room itself was much like the tunnel — earthen walls and ceiling, reinforced by wooden beams. A collection of soiled animal furs were strewn across the floor. The only break in the drab interior was a potted plant, drooping woefully atop a stained mat near the wall.

The chained figure didn't seem to notice Emethius. He sat cross-legged near the plant, plucking at its leaves one at a time. He would crease each leaf down its center, then with slow, purposeful motions he would peel away each segment of the leaf until nothing remained but the stem.

How is this my prince? Emethius had to fight the cold panic that was working through his body. Only a few months had passed since Emethius saw Meriatis. How could he have deteriorated so quickly? *You put a blade in his gut, remember?* nagged a voice in the back of his head.

"I need to be alone with my patient," said Emethius, doing his best to keep his voice calm.

The hazel-eyed guard shook his head in response. "It's not safe, master."

"The gods watch over me, I will not be harmed." Emethius crossed himself in the gesture of the faithful. "There is a sacred trust between patient and healer. It would not be appropriate for others to be present."

"Master Fayec never wanted to be left alone with him."

"Aye? Well look what Master Fayec's ineptitude has accomplished." Emethius pointed at Meriatis, his finger quivering with genuine rage. "Out, all of you! I need silence and solitude to work my craft."

Hazel Eyes nodded to the two guards tasked with watching Meriatis. They both shrugged with indifference and exited the room. "I warn you, keep your distance from him," said Hazel Eyes as he shut the door.

Emethius waited until he heard the men strike up a conversation in the hall. "Meriatis," he whispered. "Can you hear me, friend? It's me, Emethius."

Meriatis made no response. He was focused on the newest leaf he had plucked from the plant. The Blackheart was a disease that poisoned the mind, but not the body, leaving behind a vacant shell that could live long after the soul was gone.

Is there anything left of Meriatis behind those cold dead eyes? Emethius cautiously edged closer to Meriatis, uncertain how dangerous his friend had become. "I'm here to help," said Emethius.

Meriatis slowly turned, revealing features so different Emethius hardly recognized him. The prince was shrunken and malnourished. His cheekbones stood out against pale and blotchy skin. His hair was matted, and clumps were missing in places. But the most striking feature was his eyes; they had turned from a radiant hazel to a sickly black.

"I... I hear y-y-you," said Meriatis. His voice was foul, and drew from his throat in fits and starts. Meriatis's hands groped in Emethius's direction. When his grasp met nothing but empty air, a look of rage came over him. "Come! Come to me!" he screamed, his voice screeching like a dying pig. He frantically swung his arms, until finally his hand came to rest against the potted plant. He seemed to find some comfort in this, and resumed plucking at the leaves.

"He is not your maker, but your master all the same," sang Meriatis. "You will face him in time, and all will be brought to shame. He will smother the land with brimstone and spoil, and all who remain will bend their backs in toil."

Emethius watched Meriatis continue on like this for several minutes, plucking leaves and singing his cryptic song. Finally, Emethius couldn't take it any longer. He reached within his cloak and pulled out the vial Ftoril had given him. Particles of what Emethius assumed were dragon horn had settled to the bottom. He gave the vial a hard shake, causing the white flakes to stir like snowflakes.

"I need you to swallow this," said Emethius, placing his hand on Meriatis's back. The sudden stimulus was too much for the prince. He leapt atop Emethius like a cat pouncing on its prey. He growled viciously and bit down on Emethius's shoulder.

Emethius impulsively opened his mouth to cry out in pain, but he caught himself. He couldn't alert the guards outside. Instead, he threw his weight backward, slamming Meriatis against the wall. The air burst from Meriatis's lungs in a loud *umph*. His body fell limply to the floor. Emethius quickly subdued Meriatis by putting a knee on either of his wrists. Meriatis howled and spit and champed his teeth, but it was simply no contest; in his current state Meriatis was weaker than a child.

Emethius pried open Meriatis's jaw and forced

the vial into his mouth. The liquid poured in, causing Meriatis to sputter and choke. Emethius clamped his hand over Meriatis's mouth so none of the elixer would spill back out. "Drink it. Drink it!" he hissed. Meriatis's resistance weakened then stopped altogether. His ragged breathing eased. His eyelids drooped. The tonic was taking hold.

Emethius cautiously released Meriatis and stepped back. "I have given you a healing tonic that will drive away the madness for a while. Do you understand what I am saying?"

Meriatis groaned and blinked with surprise. "Emethius? Why are you here?" He tried to crawl forward, but was halted by his chain. Dumbfounded, Meriatis stared at his shackles and tugged weakly at the chain. "Why am I here?"

"You're sick, Meriatis," said Emethius. He was suddenly seized by an over-powering feeling of pity. How was it possible that his friend had been reduced to this. Emethius looked away and tried to explain what had happened. "It's the Blackheart. You've been like this for some time. The dragon whelp Ftoril said you were alive. I didn't believe her, I didn't want to believe her. Yet here you are."

A light of recognition showed in Meriatis's face. "The Sage sent you." Meriatis frowned, as if he had just made a horrible realization, and he began to paw at Emethius's cloak. "I have been poisoned, Emethius, and it grows stronger every day. I fear I'm losing myself."

"The Sage and the Sorceress offer a cure, but we haven't much time," said Emethius. "Ftoril claims you stole something, a sword. You must tell me all you remember before the tonic wears off."

"Shadowbane." Meriatis snickered at the name. "They weren't willing to use it. I was. So I took it from them. I... I..." Meriatis doubled over, grabbing at the side of his head. An expression of pure agony contorted his face. "There were so many of them. Tentacles, black as night. They were everywhere!" His eyes flickered about the room in terror. "Behind the walls, above the ceiling, beneath the floor. Inside me!" He lowered his face against the floor and sobbed.

There was a sudden rush of footsteps beyond the door. The guards were running away from their post. Something was amiss. The urgency of the situation fell on Emethius like a sack of stones.

Emethius lifted Meriatis's chin so that he had no option but to meet Emethius's eyes. "Listen to me, Meriatis," whispered Emethius. "The sword you tried to kill me with at Imel Katan, where is it?"

"Tried to kill you? What are you talking about, Emethius?" Meriatis's eyes lolled backward. His eyelids fluttered. His voice took on a drunken drawl. "Do you remember what I told you at Imel Katan?"

"Meriatis..."

"The Calabanesi," continued Meriatis. "We bow and we pray, granting them the undeserved title of god. And in doing so, we have become slaves to our own creation. They are poisoning us with the Blackheart, Emethius. They plan to harvest us all like pigs."

"Meriatis, there isn't time," urged Emethius.

"But it can be undone, Emethius. We just need the right tools. The right weapon. The right blade."

"Yes, the sword! Where is the sword?"

Meriatis pounded his fist into the ground. "We can destroy them. We must destroy them. It's the only way to keep the Shadow at bay."

The hiss of drawing steel resounded beyond the door. The door's heavy latch began to turn over. The guards had returned.

"I must know," pleaded Emethius.

For a moment Meriatis's eyes were once again hazel, but the expression on his face was so pained and sad. "They took it, Emethius. The voices took Shadowbane from me. It is lost."

A guard burst into the room.

"You need to get out!" It was the guard with the

western drawl. His sword was drawn.

"But the healing is not finished," stammered Emethius. He waved his hands in the air, copying the motions he had seen true Tiber Brothers make when they performed blessings. "I need a few more minutes..."

"You'll leave now or I'll run my sword through your gut," growled the guard, clearly in no mood to negotiate.

Something was terribly wrong. *They know I'm a fraud.* The thought tore through Emethius's nerves like a bolt of lightning. *They know I'm a fraud, and I don't have a way to defend myself.* He eyed the guard's sword.

Even if the guard knew Emethius wasn't a healer, he likely didn't know Emethius was a trained soldier. Emethius might be able to overwhelm the guard with a sudden attack and wrestle the weapon from his hands.

Emethius rose to his feet and slowly turned to face the guard. His attack would have to be quick and devastating. But just as he was about to pounce, Meriatis grabbed both of Emethius's ankles and pulled his legs out from underneath him. Emethius fell flat on his face, and before he knew what was happening, Meriatis sat astride his back. Ftoril's tonic had not lasted five minutes!

The crazed prince raked Emethius's face with his nails, scratching him from forehead to cheek. Emethius rolled and tried to shove Meriatis off. Meriatis responded by reaching inside of Emethius's shirt and clawing as his abdomen; it felt like Meriatis was trying to rip out his entrails. Emethius kneed the prince in the groin, but it had no effect. Finally, the guard intervened, yelling and cursing as he pulled Emethius and Meriatis apart. Meriatis collapsed back into his corner, growling like a wild beast.

"Get up," ordered the guard. He smacked Emethius in the back with the flat of his blade to emphasize his point.

"I've done nothing wrong," cried Emethius. He pointed at Meriatis. "If you stop the treatment now you will condemn the patient to madness."

"He already is mad," growled the guard. "And we have bigger problems to deal with today. Let's go."

Two more guards were waiting out in the corridor. They took up position behind Emethius. Emethius looked over his shoulder to see if there was a friendly face among the pair. He was greeted by menacing stares. Outnumbered and without a weapon, there was nothing for Emethius to do but comply. If they let him live, he might be able to get word to High Lord Valerius and plead his case. That wasn't likely though. The guards would probably execute him in the courtyard, that is, if they didn't question him on the torture rack first.

They led him straight to the grotto's exit. Emethius was pondering whether that was a good sign or a bad one when he was greeted by the most unexpected sight. A burly dwarf stood in the middle of the abbey's courtyard holding a bloody cloth around his hand. He paced to and fro cursing wildly. Emethius's eyes widened. *I know this man.* The stricken dwarf was Sir Rupert, the master-at-arms of House Benisor.

Emethius ducked his head, hoping to conceal his face from the master-at-arms. Sir Rupert had known Emethius since he was just a small child chasing Meriatis around the palace grounds. The knight was the first person to show Emethius the proper way to hold a sword. There was zero chance Emethius could pass by Sir Rupert unrecognized. *I'm absolutely and truly screwed.*

"The little bastard got Ol' Rupert's thumb," snickered Slant Jaw, pointing to the opposite side of the courtyard.

There, snarling like a cornered dog, lay Ftoril trapped beneath a weighted net. Half-a-dozen guards, all draped in cloaks as black as night, ringed

Ftoril with leveled spears.

Ftoril began to gnaw at the netting, fraying it to ribbons in a matter of seconds. She managed to snake her snout through the gap. A guard tried to correct the behavior by bringing the steel toe of his boot across her snout. This set Ftoril into a berserk rage, and she probably would have torn through the netting had Sir Rupert not yanked a spear out of the hands of a subordinate and cracked Ftoril squarely across the brow. The hard oak staff broke in two from the force of the blow and Ftoril immediately went limp. Sir Rupert spit on the unconscious dragon and clutched his thumbless hand.

"Get out of here," hissed Sir Rupert, redirecting his rage toward Emethius. "We've arranged boarding for you at the Sallyport Inn. I expect to see you back here at first light."

Emethius kept his face pointed toward the ground, hoping the darkness of night would continue to conceal his true identity.

"Look at me, boy."

Emethius lifted his head and their eyes met.

"Say not a word of this to anyone," said Rupert. "Not a word about the abbey, not a word about your patient, not a word about the dragon. Got it?"

"Y-y-yes, sir," stammered Emethius.

Rupert turned away, preoccupied with his missing thumb.

For a moment Emethius stood paralyzed to his spot. He didn't know what to do. Ftoril was the key to Meriatis's rescue. Without the dragon to carry his message, how would this mysterious Sage and Sorceress ever know of Meriatis's condition? They wouldn't, Emethius surmised.

A second dark thought entered Emethius's head; Meriatis wasn't the only life at stake. A master healer was tied up in a cave somewhere waiting to be set free. The healer would die without Ftoril. Emethius's only option was to turn himself in and reveal to Sir Rupert that Ftoril had kidnapped the healer. In doing so, he would doom Meriatis, but the prince was probably doomed either way.

Emethius took one step forward and opened his mouth as if to speak, but as he did, cowardice seized him. The words tumbled from his mouth in a single indiscernible croak. All eyes turned on Emethius.

"You got something else to say?" demanded one of the guards.

Emethius shook his head and walked away, turning his back on Meriatis, Ftoril, and the healer he never met. It was the most selfish thing Emethius had ever done in his life, yet he hadn't the strength to act otherwise.

He mounted the healer's horse and rode north along the wooded path. As soon as he fell out of earshot of those at the abbey, he kicked his heels into the horse's flanks, driving the beast into a blinding gallop. Overhanging branches raked at his face, the wind tore at his ears, but still he drove the horse faster and faster. He had to get as far away as possible, or the horror of what he had just done would force him to turn around.

The scar in Emethius's back began to itch. *No, something is actually scratching me,* Emethius realized. Something coarse was tucked into the hem of his pants and was rubbing against the small of his back. Emethius reined in the horse, drawing the beast to a skittering halt. To his surprise, he discovered a piece of folded parchment shoved halfway into his pants. His mind raced back to the moment when Meriatis attacked him in the grotto.

"Meriatis placed a message on me in the scuffle!"

He squinted, straining to see what was written on the parchment. Moonbeams suddenly flared through the tree, and for a moment the parchment was cast in light. Emethius was forced to stifle a gasp.

The parchment contained an image drawn with

blood. It was a poor illustration, but even so, Emethius recognized the image immediately. It was nearly identically to the map he had discovered in Herald Carrick's journal, save one exception. There was a large 'X' drawn near the western coast of Eremel. Four words were written beneath the 'X', the very sight of which chilled Emethius's heart.

'*Wasa vapaj*, w*asa tupwae*,' it read in the ancient tongue.

The message was clear. *Find the Sage, find the cure.*

CHAPTER
XI
MALRICH

Ali watched intently as Malrich worked the peas into mush with a spoon. She treated Malrich with a rare gummy smile and crept to the edge of the bed for a closer look. Just before she was able to reach him, the leather thong that tied her to the bedpost drew taut. The restraint always puzzled her, and she looked at it nonplussed.

"I'll take it off in a minute," Malrich reassured her as he added chopped carrots to the bowl. *Food suitable for a baby*, thought Malrich glumly. But it was all his wife could eat.

Malrich had to start putting his wife in restraints after she randomly attacked him in the middle of the night with a red hot fire poker. Fortunately, he managed to wrestle the searing iron bar from Ali's hands before she inflicted any permanent harm. That incident marked the end of Ali having the freedom to roam about the house at will. The affliction had polluted too much of her mind for her to be trusted.

Ali's mother moved into the house a few weeks after the incident, asserting that Malrich was not capable of caring for his sick wife. *She was probably right about that*, thought Malrich as he eyed his emaciated wife. Ali had no muscle or fat to speak of. Every bone in her body stood in stark relief against her liver-spotted skin. Malrich had grown used to how frail she looked — she'd been like that for over a year now. What troubled him were her eyes. The pupils had somehow consumed the iris, leaving behind black pits as dark as jet. It was inhuman, almost bestial. When their eyes meet, he found himself looking away more often than not.

Malrich tried a spoonful of the carrot and pea puree. It was hardly palatable, but it would suffice. Satisfied, he upturned a small vial of tar colored fluid into the bowl. He had purchased the vial of poppy milk from the apothecary earlier in the day. The apothecary wasn't precise on the measurements. Malrich added a dash more just to be sure it served its purpose.

He removed the restraint from Ali's wrist, finding that the flesh beneath was pale and sweaty. He massaged her wrist, working the flesh until the blood flow returned to normal. When he finally released her, Ali spun about on all fours atop the bed, like a dog let loose from its kennel. Finally, she settled, and sat cross-legged atop her soiled mattress. A low cackle issued from deep in her throat as she watched the food with keen focus.

"Dinner is served, my love," said Malrich, trying to ignore the unsettling noise his wife was making. He held out the puree, wondering how his wife would respond. Half the time she would grab a handful and throw it in his face. Other times she would refuse to take a bite. Thankfully, she grabbed the bowl as if it were a prized possession and began to slurp down the puree in noisy gulps, groaning and growling as she consumed every last bit.

Within minutes the poppy milk began to take hold. Ali's motions became slow and feeble, until finally, she curled fetal and clamped her afflicted eyes shut. She reached out to Malrich and made a pitiful noise that might have been an attempt at speaking. He held her hand and pulled her body against his own.

"I will sit beside you until you fall asleep," said Malrich, as he cleaned the food from her lips and chin. He hummed softly and then began to sing.

> *"O' where have you gone*
> *Sweet lover of mine*
> *To the white misty bay*

Or the eternal forest of time

Rest easy my love
I forget not my word
Your shadow does linger
Your light shines in my world

The echo of soft laughter
A smile on your face
The touch of your skin
Your warm loving embrace."

He gently stroked her fevered brow, humming and singing in turn. Ali closed her eyes and her breathing slowed. He noted she had picked open a half-healed sore above her left eye. *I'll have to remember to put ointment on that before I depart*, thought Malrich as he continued to sing.

"Though fate had decided
For us to part ways
When weary my bones be
We'll meet again one day

Seasons come and seasons go
But do not lessen the loss
Gray stone and graven words
Are now greened over with moss."

Ali's chest began to rise and fall in regular

intervals, and she started to softly snore. Malrich stayed at his wife's side a while longer, clasping her withered hands. They were no longer the firm hands that had once held their son. Hideous scars ran from her fingertips to her elbows, burns she received the day her mind finally succumbed to the madness.

Certain that the poppy milk had done its job, Malrich eased himself out of bed. He gently rolled her on her side, just in case she got sick in the middle of the night, then slipped mittens over Ali's hands to keep her from scratching herself while she slept. He added fresh coals to the brazier to make sure Ali would stay warm. Lastly, he reattached the leather binding, this time fastening it to her right ankle. He made sure to switch between her wrists and ankles every other night. The binding would gall her flesh if left in one place for too long.

He walked out into the common room. Ali's mother sat perched in an old rocker by the hearth, working at her stitching. "She's set for the night, Minelle," reported Malrich.

Though in her late middling years, Minelle still possessed a certain grace and beauty. She had a full figure, olive skin, and short-cropped blonde hair. Her blue eyes were piercing, which she used to great effect whenever she was mad at Malrich, which was often.

Minelle made it readily apparent that she blamed Malrich for her daughter's sickness. She did not believe Malrich was good enough for Ali, and it was his corrupting influence that led to Ali's affliction. Never mind that Minelle's husband had died of the Blackheart a decade earlier. If anything, the sickness ran in her family's blood, but no sensible words would change Minelle's opinion on the matter.

Malrich almost believed that Minelle had moved into the house just to haunt him. The resemblance between mother and daughter was uncanny, and Minelle's mannerisms and intonation reminded Malrich more of his wife than he would like to admit. Minelle was what Ali would have become had the Blackheart not driven her to madness. Sometimes, when Malrich came home at night he would spot Minelle's silhouette against the window, and for a split second he would imagine Ali was waiting for him on the opposite side of the door.

Minelle didn't bother to look up from her stitching when Malrich entered the room. She was adding a red trim around the edge of a wool blanket she had been working on all winter.

"Red agitates Ali." Malirch thumbed at the spindle of thread she was using. It was the color of blood.

"Red has been her favorite color since she was a babe."

She's not a babe anymore, Malrich wanted to say, but neither was she an adult. So what was she? *A shell*, thought Malrich glumly. "It will upset her, is all. I think somewhere deep down it reminds her what she's done." He made his rounds about the house as he talked, shuttering the windows and adding a fresh log to the fireplace.

"Don't try to be sly," said Minelle, pointing a wooden sewing needle at him. "I see what you're doing, checking to see if everything is set for the night. Where do you think you're off to at such a late hour? There are ill humors in the air."

"No more so than there are in here," said Malrich, grabbing his coat. Malrich had heard the rumors, too. There was a pox out of Tremel. A Tremelese galley had crawled into port the other day with half of its crew dead. The port wardens had quarantined the vessel and forbidden anyone to come ashore. "I'm not going anywhere near the docks. I'm going to get a drink."

"Isn't that a surprise. You've already killed my daughter and grandson. I have no problem in you speeding up your own demise."

Malrich didn't feel clever enough to respond. He

grabbed his coat. "You know where to find me."

Minelle snorted and returned to her stitching.

•　•　•

Malrich took a seat in a booth at a tavern in the southern district near the Royal Port. A great open hearth heated and illuminated the space. Ventilation was poor, and the tavern's half-rotten ceiling was stained black with soot. There were more names carved into the tables and walls than there were men in the second legion. Malrich's own name was carved into a stall located near the back of the establishment. That was where he usually sat, but tonight he chose a table by the front door, positioning himself so he could keep an eye on the tavern's lone window. The window overlooked one of the few canals in the city that wasn't locked up with ice, thus making it the only sensible route a small watercraft could take if it were returning from the southern end of the bay. Emethius would have no choice but to return this way from the abbey.

The tavern was packed, filled with a sundry mix of Emoni and Tremelese sailors. On any other night, Malrich would have spent the evening telling jokes, sharing stories, and drinking until he was sufficiently drunk; but not tonight. He kept his head down, eyes trained on the window. Even so, he couldn't help but overhear the conversation from a nearby table.

"The Shadow has been especially bad along the Barren Tracks this year," reported a sailor out of Ulmer. He had the strong muscular forearms of a rigger. "The Stygian mines have been closed for the season. Mark my words, the price of silver is going to spike."

"I'd rejoice if I had a single coin to my name," said a one-eyed riverboat captain. He was a regular at the tavern and rented a room upstairs. "But work has been hard to come by. The Estmer's still icebound north of the Bend. Half my men have broken contract and joined up with whalers. I'll be lucky if I can pay my port fee come spring."

"The ice will free up soon, and you'll wish it hadn't," said the rigger. "Cul raiders were spotted on the south shores of Lake Virta last fall. By now they've likely moved into the foothills of Mount Calaban."

"Lies, lies, and more lies," said the one-eyed captain. "The Cul haven't been spotted west of the Morium in a thousand years."

"Have you been alive long enough to know that for certain?"

"I've been alive longer than you, you green-eared bastard."

"That's true, and you have the senility to prove it!" The other men at the table laughed.

"You'll find boys to man your oars once the season turns," said a sere old trader who spoke with a thick Chanselese accent. "Work's drying up everywhere. I just led a team along the Silverway. There are thousands of homeless wintering in the ruins of Estri, and enough displaced farmhands in the Estero valley to man every ship in the Elyim fleet ten times over. They'll all come south looking for work once the snow melts. A day's work won't fetch a man a penny by the time summer comes."

"That is, if the pox doesn't arrive here first," said a dwarf from a nearby table. He was so hairy, the only part of his face Malrich could see were his eyes and bulbous nose. "It'll cover you from head to foot in weeping sores, and your lungs will be so clogged with phlegm you'll drown on dry land."

The old Chanselese trader nodded gravely. "Karl Moch had just recalled his fleet to Morsegoroth when I departed. My guess is that he's trying to outrun the plague."

"There's no doing that," reported a young dwarf who looked half sick himself. His brow was covered in a fine sheen of sweat and the whites of his eyes were twinged with yellow. "The pox is running rampant in Hearstead and Delos, killing highborn and lowborn alike. Before we set sail, King Calmer was threatening to shut down trade until the plague abated. The cap'n said we were the last ship out of port. We made calls at Mier and Inglestead, and found much the same. Mass graves, bodies being burned. The pox will make its way across the Sea of Ro, sooner than later, I'd wager."

"The gods have already given us a plague," muttered Malrich from his stoop. All eyes shifted upon Malrich. "Your pox sounds like a godsend compared to the nightmare that haunts the homes of Merridia, a sweet release from the ravages of the Blackheart. Should we be so fortunate." Malrich took a long draught from his mug.

"*Hear, hear!*" called the one-eyed captain. Many of the other talsani within earshot nodded their heads in grave agreement. The Tremelese sailors grumbled amongst themselves in their own tongue, sounding their disapproval, and one dwarf was even so bold as to spit at Malrich's feet. Malrich shrugged the insult off. They would never understand. The dwarven people were somehow immune to the Blackheart, although no one could say precisely why. They would never see their loved ones driven to madness. They would never have to make the stark choice of life or death, to allow the madness to worsen or condemn their loved one to the headsman's ax.

Malrich finished his beer, then ordered another, and then another after that. *To hell with staying sober*, he thought, as he finished his fourth. At some point in the evening, he must have fallen asleep, because he awoke under the heavy glare of the tavern owner's eyes. One quick survey of the room revealed that Malrich was the only patron left.

"What are you still doing here, Mal?" growled the owner. The owner's nose was twisted sideways, the result of his propensity for instigating fights. He clenched his hand into a fist, causing his big flat knuckles to take on the shape of a gavel.

Malrich groggily wiped the sleep from his eyes, looking from crooked nose to clenched fists and back again. "I ought to be going."

"Aye? And I ought to pummel you for loitering around my tavern all night," said the owner. "Get out, now!"

"My apologies," said Malrich. He fumbled blindly in his pocket for some coins and threw whatever he had on the counter. He stumbled from the tavern half-asleep. His joints were stiff, and his mind was foggy from a hangover, but the cold air sent a sudden jolt of wakefulness through his body.

He had not meant to spend the entire night at the tavern. Minelle would be furious with him, and rightfully so, but he couldn't go home, at least not yet. He had to make certain Emethius was all right. He hurried down the street toward Emethius's house.

Three years earlier, on a not so dissimilar morning, Malrich had stumbled home hungover and sore from spending the night asleep in a cramped barroom stall. When he opened the front door of his home, he discovered the entire house reeked of charred meat. At first, Malrich thought Ali had simply overcooked breakfast, but when he looked into the fireplace his heart broke.

Sometime in the middle of the night Ali's mind gave way to the madness of the Blackheart. There was no telling how long his little boy had been lying there in the hearth, and in truth, it didn't really matter. His son was gone.

Malrich would have killed Ali that awful winter morning had the neighbors not intervened. By the time they finally broke down the door and pulled Malrich off of Ali, he had beaten her face bloody. But when they saw what she had done, all judgment left their eyes; they couldn't fault a father for acting as he did. They left Malrich alone to finish what he started.

But he couldn't finish it. Not Ali. Not the love of his life. She lay on the floor, her swollen eyes filled with terror. She didn't understand what she had done to deserve such punishment. That was the way it was with the Blackheart.

His neighbors' intervention had brought with it a stark sobriety. He sat there all day, a bottle in one hand and a knife in the other. "*It will be quick*," he kept telling himself. "*It's either my knife or a headman's ax.*"

Finally, with the setting sun casting light across his broken home he did the only thing he had the courage to do. He carried his battered wife to bed, tucking her in like an invalid. Then he carried his son to the Soul Weigher to receive his final sacrament. It was the last time Malrich set foot in a temple.

Malrich was not without blame. He should have never trusted her alone with their son. Ali showed symptoms of the Blackheart long before the incident. The blanching of her olive skin. The darkening of her blue eyes, that had once been the color of ice. He shook the image from his head. It was easier to remember her as she was now. *Ali is dead, it is only her body that remains.*

• • •

The streets of Mayal were nearly barren as Malrich hurried toward Emethius's home. A fishmonger walked by, eager to haul in his lines and see what the night had brought. A Tiber Brother rushed past, running late for the dawn prayer. His bald head steamed in the chill morning air. In the distance a bell tolled, welcoming the arrival of the sun. The gray stone pavers took on a fiery hue.

What Emethius didn't know, what he could never know, was how close Malrich had come to joining the rebellion himself. The ideas that led to the rebellion had been simmering just below the surface for as long as Malrich could remember. One only needed to visit the watering holes near the docks to hear that the people were not doing as well as the lords and priests would have everyone believe. The Blackheart was running rampant, and the common folk were losing faith. They were losing faith in High Lord Valerius, who claimed that the Blackheart was a scourge sent by the gods to separate the sinners from the saints. They were losing faith in the theocratic system, with its six holy dioceses and the venal aristocracy that propped them up. But most importantly, they were losing faith in the Calabanesi.

In taverns late at night, Malrich often gave a sympathetic ear to men and women espousing the virtues of the rebel cause. He understood their anger and frustration. But when swords were finally drawn, he stayed loyal to the oath he had taken when he became a Soldier of the Faith. But that was when he still thought Herald Carrick was the leader of the rebellion. Had he known about Prince Meriatis, things might have gone differently. *The whole damn war might have gone differently.* Thousands upon thousands would have rallied to the banner of the young and charismatic prince. The old order would have fallen. Malrich could only wonder what would have risen in its place.

He rounded the corner of Emethius's street and stopped dead in his tracks. Three city watchmen were loitering near Emethius's front door. A sudden fear welled in Malrich's heart. What if Emethius was captured? His panicked mind raced through countless scenarios. Would Ftoril be on the hunt to quiet anyone who knew about the prince? Would Emethius give them Malrich's name? And if Malrich was arrested, what would the court do with Ali? The thought gave him shivers.

Malrich lowered his head and pulled his cloak flush with his cheeks in a vain effort to conceal his face.

One of the watchmen stumbled into the middle of the street and began to make lewd gestures toward his companions, all the while shouting about his conquests at a brothel. The other watchmen laughed. No one so much as lifted an eye in Malrich's direction.

Malrich swallowed the knot in his stomach and walked past the watchmen.

He was a coward in many ways, giving in to fear while greater men led the way. He was too afraid to help Emethius with Prince Meriatis, fearful that Ftoril was a two-faced fraud. He was too hesitant to join the rebellion, although he believed in the very ideas for which they fought. He was too weak to do right by his wife when she was healthy, or to do what was necessary to protect his son after she became sick.

A wise man once told him that fear made men do the sensible thing. The older he got, the more he realized sensible was just a kind word for cowardly. Sensible men never changed the world. Sensible men righted no wrongs.

Arriving to Emethius's house, Malrich knocked on the door. There was no response. He attempted to peek through the window Ftoril had crashed through, but Emethius had done a thorough job boarding it up. Finally, he tried the handle. He was surprised to find it unlocked.

Malrich cautiously peered inside, half expecting a trap.

"Get in here, you oaf, and shut the door."

Emethius was sitting at the dining table with a collection of parchments strewn out before him.

"I thought... I thought... well, I'm not exactly sure what I thought. But..." Malrich trailed off as he caught sight of the new map that lay side-by-side with the map Emethius had found in Herald Carrick's journal. "What exactly happened at the abbey?"

"The mission was a complete and utter failure," reported Emethius, with a noticeable waver to his voice. "Meriatis doesn't have a clue what happened to Shadowbane, and even if he did, it wouldn't be of any help. Ftoril was taken captive."

"Gods help me," muttered Malrich. "Did they kill her?"

"Not that I saw, but there's no telling what they'll do to her. Sir Rupert is the one who finally subdued her. Ftoril took off his thumb before he knocked her out."

Malrich would have found that funny if the stakes weren't so dire. "Do you think she'll talk?"

"Did she talk when we had her tied up?"

"No, but we didn't start lopping off body parts."

Emethius shrugged. "I'm guessing we're safe, but only time will tell for certain."

"Where did you get the map?"

"In a brief moment of lucidity, Meriatis slipped

me this map." Emethius rubbed his hands together, but it did little to hide the fact that he was trembling. "It answers an important question; I now know where the cure to the Blackheart is located. But that knowledge is more of a curse than a blessing."

Malrich had never seen Emethius so shaken. He sat down and examined the blood-covered parchment. The image was clear enough — two lone peaks stood on the western coast of Eremel bisected by a river. At the head of the river was a large "X" and some words written in the ancient tongue. Malrich had a hard enough time reading and writing in the common tongue — he had never learned a word of Talsa Ew. In this case it didn't matter. There was no other location in the world the mark could be indicating.

"Bi Ache, the Sin of Atimir, the city of the damned," said Emethius. "That's where the cure is hidden. And that's where I must go."

Bi Ache was once the greatest city is the world. A thousand years ago it was overrun during the resurgence of the Cul. Its citizens were slaughtered or forced into slavery. No sane person had ventured there since.

"No," was all Malrich could manage in response.

"It's not an option," said Emethius solemnly.

"Oh, isn't it?" challenged Malrich. "You'll die, you know you will. No one has set foot west of Terra Falls since the Cul burned Bi Anule."

"Superstition has kept them away, not fact," countered Emethius. "No one knows where the Cul are hiding."

"Here, there, and everywhere in-between," said Malrich, pointing to the crudely drawn mountains that ran the length of the western coast. He narrowed his eyes sternly. "Meriatis is mad and that little dragon friend of yours is as wretched as they come. What do you think you are doing? What's going on in that head of yours that makes you think it's your responsibility to cure Meriatis of an incurable disease?"

Emethius's eyes glimmered, betraying the hidden turmoil in his mind. "Yes, Ftoril is wretched, but not wicked. I believe she cares very little about Meriatis's fate, and the end she sought would not have been the same as our own. But when she said there was a cure, I believed her."

"You want to believe her, is more like it."

"Meriatis's map all but confirms Ftoril's claim."

"Aye? Ftoril may have told Meriatis the same lie."

Emethius pushed himself away from the table and began to pace. "Life is a battle between right and wrong, and the easiest path is not always the most righteous. Meriatis may have fallen from grace, but he does not deserve to be condemned to madness if there is a cure. No one does. And if that does not convince you, it is as simple as this; Meriatis is my friend. That's justification enough in my opinion."

Malrich visualized the journey Emethius would have to take to reach the ruins of Bi Ache — all paths led along dark roads haunted by an even darker enemy. "You could sail to Terra Falls, but there's not a captain in the world that will take you a league farther. From there it's a hundred and fifty leagues as the bird flies, but the route you will be forced to take will never be straight. For every step of the journey you will be hunted by the Cul. I see only doom in that route."

"No, there is another way." Emethius pointed out the route on the map. "I can take the Barren Tracks into the Great Northern Ador — the Dunie still guard the way. The Cul fear that forest as much as any talsani."

And for good reason, Malrich knew. The forest was haunted by the ghosts of the dead. The gods forbid the living to enter.

"If the maps of old still bear any truth, the Northern Ador comes within fifty leagues of Bi

Ache."

"Fifty leagues in the Cultrator is still a death sentence."

"The Cul rule the night, but in the open wastes of the Cultrator there will be no refuge from the sun. They will stay hidden by day and I will stay hidden by night."

It was possible, Malrich knew, but not likely. He threw himself down on a bench, half out of exhaustion, half out of distress. Of all the possible destinations in the world, why did it have to be Bi Ache?

A heavy silence hung over the room, save for the odd pop of firewood crackling in the hearth. Malrich grappled with the implications of Emethius's plan. If there actually was a cure for the Blackheart, it was a hope beyond anything he had ever thought possible. But his heart sagged at the realization that it was probably just that; a hope. *A false hope that will mislead, and draw us like a siren's call into the most forsaken place in the world.*

"To think, we now take council from a madman, a dead herald, and a duplicitous dragon," scoffed Malrich. He wrung his hands nervously and chewed at his lip. Finally, he sighed, accepting the burden in full. "By the gods, I pray that you are right, because you will be condemning us both to death if you are wrong."

"I ask nothing of you, Mal."

"That is because you needn't ask. One alone stands little chance in the wilds of the Cultrator, but two, well..." Malrich smiled. "Besides, it's not your decision to make. My home has been burdened by the Blackheart as much as any. If there's a cure..."

"You owe it to Ali to seek it out." Emethius nodded his head. He misunderstood Malrich's motivation, but Malrich didn't bother to correct him. Emethius jumped from his chair and gave Malrich a hearty hug. "You are a true friend, Mal. We have countless leagues yet to travel, and nothing but uncertainty between us and our destination. But, if at journey's end we find ourselves once again in Mayal, may your wife be cured of her affliction, and may you both live a hundred years blissfully wed."

"May it be so," said Malrich, not really meaning it. Because the truth was, no cure would ever bring Ali back; the woman he loved had died long ago. He was undertaking this journey for the ghost of his son, and for every other Merridian who had suffered the ravages of the Blackheart. He had to find out if there was actually a cure, and whether or not the gods were purposefully withholding it from the masses. For the truth, Malrich would walk to ends of the earth. For the truth, Malrich would sacrifice his life a hundred times over.

CHAPTER

XII

TRANSFUSER

Leta stood in the inner ward of the Vacian Monastery looking over the rows of neatly arrayed beds. The beds were empty for now, each prepared with fresh white linens and a down pillow. They almost looked inviting, were it not for the wrist and ankle restraints fastened to the frame of each bed.

There had been a lull in the influx of new patients over the past few weeks. *A reason to be grateful,* thought Leta. Still, here the beds stood, awaiting the inevitable. More patients would come, they always did, and eventually someone would be sent to the headsman.

Leta had always regarded her duties within the Vacian Monastery with a sense of pride. Helping the afflicted was godly work, and if she needed to assist in separating a soul from its tainted body, then so be it. Death could be a mercy, or so her father taught her. But the death of a clean soul was simply murder.

Is my soul tainted by my actions? Will the gods hold me accountable for sins I did not purposefully commit? She had no answers, only doubts, and an incurable guilt that gnawed at her soul.

"*I have only spoken the truth.*" Those were the heretic's last words. He had not seemed as demented as the other patients, but he wasn't of sound mind either. Leta could only come to one conclusion — Lady Miren was somehow poisoning the minds of the heretics she sent to the monastery. There were a handful of poisons that would cause a patient to demonstrate symptoms similar to the Blackheart, but all would wear off within a matter of hours.

That troubled Leta even more. Someone in the monastery had to be continuously administering the poison, which meant there was a traitor in Leta's flock. The thought caused her stomach to roil anew.

The door to the monastery opened, and in trotted Orso and Lady Miren's three wards. The noon bell tolled, marking that the four children were right on time for their evaluation.

"Good morning, priestess," said Awen and Bree in unison. They each curtsied. Leta couldn't help but notice that their form had improved significantly. They had clearly been practicing.

"Lady Miren sends her regards," said Ionni. Her curtsy was stiff and awkward. Her left leg didn't seem to rotate properly at the hip.

Orso didn't bother with such formalities. He pushed his way to the front of the gathering and wrinkled his nose. "What's that smell?" asked the boy. His eyes wandered to the row of empty beds.

The fresh sheets hid the stains on the mattresses, but did little to lessen the scent of excrement and bodily fluids.

"What do they do here?" asked Awen, staring at the empty beds.

"This is where they treat the affliction," said Ionni, answering before Leta got the chance.

"My cousin died of the Blackheart," announced Bree with far too much excitement. "He was only five."

Ionni ribbed Bree with her elbow.

"It was very sad," added Bree. She looked down at the floor.

Leta smiled. Being the oldest of the three girls, Ionni had clearly taken on the role of big sister.

"You look very similar to him," said Awen. She was squinting at Leta's face.

"Similar to who?"

"Prince Meriatis," said the girl, as if that answer was obvious. "I mean, you're very pretty, like a princess from the stories. But Prince Meriatis was more handsome."

Leta decided to take that as a compliment. She knelt down before the small girl so that they were eye to eye. "And how would you know what my brother looked like?"

"I met him."

"Me too!" said Bree happily.

"He worked with my father on the senses," said Awen.

Leta raised an eyebrow. "Do you mean the census?" A census was conducted every fifty years to measure the population of Merridia. It was one of the last things Meriatis worked on before the onset of the rebellion.

"Uh huh. That's right," said Awen nodding vigorously.

"Me too!" Bree declared, even more happy than before.

Was that why these poor children were here? Because their fathers had helped Prince Meriatis perform his civic duty to the throne? That seemed hardly a treasonous act. Leta noted that Ionni remained silent during this interaction. Ionni wasn't a carefree child like the other two girls; she would be harder to crack.

Leta waved the children along. "Follow me. Let's not linger here. I'm sure you are all excited to begin the evaluation." Leta guided them to the testing area — a small chapel dedicated to the Weaver. A marble statue crafted in the likeness of the winged goddess stood overlooking a small altar. Atop the altar sat a cage covered with a red cloth.

"What's in the cage?" asked Orso. He ran up to the altar and tried to peek under the cover.

Leta withdrew the cover, revealing a large white snow hare. "This is Saddy," said Leta, lifting the hare out of the cage. Saddy was accustomed to being handled, and didn't resist. She stroked the hare along its ears and back, which Saddy seemed to like. "Saddy is going to assist us with our test."

"A rabbit? That's silly," said Awen, the youngest of the three girls. "How is a rabbit going to help us?"

"She's a nice rabbit. Soft and friendly. She especially likes lettuce. Here, hold her." Leta passed Saddy into Awen's outstretched arms. Awen's cynicism seemed to disappear immediately. She giggled like the little girl she was.

"Let me hold her," said Orso, reaching for the hare.

"Each of you will get your turn," said Leta. She

motioned for Awen to pass Saddy to Bree. "Today you will each be evaluated to see if you bear the Weaver's Blessing. Those who possess the gift can perform the miracle of transfusion. They can manipulate the power of life. They can bring fruit to a barren tree, they can sow a barren field with grain, or they can mend the wounded and heal the sick. Those blessed with the gift have ascended to some of the highest seats of honor in our land. My father bears the gifts, as does Herald Cenna."

"But you don't," said Ionni. She collected the hare from Bree, who seemed eager to part with the animal.

"It's true, I do not possess the blessing," admitted Leta. "The gift often skips a generation, and has even become extinct within some bloodlines, as is the will of Calaban.

"As is the will of Calaban," echoed the children in unison.

Orso yanked Saddy out of Ionni's hands and clutched the rabbit to his chest. "When do we begin this test?"

"Actually, we already have," said Leta. "Now that everyone has had a chance to get acquainted with Saddy, I would like you all to put a hand on her back. Orso, you can continue to hold her. Girls, gently place your hands behind her ears. Now focus your attention on Saddy's body. Consider what she hears, what she sees, what she feels. Imagine her heartbeat and the air drawing into her lungs." Leta waited a moment for the children to comply. When they each appeared deep in thought, she asked her next question. "Do any of you feel Saddy's life force?"

The three girls contemplated the question for a second. They each shook their heads.

"I felt something," declared Orso with pride. "A tingling in my fingertips. Do you think I have the gift?"

Leta replied only with a smile. Orso was lying. The Weaver's Blessing didn't work like that, but the boy was too ignorant to know any better. Leta's question was meant to get the children to hone their senses, to focus solely on their physical connection with the hare and nothing else. It helped to enhance the feeling of shock they would all soon encounter.

Leta reached into her pocket, grabbed a razor blade she had hidden there, and promptly drew it across Saddy's furry neck.

At first, the children simply thought Leta was stroking the hare's neck. It wasn't until the first trickle of blood emerged that anyone knew something was wrong.

"You hurt Saddy!" screamed Awen. She released her hold on the rabbit and began to flap her hands in distress.

"You have to keep in contact with Saddy for the entirety of the test," said Leta, her voice purposefully calm.

Awen shuffled farther away.

Leta couldn't blame the girl. She always used snow hares when administering the test. The white fur caused the blood to stand out in sharp contrast. The impact on the children was more visceral, and therefore more likely to provoke a response. Awen's response was horror. An acceptable reaction, but not the one Leta was seeking.

Bree backed out of the test next with tears rolling down her cheeks.

Saddy's eyes flared, and her little nose began to frantically twitch.

Bree squealed and turned away, unable to bear the sight.

Saddy's body began to convulse. The poor animal's motor functions were starting to break down.

Ionni and Orso kept their hands on the rabbit. Orso's mouth hung agape as he watched the blood course down the length of Saddy's body, running over his fingers and the back of his hand. Only

Ionni appeared unfazed. The girl was much older than the other three children. She likely knew what the test entailed and was mentally prepared for the macabre experience. Some evaluators used rabbits. Others used hens, lambs, or piglets. Besides the animal, the methodology of the test didn't change. Give a child a cuddly animal, then kill it in their hands. If the child was a transfuser, the test should induce a reaction.

Leta could only watch and wait. In the next minute one of two things was going to happen — Saddy would either bleed to death, or one of the children would manifest the powers of a transfuser; in the dozens of evaluations Leta had administered, she had not once seen the latter happen. As far as she was concerned it was a foregone conclusion — the rabbit would die. It always did.

Leta wasn't sure why they still bothered administering the evaluation. The Weaver's Blessing was becoming an extraordinarily rare gift. It was not exactly a mystery why. The power seemed to be hereditary, and there were desperately few transfusers alive to pass on the gift to their children. In an age long since past, nearly every city, town, and backwater in Elandria had a resident master healer. The emergence of the Blackheart changed all of that.

When the Blackheart first emerged, people's understanding of the affliction was limited, and the attempted remedies only worsened the problem. It was not uncommon for master healers to perform transfusions on Blackheart victims. What no one realized until it was too late, was that the act of transfusion passed the affliction to the healer. As more and more people got sick, more and more transfusers succumbed to the Blackheart as well. Master healers were eventually forbidden from practicing their powers on the afflicted, but by then the damage was done. An entire generation of healers was already dead or dying. The number of master healers had not recovered.

To make up for the shortage of capable healers, those few transfusers who remained were actively recruited by the Tiber and Vacian Orders. This only exacerbated the problem. Members of the Tiber Order swore an oath of celibacy, and although Vacian Sister's were allowed to marry, they seldom did. By Leta's count, there were only eight active transfusers within the Vacian Sisterhood. Sister Beli, Leta's assistant, was one of them. The gift was slightly more common in men — there were a little over fifty transfusers within the Tiber Brotherhood. Unfortunately, almost all were past middle age and none had children.

Within a generation or two the Weaver's Blessing would likely become extinct.

High Lord Valerius possessed the gift, but neither Leta nor Meriatis inherited the power. There was hope that Leta's son, Nysen, might possess the Weaver's blessing, but he failed the test just like everyone else. That memory in particular caused Leta great pain. Nysen didn't care that he wasn't a transfuser. All he cared about was that he couldn't keep the rabbit alive. Several days after the test, Leta walked into her son's room and found him crying on the floor. He had cut open the throat of one of his stuffed animals and was trying to sew it back together. He couldn't understand that it wasn't his fault that the rabbit had died.

It was only a few weeks later that Nysen's skin began to spot. By the end of the year he would be dead, another victim of the Blackheart. Leta always felt awful that she put her son through such a cruel test. The failure haunted him, and even on his deathbed he was asking about the rabbit. "*Will Saddy be angry with me when I meet her in the afterlife?*"

"*No, of course not,*" Leta remembered saying as she placed a damp cloth on her son's sweltering brow. "*Saddy will love you because you tried to help her. Caring for others is the most important task the gods ask of us. Sometimes we succeed, sometimes we fail. But we must always try."*

Leta had learned since then to cut the rabbit's throat deeper. It sped up the process and shortened the creature's suffering. It was the prolonged suffering that seemed to traumatize the children the most.

Saddy began to twitch — her final death throes. The test would be over soon. Leta could go on with her day, and these poor traumatized children could wander home and worry about their own failings. *Just one bad memory in a life that will be full of nightmares*, thought Leta.

The rabbit suddenly squealed — an unusual noise given the fact that its neck was cut wide open. It began to frantically kick its hind legs, trying to free itself from Ionni and Orso's grasp. Something was happening that Leta had never seen before. The flow of blood had inexplicably stopped.

Leta dug through the rabbit's fur with her fingers, searching for the wound. It was gone. Leta was dumbfounded. "Who did it?" blurted Leta in disbelief. "Which one of you healed the rabbit?"

Ionni released the rabbit and raised her hands. "I don't know what happened, priestess."

"Um, Priestess Leta." Awen was pointing at Orso.

The boy was trembling. He dropped the rabbit, and the blood slick critter went bounding off through the hall, searching for a place to hide. Leta paid the creature no mind. Something was terribly wrong with Orso.

"My... my neck," managed the boy, his face turned pale. He reached toward his ear. When he withdrew his hand, his fingertips were wet with blood. The skin along the boy's neck was slowly separating, as if it were being pulled apart along a hidden seam. Blood spilled from the ensuing gap. First it was a trickle, then it came in great spurts as the artery tore open. Orso collapsed to the ground clawing at his neck.

Leta rushed to the stricken boy's side. She had to pry his blood slick and trembling hands free from his neck to inspect the wound. The laceration had nicked the main artery. He would die soon. She clamped down on the wound, hoping she could stem the flow of blood until help arrived.

"Ionni, fetch Sister Beli, High Lord Valerius, or Herald Cenna — whomever you can find first. Hurry!"

The girl nodded dumbly and ran off.

Bree began to cry. "He's going to die, isn't he?" she wailed. "Oh gods help us. He's going to die!"

Leta ignored the girl and focused on keeping

pressure on Orso's neck. Leta had only seen so much blood a few times in her life. Not once was there a positive outcome.

Ionni did not take long to find High Lord Valerius. Leta's father came rushing into the chamber, moving faster than Leta had ever seen him move.

"Let me see the wound," said High Lord Valerius as he took a knee beside Orso. Leta released the pressure on Orso's neck and the wound immediately began to spurt blood, sullying her father's robe. Valerius didn't seem to notice. He spent half a second inspecting the wound before instructing Leta to reapply pressure.

He rolled up his sleeves, revealing forearms covered in scars. "Find something we can use as a tourniquet," ordered Valerius.

Bree produced the belt from her starched robe.

"Quickly tie the belt around my arm. Make it tight."

Bree didn't budge, her feet were glued to the ground. "I... I can't." She stared at the blood like it was a pool of lava. She wasn't going anywhere.

Ionni yanked the belt out of the young girl's hand and trudged through the ever growing puddle of blood. She cinched the belt tightly around High Lord Valerius's bicep. The veins in his forearm bulged.

"That's a good lass, thank you," said the high lord, his voice purposefully calm. "Now everyone step back. Make sure you are not in contact with either of us."

Valerius closed his eyes and clamped his hand over the chasm in Orso's throat. It looked like he was strangling the boy. Orso shuddered and the heels of his shoes thudded against the stone floor. The skin along Valerius's forearm began to part, the flesh separating down through the layers of skin until red muscle was exposed. Leta felt nauseous, but she didn't look away — it was such a rare opportunity to see the miracle of transfusion in action. Valerius released his hold on Orso's neck. The laceration on the boy's neck was gone, leaving behind a thin red scar that trailed from ear to jugular.

Bree wiped back her tears. Awen simply stared slack-jawed at the now healed wound in Orso's neck. Only Ionni seemed to understand what she had just witnessed — she edged closer trying to get a better look at the wound in High Lord Valerius's forearm.

"There is no need to be afraid, girls," said Valerius, letting a rare smile crease his lips. "Young Orso will be back to full health in a few days."

Valerius cleaned his bloody hands on his already sullied robe.

Orso appeared to be asleep — his eyes were closed, his breathing was steady.

"B-b-but how?" stammered Awen, clearly still confused.

"I gave Orso some of my vitality," explained Valerius. "In exchange, I took some of Orso's hurt into myself. You see, transfusion is a balancing act. The wound must go somewhere." He held up his forearm so the girls could see.

"Yes, I've seen a transfusion before," said Ionni, "but what I don't understand is why Orso was injured in the first place."

"Priestess Leta's evaluation is designed to instigate a reaction from people who possess latent powers," explained High Lord Valerius. "Orso, it appears, is blessed with the gift of transfusion. Unfortunately, the boy's abilities are instinctual. His emotional reaction to the sight of suffering caused his powers to manifest, but due to his lack of training, he did not possess the ability to redirect the wound. He simply took the wound from the hare and mirrored it within his own body. A skilled transfuser can redirect the wound to a less vital part of their body." Valerius pointed to the laceration in his own forearm. Despite the severity of the injury, only a small trickle of blood emerged from the opening.

"Or they can impart the wound to a third party," added Leta. "I'm sure you've heard of a leech boy."

"Treves, Herald Cenna's assistant, he's a leech boy, isn't he?" said Bree. Then, as she realized what the title entailed, she scrunched up her face with disgust. "Oh, that poor boy. How cruel."

"Indeed, it is," said High Lord Valerius. "But it is one of the stations an acolyte must complete on his path to becoming a Tiber Brother."

"Why don't you use a leech boy, high lord?" asked Awen.

High Lord Valerius raised his hands, showcasing the innumerable scars that crisscrossed his forearms. "To serve others, one must share in their suffering, so the Book of Requiem teaches us. A man of my station must feel his people's suffering most of all. But that's enough for one day. Look, the brave lad is waking up."

Orso began to stir.

"How do you feel?" asked Valerius, helping Orso sit upright

"Cold. Achy." Orso gingerly felt at his neck. "Where did all of this blood come from?"

Valerius didn't bother to answer. "Girls, help Orso to the infirmary. Sister Beli will know what to do."

Ionni took the lead in hoisting Orso to his feet. The other two girls each grabbed an arm. Orso's legs were wobbly, but he managed to remain standing. They led him away through the hall, leaving bloody footprints in their wake.

"I put more of my vitality into the boy than I let on," admitted Valerius, once they were alone. "I feel lightheaded. Bring me a chair."

Leta quickly brought her father a stool.

Valerius settled onto the stool with a groan. His eyes wandered to the blood that was coagulating on the floor. "You cut the rabbit too deeply. That was careless of you. I've warned you of the risks."

"How was I to know that the boy possessed the gift?" said Leta, struggling not to sound overly defensive. "I've performed this test dozens of times, and not once has one of my subjects manifested the ability to perform a transfusion. I guess I just got tired of watching rabbits suffer. A deep cut means a quick death. I made a mistake."

"That you did, and you almost killed the boy. And not just any boy, the only son of one of the most powerful families in Merridia. A family to whom we owe a great debt of gratitude. Were it not for the efforts of Praetor Maxentius and General Saterius, I may well be dead."

"And Meriatis would be alive," muttered Leta under her breath.

"I'm going to assume I did not hear you correctly."

Leta did not repeat herself.

Valerius's eyes narrowed. "You are taking all of this much too lightly. Over a thousand children have been tested in the past year. Orso is the first to possess the gift. This is no coincidence; this is a message from the gods. They favor the boy."

"They favor him for what?" asked Leta.

"A transfuser with such a noble bloodline could make a compelling claim for the throne."

"The Throne of Roses already has an heir," snapped Leta, unable to hide the irritation in her voice.

"You?" Valerius shook his head. "We have spoken of this matter to exhaustion. You already know my answer. A woman has never sat upon the Throne of Roses and never will. The gods will not allow it. Now please, go fetch me a thread and needle. I need to close up this wound."

Leta scowled, and walked off to acquire the requested tools. Her father was right about one thing — no woman had ever sat upon the Throne of Roses. But he ignored an important fact. Orso wasn't the only one touched by the gods. Leta had the scars to prove it.

CHAPTER
XIII
GREENSTONE

Emethius regarded his childhood home with an aloofness he found surprising. It had been years since his last visit, and the main structure seemed smaller and infinitely older than he remembered. It was a cold, uninviting building. Water seemed to seep from the walls, and moss covered every inch of the structure. Emethius could sense the stale taste of mildew on the back of his tongue, even from afar.

I shouldn't have come here, thought Emethius, for a moment hesitant to approach the door.

Greenstone was built at a time when the Cul still threatened the lands west of the Morium. One of Emethius's ancestors attempted to construct the keep in the style of the dwarven master masons by dry fitting interlocking stone. Outwardly, the results were impressive. High walls made the keep all but impenetrable. Unfortunately, the whole structure tilted to the left. The foundation was rotten, and probably had been since the day it was built.

The main culprit was the cellar. It was constantly flooded by groundwater, and there was no easy way to keep it dry. As a child, Emethius devised a plan to siphon the water out of the cellars using a series of pumps. He still remembered his father's response. *"Greenstone has stood for a thousand years, and it will likely stand for a thousand more, with or without your help,"* his father had said, as he threw Emethius's plan in the fire. *"Don't waste any more parchment with your sketches."*

Emethius never bothered to show his father any of his other plans after that, be it his plan to run an irrigation canal to the bone dry southern fields, or his schedule for a crop rotation that would double their annual yield. Emethius learned early in life it was simpler to keep his opinions to himself, rather than challenge his father and face the repercussions.

To avoid his father's brooding temperament, Emethius spent a lot of his childhood outside. Back then, the Lunen family estate was one of the largest in the Henna Lu diocese. Emethius could walk all day and never leave his family's property. Fields of golden grain seemed to go on as far as the eye could see. There was a forest to the east filled with wild game, and a stream that bisected the land, teeming with trout. The sea was only an hour ride, and Emethius would often go sit by the water and listen to the waves crashing against the shore.

Looking over the land now, Emethius wondered if any of these boyhood memories were real. Most of the winter snow had melted, leaving behind a muddy soup. The fields were unfurrowed — no one had bothered to turn over the soil for the upcoming planting season. The crofter huts that dotted the fields like molehills appeared abandoned.

"Go for now," whispered Emethius into his horse's ear. Manos exhaled loudly and wandered off to munch on the fresh sprouts that were just beginning to emerge from the mud. The gelding was born in these fields, the offspring of his father's old warhorse and a tractable mare named Baylilly. Emethius trusted Manos not to go far.

As Emethius approached the keep's sole entry portal, he passed the stump of an ancient elm. As a child, Emethius used the stump as a chopping block for firewood. The rusted head of an ax was embedded in the stump, probably deposited there the last time Emethius had used it. He swore the stump still bore a blood red tint. He tried to ignore the disconcerting thought and knocked on the keep's heavy wooden door.

The door opened slowly. Emethius was not surprised that Sir Bastin, the estate's master-at-arms, was the one who answered. For a second the old dwarf's eyes lit up like he was seeing a ghost.

"Emethius!" cried Sir Bastin in disbelief. "It has been some time. Years, in fact! Come, come, please." He motioned for Emethius to enter. "How have you been, my boy?"

"It's good to see you, Bastin," said Emethius, giving the dwarf a warm hug. "And I am doing well. I'm alive after all, and that wasn't always a guarantee."

"Being alive is a fair bit better than being worm food," said Sir Bastin with a soft chuckle.

Sir Bastin had served as the master-at-arms for Emethius's father, his grandfather, and even his great-grandfather before him. Emethius's father would often joke that Sir Bastin came with the property. The old dwarf knew enough secrets to sully the Lunen family name a dozen times over, but he had always stayed loyal, even after Lithius Lunen was publicly disgraced and stripped of his lordship.

The Lord of Greenstone had once claimed dominion over the entire Eastern Angle, a spur of land that jutted into the sea of Ro a few leagues north of Henna Lu. Unfortunately, Emethius's father had put an end to that. After his shaming during the False Prophet's Rebellion and his now infamous last charge, Lithius Lunen took hard to gambling and drinking. He leveraged his land to pay off his debts, but eventually, even that wasn't enough. When Lithius failed to pay his annual tithe for the fifth year in a row, Praetor Maxentius settled the matter by reclaiming the majority of the Lunen estate and partitioning it out to men who would pay their dues. As a final insult, Praetor Maxentius stripped Lithius Lunen of his lordship. Now, all that remained in the Lunen name was the keep, a few hundred acres of land, and a lighthouse on the coast.

This disgrace also meant Sir Bastin was no longer obligated to serve House Lunen. Knights of Niselus only served households that were granted lordships by the Throne of Roses. Given a choice, Sir Bastin decided to retire from the brotherhood and stay on as the estate's master-at-arms.

Although Sir Bastin had technically retired, he still wore his brotherhood uniform — a hardened leather cuirass embossed with the symbol of a burning tree, brown leather greaves, and a red tunic that stopped just short of his knees. He even wore a short sword at his hip, although Emethius doubted the old knight still had the strength to wield it. His skin was like wrinkled leather, and only the slightest wisps of white hair remained atop the knight's otherwise bald pate.

Sir Bastin examined Emethius from head to foot. "Some of the men from the Red Company returned south shortly after the war. I've heard quite a few versions of what happened at Imel Katan. How has your wound healed?"

"The memory haunts me more than the wound," said Emethius, allowing himself to be led into the parlor. It was just about the only room in the house that appeared to be in use. Everywhere else he looked he saw furniture covered in sheets and cold, empty fireplaces. In the parlor the hearth was crackling, illuminating the room in orange light. Emethius seated himself in what used to be his father's favorite chair, and kicked off his riding boots. His damp and tired feet were grateful for the sudden heat.

"How is she?" asked Emethius, when it became apparent his mother would not be joining them.

"The same as the last time you paid us a visit," said Bastin. "She takes all of her meals in bed, and wanders downstairs rarely. On some days, only to use the privy. She probably hasn't stepped outside since the first snowfall last fall." He sighed wearily.

"I'm too old to be anything but frank, so I'll come right out with it. Why have you come home?"

Emethius handed Sir Bastin a letter sealed with candle wax. Bastin gave Emethius a queer look as he broke the seal. His lips moved as he read over the message. He gave a curt nod at the end. "Praetor Maxentius has granted you mastery of Greenstone." His face remained a staid mask, betraying nothing of his opinion, but Emethius sensed this came as a relief to the old steward.

"It's not a lordship," explained Emethius. "None of the property my father lost has been restored to the estate, but it's a start."

Sir Bastin frowned ever so slightly. "Your mother will not be pleased."

"I didn't ask for this," said Emethius. "But this was my reward for my service during the war. Kill a prince, earn a title. If I had known it was that easy I would have stabbed Meriatis in the back long ago." He gave a quiet laugh.

Bastin did not share in his amusement. "Master Emethius. I'm not saying the title isn't well deserved. It's just... um... atypical for a son to inherit an estate while his mother still lives."

Emethius agreed, but it was better this way. "When was the last time my mother surveyed the property? Does she have a clue that squatters have settled near the greenwood? And when was the last time she rode down to the coast? I'd imagine the lighthouse beacon hasn't been lit in a decade."

"Be that as it may, she will contest this."

"Don't tell her. She doesn't need to know that anything has changed."

"I don't understand. Is it not your intention to move back in? Isn't that why you have come home?"

"No, Sir Bastin, my intention is to guarantee that my affairs are set in order." He paused, unsure how much he should reveal. "I may not be returning home for a long time, and I can't afford for people to be looking for me. Everything must be set in order — the fields, the lighthouse, our family debts, all of it. It doesn't take a farmer to note that the fields have not been prepped for the upcoming season."

Sir Bastin sighed wearily. "Your mother evicted most of the crofters. She lost her mind after she learned you were injured in the war. She began to accuse anyone who disagreed with her of being a rebel. It went on like this for several weeks, then she caught a fever and became convinced someone had poisoned the well. That was the final straw. The first thing she did once she got better was evict everyone."

That would explain the squatters down by the greenwood, thought Emethius. His uncaring mother had evicted two score people right before the onset of winter. Of course they took refuge in the greenwood. They had nowhere else to go.

"This is unacceptable," snapped Emethius, letting his anger get the better of him. If a tax assessor noticed the fallow field, Emethius would be called to court to answer for his dereliction. That was a risk Emethius could not afford. Emethius planned to be half a world away in the depth of the Cultrator by the start of the growing season. "Offer the farmers my apologies for their hardship, and ask them to return to their homes. If need be, tell them they only owe half their annual tithe for this year's harvest. But get them back. I won't have my fields lying fallow all season. A single missed season and we'll be making up our debts for years to come."

A bell chimed from the second floor. Emethius's mother must have heard his outburst.

"I'm coming, madam!" called Sir Bastin, then, turning to Emethius, "I mustn't make her wait." Sir Bastin hobbled up the stairs as quickly as his aging legs would take him. When he reached the upstairs landing, he opened the double doors leading into Evantia Lunen's bedchamber with a flourish.

"What may I do for you, Madam Evantia?"

The voice of Evantia Lunen wafted down from above, weak and sickly. "I thought I heard someone else. For a second there, it sounded like Lithius. Am I hearing ghosts? Who's down there with you?"

"My apologies for disturbing you, madam. We were being too loud. A banker from Henna Lu has paid us a visit. He's concerned about the barren fields. Do you feel well enough to meet with him?" Emethius smirked. Sir Bastin knew how to play his mother. Not in a thousand years would she want to meet with a banker.

"No, not today. Come inside and shut the door."

Sir Bastin gave Emethius a sly smile and disappeared into the bedchamber.

Emethius walked into the adjacent room. It was his father's study. Greenstone had accumulated quite the library over the years, although Emethius had never seen his father open a book. He kept them there as show, something to brag about when he entertained visiting lords. Emethius would sneak into the study and read whenever his father was away. His favorite book was the *Lay of Etro*. It told of Ateasar and his forbidden love for Ierra, Princess of Merridia. Emethius found the book on a low shelf, likely where he had left it years earlier. The book was covered in dust and its pages were warped from humidity, but the words on the pages were still clear.

"*Ateasar ise Ierra, vep'horan pepsi sitape,*" said Emethius, reading the opening line. It was the first book he read in the ancient tongue, and although it took him half a summer to get through the archaic text, it was worth it.

Beside the bookshelf, the plaster wall was cracked, serving as a dark reminder of less happy times. Emethius's father had thrown Emethius against the wall during one of his drunken rages, breaking Emethius's collarbone in the process. After the incident, Emethius rarely returned home from school, and when he did, he kept his visits purposefully short. In Emethius's absence, Lithius Lunen began to direct his rage toward Emethius's mother. One summer, when Emethius came home from an unusually long stint at the Royal Academy, he found his mother bedridden with broken ribs and a face that was bruised so badly she was hardly recognizable.

"*He's afflicted with the Blackheart,*" Emethius had proposed, hopeful his mother would take the bait.

"*No, of course not,*" Evantia Lunen had reassured him. "*I made a mistake, that's all. You know how your father is.*"

That, Emethius did.

When his mother refused to commit Lithius to a local Vacian Monastery, Emethius took matters into his own hands. He imagined his mother would see the death of her husband as a second lease on life. Instead, she spiraled further into depression. Emethius couldn't help but feel responsible. *I only tried to do what was right, what was just.*

"Ahem."

Emethius turned to discover Sir Bastin standing at the entrance to the study. He nodded toward the broken plaster. "Your father instructed me to hire a carpenter to fix that wall half-a-dozen times, but I never did. I wanted to leave it there as a reminder, something he could stare at while he sat in here nursing a bottle. He was a rotten father and an even more wretched husband. I don't fault you for what you did."

"My mother does."

"He came close to killing her more times than I would like to remember," said Sir Bastin with a sad shake of his head. "The only reason I continued to serve this house after your father lost his lordship was to protect you and your mother. But in the end, it was you who saved her life. What she has chosen to do with the extra time is her choice, and

I give it little thought. What concerns me now, is what you intend to do."

Emethius wished he could give Sir Bastin an honest answer and tell him he was off to find a cure to the Blackheart and to save Prince Meriatis's life, but he couldn't.

Before he departed, Emethius raided the household larder, collecting what was needed for the long journey ahead. With his saddlebags packed almost to the point of bursting, he ventured down to the stables to fetch Manos. He was pleasantly surprised to find his gelding happily chomping at a pail of oats right beside Baylilly. Sway-backed and a little bony, the old mare was long past her prime. Even so, Emethius needed a pack horse to carry supplies, and for that task, Baylilly was perfect.

"How about one last ride and a wee bit of adventure to boot?" said Emethius to Baylilly, as he strapped the saddlebags to her back. The mare answered him with a soft nicker and a nuzzle from her nose.

Emethius departed at dusk. Once again, he rode past the rotten elm stump that stood before the keep. The ax head embedded in the stump glowed as red as blood, set aflame by the dying embers of the setting sun.

"Lithius Lunen," said Emethius, giving a name

to the first of four grooves dug into the hard leather vambrace he wore on his left forearm. Eager to put physical distance between himself and the specter of his father's memory, Emethius spurred Manos into a gallop and went charging into the dusking night.

• • •

The last of the snow had melted by the time Emethius reached Vel Katan four days later. Everywhere he looked, people were shaking off the last vestiges of winter. Farmhands were tilling fields, grapevines were sprouting buds, and young foals were taking their first tentative steps outside. The land seemed oddly rejuvenated, and with that, Emethius felt a glimmer of hope.

"I embark on a righteous journey," Emethius reminded himself as he crossed himself in the gesture of the faithful. "All matters are fated by the Weaver. The gods will watch over me."

Vel Katan was one of the largest cities in Merridia. It was the seat of the third diocese, and home to a grand temple dedicated to the god-saint Ilmwell. It was also the location of the only bridge that spanned the Osspherus River south of Burrowick.

A stone wall constructed of black volcanic rock

ran the town's perimeter. Emethius was forced to dismount to fit through the low archway that granted entrance into the town. He found himself standing amongst a maze of homes that were painted in a wide variety of hues; cherry reds, deep oranges, rustic browns.

Vel Katan was named after the ruined Cul fortress that glared menacingly down upon the city from its perch atop the river's far bank. Emethius spied the fortress with disdain. He despised all things associated with the Cul, and thought it odd that the structure remained standing when so many others had been torn down. It likely remained untouched as a warning — the deserted Cul fortress was on the far bank of the river, placing it within the kingdom of Emonia. The vile structure served as an unfriendly reminder to the people of Merridia; *do not enter, there are enemies beyond.*

Emethius left Manos and Baylilly with the stable master, flipping the man an extra copper coin to guarantee the horses were treated well. He then entered the city's central inn to seek out a bed for the night. He was shocked to discover Malrich had already arrived.

It was planting season, and most Soldiers of the Faith took leave to tend to their plots of land during this time of the year. Even so, Emethius and

Malrich decided to leave Mayal at separate times, worried that if they left together it might draw unwanted attention. While Emethius dealt with his affairs at Greenstone, Malrich remained in Mayal to make arrangements for the care of his sickly wife. Things must have gone smoothly — Emethius wasn't expecting Malrich to reach Vel Katan for another two days. Malrich was hunched over at the bar in the common area. He was engaged in a loud debate with the innkeeper over the qualities of a good wine.

"I like them tart and dry," said Malrich, smacking his lips. "Give me a good Estero Ruby red and I'll be happy all day."

"You folks are pampered in Mayal. Out here we have two types of wine. The red stuff and the white stuff. Which will it be?"

"How about the hard stuff," said Malrich, pointing over the counter to a bottle of brandy.

The innkeeper grinned. "That I have aplenty." He uncorked the bottle and filled a shot glass to the brim. Malrich drank the shot in one gulp and motioned for the innkeeper to fill it again. The innkeeper was about to pour Malrich a second glass when Emethius caught his eye.

"He's had enough of the hard stuff, thank you," said Emethius, tossing the innkeeper a copper

Merridian. "Please fetch us two ales instead." The innkeeper nodded graciously, corked the bottle, and hurried off with two pewter mugs in hand.

Malrich spun around on his stool, his nostrils flaring like a man looking for a fight. "Who are you to tell me I've had enough... oh, Emethius. Sorry. I didn't expect you here so soon." His breath stunk of wine and his speech was slurred.

"I was going to say the same to you," said Emethius. The innkeeper clacked a pair of mugs on the counter, each brimming over with beer foam. Emethius decided not to address his friend's inebriation and slid Malrich a mug.

Emethius briefly went over their plan, keeping his voice purposefully low. He repeatedly reminded Malrich to do the same. Emoni soldiers were regulars at the inn. If they got word that Malrich and Emethius were Soldiers of the Faith things might go poorly when they crossed the border into Emonia.

Near midnight, some of the bolder patrons began to tell tales. The first to rise for the occasion was a merchant from Chansel. He did a rendition of the Voyage of the Chosen, which told the story of how King Hearstock and King Merridir led the pilgrims over the sea to start a new life in Elandria. Next came an Emonian soldier who sang a song about Adelius, the third king of Emonia, and his fall at Vas Perloh. He was followed by a very drunk Merridian who lampooned King Clement, who was the current Emoni king, with a series of cruel and lewd jokes. By the time he reached his fifth joke he was shouted down by a group of Emoni soldiers who were gathered around a table in the back.

A dwarf dressed in rich silks rose next. Emethius noticed a Tremelese caravan locked up behind the inn when he stabled Manos and Baylilly and assumed the dwarf was the owner. The dwarf had a cohort of companions egging him on. They smacked their mugs against the table, chanting and hooting. This came to a sudden stop when one of the dwarves broke his mug. Beer spilled all over his companion's lap. Everyone thought this was quite funny, except the dwarf who was now drenched in beer. He responded by knuckling his companion in the head. This resulted in more laughter, until finally the dwarf who had risen to speak barked out some harsh words in the Tremelese tongue. The laughter died in his companions' throats. He turned to the crowd and bowed.

"I apologize for the buffoonery of my comrades," said the dwarf. He spoke the common tongue fluently, although he pronounced the words more harshly than any Merridian ever would. "My name is Biriss. I am the captain of this fine crew. If it pleases the audience, I would like to entertain you with a song." Tankards clacked against tables with approval. "Very well. Gentlemen, if your drunken tongues are still capable of carrying a tune I would be most obliged." His dwarven companions began to hum, setting a tune to Biriss's words.

"We have heard three tales for Talsani ear
so I will share one of Dwarven deed.
Many centuries have passed since noble castes
freed the land of tyranny.

In the northern lands near Midich Heights,
a terror held its abode.
The peasants fled and the warriors bled,
no one dared go where the dragon strode.

Heeding the victims' call, came a dwarf quite tall,
a man of noble breed.
Ingel Lan of Tremel, clad in black mail,
who was sown of Hearst's seed.

'Come forth,' cried the dwarf as he held up his blade
before Menalich's abode.
Smoke clouds plumed, and impenetrable shadows loomed
as the dragon bellowed and blew.

Menalich eyed the dwarf as she hissed out a curse,
    the same she spoke to all that she slew.
'Fear is my blade, and darkness my shield,
    you will know both in due time!'

At this the dwarf laughed, although it was crass,
    and told the dragon of her crime.
'You stand quite tall, with tooth, nail and claw,
    yet you hardly fit your fame.
Before this day is through, I will slay you,
    and bring an end to your reign!

Ingel sought with his blade, and Menalich with her teeth,
    their battle raged on through the day.
But scales are coarse and his sword broke from the force,
    thus he let out a woeful bay.

'So I have won,' cried the dragon unsung,
    as she looked upon him with vile eyes.
'I will eat your heart first, your blood next I thirst,
    the rest I will leave for the flies.

With those words uttered, she dove forth jaw unshuttered,
    but this was in Ingel's plan.
He dove right aside, and laid a poison prick to her eye,
    with a knife he held hid in his hand.

She lurched back in shock, and cried out her last thought,
'you have cheated me in the end!'
'I have done nothing such, only what you deserve,
and laid you with a wound that will not mend.'

And as Ingel stood there and gloated, the poison corroded,
and Menalich's heart beat one final time
And so it is told, the story of one bold,
the Tale of Ingel Lan and Menalich."

Biriss bowed low, generally pleased with himself. His comrades at the corner table held their beers aloft and cheered loudly. The Merridian and Emoni patrons rewarded him with a lackluster response; a few clapped, a few more raised their drinks in a toast, but most everyone else appeared displeased to be outdone by a dwarf.

Even after all these years, there is still no love between the races, thought Emethius.

A low murmur came over the bar as Biriss sauntered back to his table and loudly ordered a fresh round of drinks for his companions. A few patrons goaded their friends to stand up, but in the end, no one was willing to follow the dwarf's act. This seemed to please Biriss all the more, and he boastfully ordered a drink for everyone in the tavern.

Malrich leaned forward. "Those Tremelese

bastards act like there is something noble in using tricks to win a fight."

"I'm sorry," said Emethius with a raised eyebrow. "Is there something noble in dying a fool's death? Would you have preferred Ingel Lan simply let the dragon eat him?"

"There's a code of conduct in combat," argued Malrich. "Lies, poisoned blades, and sleight-of-hand — those are the tools of assassins and betrayers, not warriors."

"And cunning is not an acceptable weapon?" asked Emethius, tapping his head.

"Be cunning with sword craft," countered Malrich. "Be cunning with when and where you field your army. Then you'll have no need to cheat."

Emethius's face soured. "We Soldiers of the Faith live by a chivalrous code that demands we defeat our enemies in a civilized fashion. But it's wrong. War is not beautiful. There are no rules except this; kill or be killed. Defeat the enemy by any means necessary, be it through skill, guile, or just sheer luck."

Emethius leaned forward in his chair. "During the Culing War, it took our ancestors years to clear the Cul from our lands. The dwarves defeated the Cul within a matter of months. A Cul army fled into a forest, the dwarves burnt the entire forest to the ground. When the surviving Cul sued for peace, the dwarves threw plague rats in their wells. Unthinkable acts, yes, but damned efficient."

Malrich eyed Emethius for a moment, clearly put off by Emethius's sentiment. "I don't think you really believe those are an effective means to an end."

"I would have agreed with you a year ago, but the world has changed." *I have changed*, was more like it, but Emethius kept that thought to himself. Emethius stood, and made a short bow to the dwarven table in honor of Biriss's performance. He then lifted his mug, and finished his drink in a single long draught. Before heading off to his room for the night, he turned to Malrich. "Sober yourself. We have a long road ahead of us. If we hope to survive the journey, we may have to act more like the dwarves than you would like."

CHAPTER
XIV
THE HERALD OF TIBER

Herald Cenna dabbed a piece of bread into his glass, letting it soak up the wine. The red wine looked like blood as it trailed up the length of the bread. Leta sat across from him, her legs primly crossed, her fingers steepled on her knee. Her breakfast remained untouched on the table.

"Isn't it a miracle what happened with Little Orso?" said Herald Cenna, plopping the piece of sodden bread in his mouth.

Leta raised an eyebrow. To discuss Orso Petrius was certainly not the reason she had asked Herald Cenna to meet. She had been trying to speak in private with Herald Cenna for nearly a fortnight, but every time their paths crossed he was always in the company of others. By day, his gaggle of students was never far away, be it the children he lectured in the morning, or the young acolytes and Tiber Brothers he trained in the afternoon. At night, Lady Miren was at his side so often one might have thought Herald Cenna was courting the old widow, were it not for his oath of celibacy. To win a moment of his time, Leta had arranged for Sister Beli to take his morning class on a tour of the Vacian Monastery.

Unfortunately, Herald Cenna and Leta were not entirely alone. Treves, Herald Cenna's leech boy, sat in the corner. For once Treves wasn't jotting down notes on his scratch pad. His hands were wrapped in gauze. Apparently, Sir Rupert had badly injured his hand in a training accident, and Treves was nice enough to volunteer a bit of his vitality to save the old knight's hand. Leta would have felt sorry for the boy if she wasn't so frustrated by his presence.

"It's a miracle that Orso didn't bleed to death, if that's what you mean," said Leta, trying to keep her irritation from showing. "My father already lectured me on the topic. I shouldn't have cut the rabbit so deep. I'll admit it was my fault."

Cenna gave her a dismissive wave. "That's not what I meant. Isn't it a miracle that Orso's a transfuser! The gods have given us a gift. Merridia was rudderless and without direction. But now I see a clear path forward. He's only two generations removed from the ruling line, you know. Some say he looks like High Lord Leonius."

Leta forced a smile — it was the only way to contain her scowl. Leonius was Leta's great-grandfather. He was also Leta and Orso's last common ancestor, and Orso's only legitimate link to the Throne of Roses. "You believe Orso will become High Lord?"

"High Lord Valerius has no direct heir, that is, unless you have another son."

"I consider myself the heir," said Leta hotly.

"That is an interesting, albeit, unlikely notion." Cenna tapped his knee twice. It was an innocuous gesture that most would have missed, but it had a hidden meaning — this was a discussion for another time. Cenna shrugged. "But who am I to tell you it's not possible. In the end, it's the choice of the gods." Cenna dunked another piece of wine soaked bread into his mouth. Wine dribbled down his chin. He cleaned his face with a silk handkerchief, staining the precious fabric red.

A decadent display of wealth for a man who has sworn a vow of poverty, thought Leta, feeling rather annoyed. Of course, everything was decadent in the palace complex, even in the humble quarters of the Herald of the Tiber Order. Leta looked around the room. The marble flooring was mostly covered by precious rugs from Saterland. A Tremelese dagger hung over the mantle; the finely folded metal of its blades had ripples that seemed to shimmer and move. There was gold everywhere. Gold inlay. Gold statues. Gold trays beset with gold cups. Even the map on the wall was covered in gold leaf.

Leta stood to get a better look at the map. The borders of the six diocese were outlined in silver, and the cities were represented by gemstones. The size of the gemstone seemed to reflect the size of each city's population. "Did you ever see the results of the last census?" asked Leta, as she examined the map.

"I did, but I fear to say the results were not very useful," replied Cenna. "The numbers were inaccurate. It's my fault, really. Herald Carrick put me in charge of tabulating the results as they came in. I didn't catch how off the numbers were until your brother had already toured half of Merridia. In hindsight, I believe your brother was sending in false tallies."

That piqued Leta's interest. "Would it be possible to see the results?"

"I'll see if I can find them for you," said Herald Cenna, as he cracked open a pomegranate, letting its red innards spill down his fingers. He sucked his fingers dry between words. "A great many documents were destroyed when Herald Carrick was declared a heretic. I can't say precisely what happened to the records." He called over his shoulder. "Treves, will you go to the court archives and see if a copy of the most recent census is available?"

"Right now?" asked Treves, not rising from his seat.

"Yes, you daft child. Right now. Why else would I have asked?" Cenna chuckled to himself as he watched Treves fumble with the doorknob with his bandaged hands. Treves finally got the knob to turn and hurried out the door. "Leech boys aren't always the cleverest of lads, nor the most obedient, but we take what the gods give us."

Leta watched Treves depart from the corner of her eye, waiting until he was out of earshot. "Did you know that two of the children Lady Miren is holding hostage are from Estri?" Leta tapped her finger on the gemstone representing the city. "Both of their fathers assisted Meriatis with the census. Peculiar, isn't it?"

"Honestly, that doesn't surprise me," said Cenna. "I believe your brother was using the census as cover to recruit men for his rebellion. He spent over six months away from Mayal. The gods only know who he talked to and where he went." Cenna stared down at his plate and frowned. "Had

I only been paying closer attention to the numbers he was sending in, I might have noticed something was wrong before things got out of hand. But that's the way it is with the Blackheart. A person with the affliction can hide in plain sight for years, secretly doing the Shadow's bidding, and no one is the wiser until it's too late."

Leta couldn't ignore her own blame in the matter. She, too, had failed to detect Meriatis's symptoms. *And I'm a trained healer.* She turned away from the map and returned to her seat.

Cenna read the displeasure on her face. "We're alone now. It's time to be forthright; you didn't request a private meeting to discuss census results."

"No, I did not," Leta admitted. She thrummed her fingers against the armrest of her chair, trying to come up with a delicate way to preface her question. She decided to just be blunt. "I want to know what Lady Miren is doing with the rebels her tribunal finds guilty?"

Herald Cenna's bushy eyebrows raised with surprise. "That is an important question, and I'll be honest with you — I don't know."

"They're being condemned to the headman's ax." Just saying it, caused Leta to feel sick to her stomach. "Can't you be straight with me and admit the truth?"

"Headsman's ax — now there's a farce." Herald Cenna gave a half-hearted laugh, and for a second it looked as if he might choke on his food. "You should eat something. You look as thin as a rail." He was clearly trying to change the subject.

Leta slid her plate to the far side of the table. "I haven't had much of an appetite of late," said Leta. "My conscience has been troubling me."

"That's unfortunate, my dear," said the herald, still acting oblivious. "But a bit of guilt is not an awful thing. In the eyes of the gods we are all failures." He plucked the choicest strawberry from Leta's plate. "We must do the best that we are able, finding pleasure in the gifts the gods have granted us." He plopped the strawberry in his mouth and smiled.

Leta was not letting him off that easily. She swatted his hand aside when he reached for another strawberry. His face curled in mock umbrage.

"Will you at least admit to serving on Lady Miren's tribunal?" demanded Leta.

Cenna's face softened and for a moment he looked a bit like a child caught in mischief. He lifted his hands in surrender. "Heretics and rebels, Leta, we are convicting heretics and rebels. And yes, I'll admit it. I did serve on the tribunal." He reached for another strawberry, and this time Leta let him have it. "It was not by choice, I would like to add, but orders are orders. A man of the faith was needed to rebuke the claims being made by the heretics."

"I knew it," snapped Leta, letting her excitement get the better of her. "What happens to the men who are found guilty?"

"As I said before, I don't know precisely. It has been months since we last convened. My memory of it all is a little hazy." He waved his hand as if it were a trivial matter. "I heard one rumor that the convicts were being sent to work on Tremelese galleys. Another said they were being sold to the Citilian family in Caore to serve as field hands. I know a few men whose crimes were less severe were allowed to sign service contracts with Admiral Ferrus. A little military vigor might be precisely what those heretics need. But I can assure you, no one is receiving a death sentence. That would be a violation of God's Law."

Tell that to the headsman, Leta wanted to reply. She decided to hold her tongue. "I'm not imagining things, Cenna. The man who led the protest at the memorial service was in my monastery. I granted him his last rights."

Cenna gave her a patronizing smirk. "I fear your

eyes are deceiving you. I know for a fact that there were no arrests made at the memorial service. All of those heretics disappeared into the crowd."

"It was the same man."

"I'll humor you, let's say it was the same man. We didn't send him to you, so that means he ended up there of his own accord. Doesn't it make sense that a person afflicted with the Blackheart would be bedfellows with the rebels? Madness seeks out madness, or so they say. Your brother had the Blackheart, it stands to reason that some of his followers would as well. It was only a matter of time before some of the rebels ended up in your monastery, not because the tribunal sent them there, but because the Blackheart progressed to such a degree it was no longer safe for them to be free in our society."

"They're being sent to me!" snapped Leta. Unable to contain her frustration, she smacked her hand against the table. She couldn't stand to hear another dishonest answer slip past Cenna's lips.

Cenna leaned back in his seat and eyed the hollow pomegranate rind. "I don't know," Cenna said finally, shaking his head. "Maybe it's true, but I just don't know." He looked up at Leta, his old rheumy eyes regarding her queerly. "They are traitors, Leta, every last one of them. Lady Miren is correct when she says they are a danger to this state. The rebels would have the Line of Roses come to an end."

"That's not how I remember the rebellion," snapped Leta. "My brother intended to seat himself upon the Throne of Roses, replacing one of Benisor's descendent's with another. The line would have continued." In her mind's eye she envisioned Meriatis as a child quaking upon the throne, his face frozen with rictus. She shuddered at the disquieting memory. "Who ordered the creation of the tribunal?"

"This is something I am not at liberty to say."

"I am the priestess of the Vacian Order and daughter of the high lord. I deserve to know."

"I'll take delight in that knowledge when I'm brought before the tribunal for treason."

For a moment Leta imagined a hint of fear flared in Cenna's eyes. *Is he afraid of Lady Miren?*

Cenna sighed. "Your father's own orders, my dear. The tribunal was created on your father's own orders."

Now Leta was truly furious. Her father had asked her to take over the administration of last rights to Blackheart victims because he was too much of a coward to do the job himself. Then he ordered Lady Miren to hunt down the rebels who had sworn to his son's banner. He delegated all tasks, and took on no responsibility of his own. She was tempted to storm into the Court of Bariil and confront her father immediately.

Cenna reached out and took her hand, perhaps sensing her turmoil. "Calm, Leta, be calm. Now is not the time for rash decisions. If you truly intend to sit upon the Throne of Roses one day, something no woman has ever done, the politics of all of this are very important. Your service as the Priestess of Vacia gives you merit, and your birthright gives you a legitimate claim. But most would not suffer a women in a seat ordained by the gods for a man."

"The god-saint Tiberius granted the throne to Benisor's line — there was no reference to man or woman. As things stand, Benisor's line ends with me."

"All trees have many branches, my dear. Some limbs have grown sturdier than others," said Cenna, clearly referencing Orso Petrius and his newfound abilities as a transfuser. "All of your actions must be calculated, or you will find that your branch has grown brittle. It will only take a sharp breeze to send you toppling over once your father is gone. A degree of care now will pay dividends in the future. It is crucial that you don't look sympathetic to your brother's heresy."

"I need proof, Cenna. Hard proof that Lady Miren is sending people to my monastery," said Leta. "For those afflicted with the Blackheart, the headsman is an act of compassion. But for the heretic or rebel, the headsman is an act of murder. There is a special place in hell for murderers, and I will not be complicit. Before I grant another final sacrament you are going to accompany me to the monastery and look into the face of every man, woman, and child under my care, and confirm that none of them came from your tribunal."

"I walk the halls of your inner ward everyday," snapped Cenna, showing a sudden flash of anger. "I am old, but I am neither daft nor blind. I would remember their faces. No, if your are receiving rebels, Leta, I fear to say this is more dire than you think. Lady Miren is bypassing the tribunal and sending some men straight to your monastery without a trial."

Leta nearly jumped out of her chair. "What do you mean by that?"

"It's just the musings of an old man, and probably nothing more." Cenna stood and brushed the crumbs from his robe. "Thank you for the quick bite to eat, but I must be getting back to my students." His voice dropped to a whisper. "If you truly wish to find out the truth, you will need to follow the wolf while he is on the prowl." He patted Leta's hand and walked from the room, leaving her alone with her thoughts.

· · ·

"*Follow the wolf while he is on the prowl?*" mouthed Leta, as she mulled over the herald's cryptic words. Herald Cenna was trying to help her, she could read that plainly on his face. But there were things he was not at liberty to say. There was something that even he, the Herald of the Tiber Order, feared.

There came a light knock at the door of Herald Cenna's study. Sister Beli peered inside without waiting for a reply. "I think we are good. I did exactly as you told me, and even took the children down into the crypts. I pretended to get lost to buy more time, and I think it worked out in our favor. I just passed Herald Cenna in the hall."

"And the girl, were you able to hold her back without rousing suspicion?"

Sister Beli laughed. "There was an, ah, accident."

"An accident?"

"I dumped an entire vase of rosewater on the poor child just as I was dismissing the class. She is changing into something dry as we speak."

"Then there isn't a moment to spare." Leta

jumped to her feet and kissed Beli on either cheek. "You would have made a splendid sneak-thief. Thank the gods you're on my side." She rushed off to the Vacian Monastery at once. The only reason she didn't run was to keep from rousing suspicion.

Leta's meeting with Herald Cenna had more than one purpose. Leta had done a bit of research on the three girls Lady Miren was keeping as hostages. She found Ionni Caird to be of special interest.

The girl's father, Lord Domnic Caird, had never openly declared for Meriatis's heresy, but more than one captured rebel had fingered Lord Domnic as a man sympathetic to the rebel cause. Supposedly, Lord Domnic provided the rebels with provisions just before the loyalists put Estri under siege. If the tales were true, he was largely responsible for the rebels being able to hold out for as long as they did.

Leta caught up with Ionni Caird just as the girl was about to exit the Vacian dormitory. The poor girl's hair was wet, and she was clothed in the habit of a Vacian Sister. The attire was much too large for the girl and she looked a bit comical. Her drenched pupil's robe was clasped in a knot in her hands.

"Priestess Leta," said Ionni, blinking with

surprise. She curtsied awkwardly, showing little improvement from when Lady Miren scolded her at breakfast. "I borrowed a robe from one of the sister's lockers. I hope you don't mind." Her cheeks noticeably flushed as she picked at the ill-fitting robe.

Leta parted her mouth, feigning shock over the girl's disheveled state. "You poor thing," she cooed, drawing on her maternal side. "What happened?"

"Sister Beli was showing the class how to grant a sacrament with rosewater when she tripped." She held out her sodden robe which stunk of roses. "I took the brunt of it."

"That's unfortunate, but the gods work in mysterious ways. The robe of a Vacian Sister looks good on you, child," said Leta, lying through her teeth. "Have you considered taking the vows?"

"Ha, of a sister?" The girl gave an audible snort. "I'm the daughter of a nobleman. I could never do something so rash without my father's blessing. I'm sure my father has already vetted a half-dozen men to be my husband."

"Oh, I doubt Lord Domnic would be that hard to convince," said Leta. "I would gladly write him, if you would like. The life of an acolyte is not all bad. A bit regimented for sure. And of course, it goes without saying, you couldn't venture north with Lady Miren when she departs for Chansel. Those studying to take the vows of a sister are required to stay here in Mayal."

Ionni's eyelids lifted a bit at this last part.

Leta smiled. "And, if in a couple of years you decide the Vacian Sisterhood is not for you, well that is your choice, as well. One can rescind their vows up until the day she becomes a full-fledged sister."

Ionni eyed Leta with suspicion, perhaps sensing that Leta's offer was a trap. "I wouldn't want to do anything to make Lady Miren angry."

The girl has a healthy degree of distrust, thought Leta. *Good*. That was preferable to a child who was eager to please. Of Lady Miren's three wards, Ionni was the oldest, fourteen and nearly a lady. Leta had purposefully selected the girl, hoping she was old enough to recognize the benefits of Leta's offer.

Leta motioned toward the nearest pew. "Why don't you have a seat and talk with me a moment." Ionni sat down and crossed her arms and legs — a guarded posture that spoke volumes about her willingness to trust a stranger. *Trust is woven as delicately as the Weaver's web,* thought Leta. She took a knee before the girl so that their eyes were at the same level.

"I know the court can be a confusing place, and Mayal is so big. How are you enjoying your visit to the midlands?"

"Life under Lady Miren's care is pleasant," answered the girl. Her voice contained the slightest of wavers. "Bree and Awen both have older sisters back home and they have taken to following my lead. It's a big responsibility — they are such innocent girls; I hope I serve as a good role model. And, of course, Lady Miren has been so generous to see to our boarding and schooling. She says we will all be proper ladies by the time we go home." The girl painted a sweet picture, but she couldn't say Lady Miren's name without clenching her jaw.

There is hatred in those eyes, realized Leta. *Now I need to stoke the flame.* Leta smiled innocently. "Your father's estate is outside of Estri?"

"The ruins of Estri, yes," Ionni was quick to correct.

"Oh, I remember now. You watched the city burn, didn't you? I recall your tale from our breakfast a while back. War is a terrible thing. I am sorry you had to see that. Perhaps you can settle a debate Lady Miren and I were having the other day; did Estri burn before or after the arrival of the Chanselese fleet?"

"It is difficult for me to remember."

"I understand," said Leta, her face sagging with false sympathy. "The passage of time makes all things more difficult to recall. But if you had to say it was one way or the other..."

Ionni bit her lip and frowned. "After, priestess, the fires started after the loyalist ships arrived. There were so many masts in the bay it was like a forest had crept up on the city in the middle of the night. I remember hearing my father say, I hope the fire spreads to the ships and burns the whole damn fleet to the ground."

So the rumors were true — loyalists burned the city, not the rebels. *How many died in the ensuing firestorm?* Leta struggled to keep her anger from showing on her face. "The rebels must have been truly desperate to burn their own stronghold to the ground."

"Aye, priestess, they were truly desperate." Ionni blinked, and Leta spied the first hint of a tear in the girl's eye.

Leta took Ionni's hands within her own. She was surprised to find herself genuinely moved by the girl's pain. Nysen would have been nearly the same age as this girl, had he survived.

Ionni looked at the glove covering Leta's left hand. "Did the gods speak to you when you touched the Throne of Roses?"

"No," Leta admitted. "I was only in contact for an instant."

"I accompanied Lady Miren to the throne room the other day," said Ionni, not taking her eyes off Leta's gloved hand. "The throne was empty, and I was half-tempted to throw myself on the seat."

"Did you intend to kill yourself?"

"No, nothing so rash," said Ionni, shaking her head. "I wanted to ask the gods for justice. Justice for my family. Justice for the people of Estri."

There it was, the handle of the knife Leta needed to twist. "I am sorry about what happened at Estri. Although I had no part in the massacre, it was done in my family's name, and that brings me great shame. I wish I could change the past, but I can't. What I can do, is provide you with the justice you seek. But in order to do that, I need your help. I am looking for something specific. You are at Lady Miren's side most of the day; does she ever meet with other high officials or make mention of a tribunal?"

The girl glanced over her shoulder and surveyed the room, making sure they were truly alone. When she answered, her voice was hardly a whisper. "Lady Miren is often in council with Herald Cenna, but most of their talk concerns the building of a new temple in Chansel. She meets with your father,

I mean, the high lord, once a week for lunch. And she dines quite often with General Saterius and Lady Gwenn. But a meeting with many high officials at once? That I could not say. The only time I am not in Lady Miren's company is during my classes and on the sabbath, when she usually takes her leave around dusk to visit the Court of Bariil. She seldom returns before midnight."

Leta raised an eyebrow. She had never seen Lady Miren in attendance at the Court of Bariil. "There are many temples in Mayal. Are you sure she attends the service at the Court of Bariil and not somewhere else?"

"I'm quite certain. Where else would she go?" Ionni smiled the slightest of smiles.

This was Ionni's quiet revenge, Leta realized. The girl just provided her with the date and time of Lady Miren's secret tribunal. Now all Leta had to do was follow Lady Miren's carriage and see whom she met.

"Ahem." Ionni loudly cleared her throat and nodded toward the door. Orso was standing in the doorway.

"It's about time I found you," said the boy in a huff.

"I was just talking to the priestess about the five Virtues of Vacia," said Ionni, not hesitating for a second to conjure up a lie. She stood and straightened her over-sized robe. "The first virtue is humility, which I certainly need more of. The second is studiousness, which is something you should practice, Orso. The third virtue is honesty..."

"I know the five virtues," said Orso. "Humility, studiousness, honesty, compassion, and piety." He waved his hand dismissively and came stomping down the length of the hall. "Food is the only virtue I care about right now. We don't get to eat until Herald Cenna finishes his lecture, and he won't start until you're present. Let's go!"

"Hopefully we can speak again soon, Priestess Leta," said Ionni. "I find the Vacian Sisterhood very intriguing." She curtsied, and this time her form was absolutely perfect.

Orso grabbed Ionni by the hand before she could say another word and pulled her toward the door. Ionni hopped along on her good leg, struggling to keep pace.

He's a cruel boy, thought Leta, as she watched the children depart from the monastery. *May the gods protect Merridia if he ever becomes high lord.*

CHAPTER
XV
EMONIA

Malrich eyed the watchtower that stood on the far side of the bridge. The only sign that the lookout was manned was the green and white checkered flag that fluttered above the watchtower's turret. He half expected a troop of Emoni soldiers to come running out of the gate at any moment and bar the path with drawn swords. To his surprise, no one materialized from the tower.

"They're likely still drunk from last night's revelry," said Emethius as he spurred his horse across the bridge.

Malrich followed close behind, keeping one eye on the arrow slits that wreathed the tower. He always imagined the border between Merridia and Emonia would be guarded. Then again, why waste the money? There had not been open hostilities between the two realms in over a decade. One had to go even farther back in history, over a hundred years, to find a time when there was actually all out war between the lands.

The Emoni watchtower looked like a toy when compared to the monolithic Cul tower that stood nearby. The Cul tower leaned out over the river, threatening to fall. Crumbling buttresses wreathed its base. It seemed to Malrich that they were the only thing keeping the tower upright.

Emethius nodded toward the Cul tower. "According to legend, so many soldiers died taking this tower from the Cul, one could climb the mound of bodies and enter through the third story window."

Malrich laughed. "There isn't a third story window."

"Nor is there a fourth or a fifth."

The closest thing the tower had to windows were narrow embrasures hardly wider than a fist. Malrich shook his head. Most stories concerning the Cul were much like this tower, apocryphal tales that crumbled upon further examination.

"Still, the foundation is solid," muttered Malrich as he eyed the bedrock upon which the Cul tower was built. He snapped his reins, driving his horse to catch up with Emethius.

"Remind me again of our little farce," said

Malrich once the watchtower had fallen out of view, and he was certain their conversation would not be overheard.

"We are traveling west searching for home remedies for the Blackheart. We're following the orders of Herald Cenna, no less." Emethius was wearing the fox tail cloak of a master healer. Where he had come upon the garment, Malrich could not say, but it looked genuine. Emethius even had all of the trinkets one might expect a healer to possess. His young age was the only thing that might draw suspicion. That, and the fact that Emethius couldn't actually perform a transfusion. *Hopefully no one asks*, thought Malrich.

"We hail from Henna Lu," continued Emethius. "There's no use in lying about our origins. Anyone with a decent ear for accents will pin us as southlanders in a second. You, sir, are my leech boy."

Malrich snorted. "My mum always thought I'd make a good Tiber Brother."

"Fitting," said Emethius, laughing at the irony. "Never have I known a more godless man."

"Oh, I believe in the gods," said Malirch. "Only a fool wouldn't. I fear the gods. I loathe the gods. But isn't that how the gods like it? Just watch, I might be the most devout Tiber Brother you've ever seen." He took a lengthy draw from his canteen and smirked.

"Hopefully we don't come across anyone who needs me to leech them a new liver." Emethius pretended to shudder, causing his fur cloak to become a rippling wave of orange, black, and white. "Your vitality, I fear, would be a bit lacking."

Not wanting to draw attention to themselves, they continued on at a leisurely pace through the morning. There were few other travelers on the road — namely traders bound for Merridia — and Malrich and Emethius mostly had the road to themselves. They rode side by side, while Baylilly trotted faithfully behind them, free of any lead.

Malrich came into possession of his current horse by claiming it off a dead rebel. He named the stallion Etso, which simply meant horse in the old tongue. Malrich had to admit it wasn't the most original name, but by that point in the rebellion he wasn't feeling especially creative. He had already lost three horses in battle. One broke its leg during a charge. The second and third were shot out from beneath him. With that record, Malrich didn't see much use in granting his new mount a proper name, seeing as it likely wasn't long for this world. Miraculously, Etso managed to survive the remainder of the war. As stallions went, Etso was a true asshole. He was prone to kick or bite anyone he didn't trust, a trait that saved Malrich's life on more than one occasion. If any horse was going to see Malrich through the harrowing journey that lay ahead, it would be Etso.

By mid-afternoon they had climbed out of the undulating hills that surrounded the Osspherus Vale, and found themselves within the treeless country known as Veren Lo. This swath of land, which fell between the Osspherus and Ulma Rivers, was under the control of the Citilian family, who were the faithful marchwardens of the Emoni king.

The hills acted as a subtle barrier between Merridia and Emonia, helping to preserve the illusion that all things were equal upon either side of the river. But once they journeyed through the hills the differences were undeniable. Serfs labored ceaselessly in the fields that lined either side of the road. The serfs were tied to the land and to the fief lord for whom they served. They tilled the soil without love, going through the motions like prisoners. Ramshackle homes made of sod brick and thatched roofs dotted the countryside. Overseers on horseback rode amongst the wretched classes, prodding with rods when coarse words did not suffice.

Malrich had never seen such a downtrodden

people in his life. He had heard stories, of course, but it was worse than he imagined. "They are not quite slaves, but they are very near to it," said Malrich, as he watched an overseer crack a whip at the heels of an elderly man. His stomach grumbled with disgust, and he took a long swig from his canteen.

"Their way is the old way, a vile custom the Emoni brought from across the sea," said Emethius, noting the shock in Malrich's eyes. "Merridia would look the same were it not for the schism. The gods never intended for Eremel to be divided into multiple realms. They brought two kings from across the sea to lord over two kingdoms and two peoples. Eremel and Tremel. One kingdom for the dwarves and one kingdom for the talsani."

"Then the gods should have protected King Ordin from that Cul arrow," said Malrich with a snort.

"It was our people who broke the line of succession, not the Emoni."

That much of the tale, Malrich knew. At the dawn of the new age, King Ordin guided the talsani pilgrims across the sea. When he was killed in battle the line of succession was unclear. Most assumed Ordin's eldest son, Fenis, was the rightful heir. But

Benisor, King Ordin's brother, proclaimed himself the prophet of Calaban and crowned himself high lord. Eremel became a broken land. One realm became two, and then two became three. Talsani made war against talsani, and the true enemy was forgotten. Thus, the Cul survived in Eremel when they should have been driven into extinction.

"We've been noticed," said Malrich. He directed Emethius's gaze to a group of horsemen gathered near a cow pen. They were conversing amongst themselves, gesturing toward the travelers.

"Press on," instructed Emethius. "If they demand a toll, we've brought coin for that reason. And if they want more than copper, we have also brought steel." He patted the pommel of his sword.

The horsemen did not accost them, but Malrich had little doubt they were unhappy to see two unknown riders crossing their land, even if one appeared to be a master healer.

As dusk neared, the fortified city of Caore came into view. It served as the region's capital, and was the seat of Citilian authority. The town was perched atop a mesa that soared hundreds of feet above the valley below. They skirted the city's north face by a wide margin, avoiding the watchful eyes within the sentry towers that wreathed the city like the prongs of a crown.

Both agreed it would be wise to avoid the local inns and taverns, and instead took shelter within a narrow grotto situated a league west of the city. The grotto was carved into the rock face of a hill and clearly served as a religious shrine. Its portal was north-facing toward the monolith of Calaban. Hundreds of spent candles littered the floor, and in the back stood a wooden effigy built in the likeness of a winged man. Folded pieces of parchment were stuffed in hollow alcoves near the statuette. Each one was a personal prayer to the gods.

Malrich lit a fire to ward off the evening chill and collected a small pile of folded prayers. He carefully unfolded each one, reading the message within. Most concerned the Blackheart.

'Save my mother, o' gods on high.'

'My father is sick.'

'My son is dying.'

'My wife's flesh has lost all of its color and her eyes are as black as coal.'

'The Shadow creeps as it ever does.'

'The Shadow creeps as it ever does.'

'The Shadow creeps as it ever does.'

"You should leave those alone," chided Emethius, as he ate his rations; a strip of dried pork that was as hard as leather and a hunk of stale bread. "Those messages weren't meant for mortal eyes."

"You don't actually believe the Calabanesi care what is written here, do you?" said Malrich. He took a swig from his canteen, filling the alcove with the pungent smell of liquor.

"Is it hard to be so spiteful of the gods?"

"No," said Malrich with a sneer. "When you beg and plead with the gods and your only answer is more suffering, it becomes obvious real quick that the gods don't give one damn about you. They've abandoned me. It wasn't so hard to abandon them back." He took another draw from his canteen. "The gods haven't time for our troubles, Emethius. They never have."

"Perhaps you're right," replied Emethius hotly. "But neither do I." Emethius snatched the canteen from Malrich's hands as he was fumbling with the cork. He dumped the canteen's contents into the fire. With an audible swoosh, the alcohol ignited in a blast of heat. He hurled the empty canteen onto Malrich's lap. "You can wallow in self-pity all you want, Mal, I won't fault you for it. But you're going to do it sober."

Malrich looked at the canteen, then Emethius, then back again. Finally, he just shook his head and continued reading the folded prayers.

Soon, Emethius was snoring, but Malrich

couldn't sleep. He read every single folded prayer, and when sleep continued to elude him, he read them all a second and then a third time. It was haunting to see how similar all of the evocations were.

'*My brother is speaking in tongues.*'

'*My wife almost killed our child.*'

'*My husband poured boiling water on himself.*'

It's as if they are all of one mind, thought Malrich. Each message darkly reminded him of his wife and the vile curse the Blackheart had brought upon their home. Unable to take it any longer, Malrich cast the lot of prayers into the fire. The pieces of parchment curled and wilted like the legs of a dying spider. Malrich settled his back against the wall and closed his eyes. Sleep never came.

I needed that drink more than I thought, Malrich realized as the night wore on. By midnight his hands were shaking and his head ached liked someone was drilling into his skull. His stomach curdled, and he cursed Emethius under his breath as he tried to keep the contents of his supper down. Malrich had always known he would have to forgo alcohol at some point in their journey. He just wasn't ready for it yet — not mentally, not physically, certainly not emotionally.

All night long ethereal visions danced in the

shadows of the grotto. He saw a woman standing over him, wagging a disapproving finger in his face. At first it was his wife, but later the shadowed figure became his mother-in-law. She held up a scorched shoe, as if it were evidence of his inadequacies as a father, a husband, a man.

A bear-faced figure visited him a few hours before sunrise. The man seemed intent upon telling Malrich something, but every time he opened his mouth it was like a thousand voices were speaking at once; all Malrich's anxiety-stricken mind could discern were growls and gasps. He counted the minutes until dawn, sweating and freezing in turns.

At first light he shook Emethius awake, grateful for companionship. If Malrich had slept a wink, he did not remember it. With eyes rimmed in black and a back bent in exhaustion, Malrich mounted Etso. They began west along the North Road before the sun had fully crested the horizon.

•   •   •

The farther west they went, the more desolate the land became. The road had once been carefully tended, as it served as the main highway linking the realms of Merridia, Emonia, and Dunis. But that was before the fall of Cella and the coming of the Cul. Few now traveled the interior of Emoni, save for the odd merchant bound for Hardthorn. The road had fallen into disuse. Its bridges were crumbling, and in places, the road was swallowed whole by the rolling grasslands of the pristine northern plains. Malrich hardly saw any of it. His body was starving for a drink.

In his youth, Malrich developed a special love for booze. But that love turned into something more severe after Ali took ill. It became a need that had to be fulfilled. Now that he was sober, his whole body ached. He bobbed atop his saddle in a sleep-deprived stupor, and on more than one occasion he caught himself about to fall off his horse. Emethius didn't say a disparaging word concerning Malrich's condition. *He's going to let me suffer through this without rubbing salt in the wound,* Malrich realized as the day wore on.

The second and third nights without alcohol were much like the first — waking nightmares broken by brief moments of sleep. But on the fourth night, when Malrich finally laid his head down to rest beneath a canopy of stars, he was taken by the deepest dreamless slumber he had ever experienced in his life. When he finally opened his eyes the following morning, he was shocked to find the sun was well above the horizon. Emethius sat beside the fire, boiling water in his canteen.

"Feeling better?" asked Emethius, not taking his eyes off the fire.

Malrich sat upright, finding that he felt shockingly refreshed. His head was clear, and all of his senses were honed and aware. He could hear birds chirping and the ceaseless rustle of the prairie grass. The brush of the cool morning breeze stirred the hairs on his arms and caused goosepimples to creep over his flesh. The sky above was bright and blue, and for the first time in several days the sun didn't hurt his eyes. He felt reborn. "Yeah, I guess I'm feeling better."

Emethius nodded and the slightest of smiles curled the corner of his mouth. "I need you at your sharpest, Mal, that's all. We'll both need to be at our best if we hope to survive this journey."

Malrich looked sheepishly at his toes. "Thank you, Emethius. I... well..., ever since Ali took sick..." He shrugged. "You know what I'm trying to say."

"I know," said Emethius, rising to his feet. "There's no need for an apology." He kicked dirt over the fire, smothering the embers, and nodded toward the horses which were already tacked. "Let's head out. It's going to be a long day and we're already getting a late start."

They reached the Ulma River as the sun neared

its zenith. The river was as old as the land itself, and meandered almost aimlessly as it flowed toward the great sea to the south, creating a vast flood plain. A month from now, the snowmelt from the Lehan Mountains would cause the river to double or even triple in size. It would be nearly impassable except at a few fords the Emoni held under guard. But the snowmelt had yet to arrive, and they only needed to ride a few miles upstream before they found a spot where the river was shallow enough to cross on foot.

Despite the calmness of the waters, Emethius and Malrich arrived to the far side of the river drenched and freezing. They disrobed, laying their clothes over rocks to dry, and started a fire. They ate lunch and sat lazily beside the crackling fire, enjoying its warmth.

"All right," began Malrich, as he rubbed his hands eagerly over the flames. "Here is the question of questions. When we return to Mayal safe and sound..." The mere mention of that concept caused Malrich to stifle a laugh.

"Do you have any doubt?" Emethius playfully hit Malrich's shoulder.

"My apologies," said Malrich waving his hand. "Let me continue." He cleared his throat. "When we return from our harrowing mission to the

Cultrator, with the cure for the Blackheart in hand, what precisely do you plan to do with it? You can't get near Meriatis, your cover has already been blown. So what's your plan?"

Emethius smiled. "For a man who doesn't believe he will live to see the next full moon, you are awfully concerned with the future."

"Logic would dictate that you should have a plan, is all," argued Malrich.

"My plan is simple. I'm going to walk up to High Lord Valerius and hand him the cure."

Malrich laughed, but quickly noted that Emethius was not smiling, nor was he even looking at Malrich. He was staring into the distance. "You're kidding, right?"

"No, I'm not," said Emethius, his eyes still set upon the horizon. "But we haven't time to discuss that right now. We're being watched."

Five horsemen were standing atop the riverbank only a few hundred paces downstream from where Emethius and Malrich had forded the river. They sat in their saddles as still as statues with their hands clutching their reins. They wore heavy tan cloaks that concealed most of their features at this distance. Still, Malrich imagined he spied swords at their hips.

"Emoni soldiers?" asked Malrich quietly, as if

the watchers might be able to hear him.

"Probably marchwardens, or hired muscle from Caore," said Emethius, although there was uncertainty in his voice. "If I had to guess, someone got wise to the fact that we crossed the Osspherus without paying tribute."

"Well they haven't a right to collect a tax any longer," said Malrich, pointing to the river that separated them. "If they're from Caore, their claim ends at the Ulma River."

"As right as you might be, one of them has a bow," noted Emethius. "If they feel so inclined, they can shoot us full of arrows and collect whatever duty they see fit off our corpses. Justification will have little to do with it."

The two quickly packed their goods and donned their wet clothes. Malrich shivered — despite having sat next to a fire for more than an hour, the sodden fabric felt colder than when he had stripped it off his body. *No*, he corrected himself. It wasn't just his clothes that were colder. It felt as if the temperature had dropped a dozen degrees. It reminded him of the air just before a storm.

He watched the riders from the corner of his eye with growing disquiet. The five riders made no motion to advance or retreat. Swords remained in scabbards. Arrows were not strung to bows. Still, the whole image brought chills to Malrich's heart. *This isn't normal,* he thought to himself, as he strapped the last of his belongings to Etso's saddle. He looked to Emethius and found he had the same worried expression on his face.

Something wasn't right, Malrich could feel it in his gut. His first instinct was to reach for the canteen at his hip. He reminded himself it was empty, and his hand wandered to the pommel of his sword instead.

"No," whispered Emethius. "Not two against five."

"I'd rather confront the bastards and have a fight than be hunted," said Malrich.

"Aye? So would I," said Emethius. "But I'd sooner live. If they give chase, we'll have a league on them before they manage to cross the river. It will be a test of endurance. We can trade off riding Baylilly to give our horses a break. They'll ride their horses into the ground before they catch us."

Malrich cursed under his breath. He had never been one to turn tail and run, but he knew Emethius was right.

"We need to find a way out of this riverbed as soon as possible," said Emethius. "Be prepared to ride hard."

They mounted their horses and headed north

along the dry portion of the riverbed, hugging the sheer earthen wall of the west bank. The five riders shadowed their movement on the far side of the river.

"I've got an ill feeling about this," muttered Malrich under his breath.

"Stay patient," said Emethius. "They have yet to show their intentions. Steady and with a purpose, look ahead, fifty paces to your left." There was a cleft in the earth wall and a narrow path leading out of the riverbed.

"Quickly now," ordered Emethius. With a slap of his reins, he spurred his horse up the incline. Malrich followed right behind him. Only Baylilly struggled with the steep grade, but Malrich managed to lead her to the top. Once they reached the open plains beyond, they drove their horses into a full gallop, putting a rapidly growing distance between themselves and the five riders.

Malrich glanced over his shoulder. The five riders had arrived parallel with the cleft in the river bank, but they made no motion to ford the river. Malrich was overcome by a sudden sense of relief; *they're letting us go*. But just as he had that thought, there was pulse of light above the lead rider. For a moment Malrich imagined he saw a pair of wings, black as onyx, sprouting from the man's back and a halo cast of shimmering light above his brow.

"I'm seeing things," muttered Malrich. He blinked in wonder and gave his head a sharp shake. The wings and halo vanished, and the lead rider was once again indistinguishable from the other four. A cold shiver ran down Malrich's spine. *What witchcraft is this?*

"Did you see that?" Malrich had to yell to be heard over the thunder of horse hooves.

"Aye, I saw it," yelled Emethius in reply. "Although what it was I cannot say. Now drop your head and ride like you've never ridden before. Ride like the gods are nipping at your heels. Ride like your very life depends on it."

Malrich dared one final glance over his shoulder. What he saw left him even more confused and terrified. The riverbank was barren. The riders had disappeared.

"The gods help us," said Malrich, finding a prayer involuntarily passing from his lips. He kicked his heels into Etso's flanks, speeding the along horse even faster.

• • •

Malrich and Emethius rode until their horses were frothing at the mouth and the moon was high in the night sky. They had entered the vast open plains of the Varen Downs and there was very little cover to be found. Finally, a wall of deep black materialized out of the gloom. At first Malrich thought it was a cliff, but as they drew near, he discovered it was in fact a grove of ancient willows. The trees stood like wardens against the wind, wreathing the base of a lone hill.

"It's best we stop here for the night," said Emethius, as he surveyed the hilltop. "There's not a higher peak in a dozen leagues. If we're being followed we'll be able to see our pursuers clearly come dawn. Get a fire going, but keep it hidden on the far side of the hill. We don't need a beacon announcing our position to the surrounding countryside."

Malrich stumbled half-blind around the hilltop collecting kindling. Emethius remained atop the pinnacle, squinting off into the seemingly endless fields of grass that glowed gray-blue in the light of the waxing moon.

"They're out there, somewhere," said Emethius. "I can feel it."

"Blasted demons, they are," huffed Malrich as he broke a branch over his knee. "I'll tell you one thing, those riders weren't Emoni."

"No, I don't think they were," said Emethius, nodding his head in agreement. "But if not, then who?"

Malrich hadn't a clue. He examined a downed log in the evening light, but decided it was too rotten to burn well. "Are we doing something so damned important that someone might want us dead? I mean, the Cul will surely want to kill us once we reach the Cultrator, but that's for a completely different reason. It's in their nature, so to speak. But to be hunted by our own kind? That's not something I expected."

"We have no reason to assume those riders want us dead," replied Emethius. "That archer could have pinned us down then and there, but he didn't." Weak laugher passed Emethius's lips. "I think by journey's end this day will rank amongst our less eventful."

Malrich snorted. "So you say." Having gathered a sufficient pile of brush, he joined Emethius at the peak. He felt exposed atop the crown of the hill and dropped his voice. "There was something unnatural about them, Emethius."

Emethius waved him off. "Don't let your imagination get away from you."

"Be serious with me," said Malrich. "You felt it. You saw it. There was a presence."

Emethius was slow to respond — he seemed to be choosing his words carefully. "There is truth in what you say, but be careful with where you let your mind wander. I agree, there was something unusual about those riders; I don't know exactly what it was, but it was powerful."

"Like a god," stated Malrich, growing more certain with every passing moment.

Emethius eyed Malrich long and hard. "I don't know," he finally answered. "When I was young, I often visited the Court of Bariil with Prince Meriatis. On most days the Throne of Roses was as cold and quiet as any other piece of metal — ordinary copper, nothing more. But every once in awhile it seemed to take on an energy, much like the air does before a spring rain. It would seem to shiver and hum. It was nothing I could actually see or hear, mind you, but it was something I could perceive whenever I drew near the throne. That's what I felt when I saw the lead rider."

Malrich shuddered at the implication. He suddenly felt like a hunted animal. "I think we should both do as you instructed, and not let our imaginations run out of control. They were most likely border wardens, tasked with seeing us off their master's land." He stifled an uneasy laugh.

Emethius patted his friend's shoulder. "We're just not that important, Mal."

"Now there is definitely some truth in that."

Malrich pulled out a sliver of flint and drew it against his dagger, sending sparks flying into the pile of brush he had collected. An ember took hold, and Malrich held up the bundle and blew softly until tendrils of smoke were curling around his fingers. He grinned, his face illuminated by the flickering flame he had just coaxed to life.

Suddenly, there was a flare to the east, and there, not more than a league away, was another campfire burning as bright and hot as the rising sun.

Malrich rapped a knuckle against his empty canteen and nodded toward Emethius. No words needed to be exchanged. Malrich snuffed the flame with the heel of his boot, while Emethius hurried off to prep the horses. Cold, hungry, and tired they walked from the willow grove and into the windswept plains beyond.

CHAPTER
XVI
A SPY BY NIGHT

Leta feared it would be difficult to sneak out of the palace complex unnoticed, but it actually proved to be quite simple. The palace was typically locked down like a fortress after dusk, but tonight was no ordinary night. It was not only the sabbath, it was also the anniversary of the Battle of Vas Perloh.

Festivities were scheduled throughout the day to celebrate the Faceless God, and the palace complex was packed with revelers. Leta joined the revelry for a few drinks, making sure to speak to the necessary court gossips so that her presence was noticed, then she quietly slipped back to her apartment. She quickly changed her attire, putting on a filthy wool skirt and blouse — an outfit she had collected from one of the afflicted patients in the monastery. She pushed her hair up in a bun and covered her head and shoulders with a drab gray shawl. With her disguise complete, she regarded herself in a mirror. She could hardly recognize the woman in the reflection. Feeling pleased, Leta set off to intercept her aunt.

Lady Miren was residing in one of the many guest houses located on the palace grounds. They were used to host visiting dignitaries and lords. Miren had, of course, selected the largest and most opulent residence for herself. Leta found an inconspicuous spot to hide near the guest house, and there she waited. It did not take long. A carriage pulled up before the front door, and out of the house stepped Lady Miren dressed in her typical black attire.

Miren boarded the carriage and the driver whipped the horses into motion. Leta followed on foot, and chased the carriage through the palace's front gate. She was happy for her disguise. Sir Rupert and his men were standing at the gate checking invitations. Neither he nor any of his guards looked in Leta's direction as she hurried past. They were too busy policing those trying to get in to give more than a passing glance at those leaving.

Once they were out of the palace, the carriage driver quickened the pace. Leta had to jog to keep up. The carriage traveled the entire width of the city before rumbling across a drawbridge and vanishing behind an iron-banded door.

Leta scowled at the pair of brass lions flanking the drawbridge; the lions seemed to bare their teeth in reply. *I should have known*, thought Leta, surprised at her own foolishness. Lady Miren's carriage had disappeared into Fort Hermsburg, the home of Praetor Maxentius.

Praetor Maxentius lived in the fortress that protected the mouth of Mayal Harbor. The fortress occupied a stone bluff that overlooked the narrow strait between the Sea of Ro and the Bay of Lares. Trebuchets lined the fort's southern battlements, positioned such that they could sink any ship that tried to enter the harbor without the praetor's permission. Meanwhile, the artillery on the western battlements were capable of reaching the only bridge linking Mayal to the mainland.

Due to Fort Hermsberg's commanding position, it was often said, 'he who possesses the fort possesses the key to the city.' For the last century, that honor belonged to the patriarch of House Leonius.

Praetor Maxentius had been the master of Fort Hermsberg for over three decades. In that time, the fort had more or less become Maxentius's own personal fiefdom within the city of Mayal. Several hundred people lived behind those high stone walls; stablemen and servants, guards, squires, and sworn knights. Plus there was a plethora of offspring from the various branches of the Leonius family tree. More than a dozen chefs kept the kitchen churning out food all day long. Fort Hermsberg was probably one of the most densely populated structures in Mayal. Because of this, the fortress was lit up like a birthday cake, with candlelight emanating from nearly every window.

Of course Praetor Maxentius is involved, thought Leta, scrunching her nose with scorn. Lady Miren needed the military on her side if she hoped to successfully complete her purge. But that still left the identities of the other co-conspirators unknown.

Leta's attention was drawn to a window on the uppermost floor of the fortress. This was the window of Maxentius's private study. South facing, it provided a commanding view of the strait. Leta visited the room often as a child, and she still had fond memories of Meriatis lifting her up onto the window ledge so she could watch the ships sail in and out of the harbor.

Leta settled onto a street bench far enough away from the fortress as to not draw the attention of the guards walking a circuit atop the battlements.

For the next hour she kept her eyes fixed on the upper floor window. Four distinct silhouettes filtered past — one woman and three men. One figure was walking a perpetual loop around the room, pacing with lengthy strides, his arms clasped behind his back. Leta assumed this was Praetor Maxentius, given the figure's somewhat round frame. The woman was Lady Miren — the frilly mourner's bonnet on her head gave Leta no doubt. One of the other men was General Saterius; she could spy the pointed snout of his wolf cloak. It was the fourth member of this clandestine tribunal who gave Leta pause. The figure only approached the window once, and then, it was to close the curtains. The brief glimpse she got was of a slender, bald-headed figure.

Leta was trying to think of someone who matched that description when the iron-banded gate swung open. Leta scurried into the shadows of a nearby alley. She peeked around the corner just in time to catch sight of Lady Miren's carriage come bouncing down the road. The carriage's sidewalls were painted a garish shade of red and were covered in ornamental roses; it was impossible to miss.

The next carriage to exit the fortress was plain and bore no house standard, which was atypical. As the unmarked carriage trundled past, Leta detected the dark silhouette of a bald figure behind the window screen. Although the occupant's face was obscured, Leta could sense eyes staring straight at her. Leta suddenly felt naked and exposed. But before she could retreat down the alley, the carriage turned, taking a road toward the core of the city.

Leta was tempted to chase after the carriage and discover the identity of this fourth secret member, but she remembered Cenna's words. *I must follow the wolf.*

Last to exit Fort Hermsberg were three riders. Saterius was at their lead, draped in his wolf cloak. A pair of lean-faced men rode on either side of him.

The wolf is on the prowl, thought Leta, *now let's see where he goes.* She followed after the three riders, trailing behind them by a few hundred feet. She was not overly concerned with being spotted; the streets were crowded with people celebrating the holy day. Jubilant music drifted from every square. Bells rang and flutes whistled, while worshipers sang and danced. Many of the revelers wore colorful masks that kept their faces hidden, emulating the gods they so revered. Some walked about with iron chains tied about their waists. The chain belts clacked and clanked, creating an electric cadence to the street.

Leta followed Saterius into Bellman's Plaza. It was one of the oldest squares in the city, named after the ancient bell tower that stood at its center. The bell itself had long since collapsed from its steeple moorings, and had plummeted through the entire structure, coming to a rest on the ground floor where it still stood today. It was cracked straight through the middle, its bronze surface turned emerald with time. It had become a favorite of the local children, and a dozen kids were crawling about the face of the bell, drumming and kicking its walls in a fruitless effort to make it chime like it did when it hung aloft in the belfry.

A man garbed in only a loincloth was perched atop the stone railing of a fountain that stood opposite the bell tower. He was loudly lecturing to anyone who would listen. "The Shadow creeps as it ever does, and the sinful bask blissfully in the sun, unaware that the total eclipse draws nears. Repent, and be glad that you were given this chance. Look upon those that have failed to heed my warning." He motioned toward a group of Blackheart victims who were wallowing beneath the lip of the fountain.

It was becoming more and more common for families to abandon their loved ones once caring for them became too much of a burden. Each night the city guards would round up such victims and bring them to Leta's monastery.

The victims lying at the base of the fountain had their hands and feet bound. They were no longer a threat to others, but that did not stop them from doing harm to themselves. One woman was gouging her thumb into an open wound in her leg, while the man beside her was grating his head against the base of the fountain. Half of his nose was missing.

Every caring instinct in Leta's body screamed that she should go and comfort these poor victims of the Blackheart. But she knew she had to refrain. Tonight she needed to tend to those who conspired to kill the innocent. If Saterius was tracking down Lady Miren's next target, then he and his men might lead Leta to their quarry. If she could identify their victims beforehand, she could protect them once they showed up at her monastery. That was the hard proof she would need if she was going to confront her father. What would happen after that, she could not guess. But her father was a good man. He couldn't possibly send people to the headsman simply because they were rebels, could he?

"One thing at a time," she whispered to herself.

The square was packed with hundreds of people. A dozen carts full of fruits, grains, and other edible goods were gathered around the bell tower, while the remainder of the square was occupied by open air drinking parlors. Drunks were belting out competing songs, causing a raucous uproar as the patrons of each parlor tried to outdo the others.

Saterius and his two companions were conversing on the far side of the square. Saterius kept motioning toward a four story building adjacent to the bell tower — more specifically the building's second story balcony. One of his men nodded in agreement, and Saterius and the other rider departed, taking all three horses with them.

The watchman that remained behind took a seat in one of the open air parlors, situating himself so that he had an unobstructed view of the building Saterius had pointed out. He sat hunched over, squinting at the building. A server brought him a drink, and there he waited, his eyes shifting from balcony to door and back again while he sipped from a flagon of wine.

Leta concluded that whoever lived in this house was one of Lady Miren's leashed rats. Saterius was probably keeping an eye on the house to see who else might show up.

Leta took a seat behind the watchman and

quickly devised a plan. A prostitute was leaning against a nearby lamppost. She was basking in the yellow glow of the oil lamp, waving her hips at anyone who gave her more than a passing glance. The woman wore a short dress, hitched up to show more thigh than was ever appropriate in public, and her bodice raised her breasts almost to her chin. Such a brazen display of flesh was rare in a theocratic state such as Merridia, and Leta was mildly surprised a constable hadn't already arrested the woman. Leta waved the meretricious woman over.

The streets had not been kind to the woman. She was bone thin, and her cheeks were pockmarked with scars. She wore gold jewelry, but the thin veneer had mostly rubbed off her necklace and bracelets, revealing dull iron underneath. A sachet was tucked into her belt, and she reeked of stale flowers.

"Does the lady like the look of things?" said the woman, as she ran her fingernails along Leta's back in a slow, long draw.

Leta swallowed her disgust and smiled pleasantly. "No, the lady does not, but my companion is in need of some company, and you seem just the woman for the task." Leta motioned to the glowering watchman.

"What is the lady trying to involve me in?" The woman puffed out her lips in a doubtful frown. No amount of makeup would cover the canker scars wreathing her mouth.

"Nothing that a Silver Merridian won't keep you quiet about." Leta offered the woman a coin that bore the image of her father's face on one side, and Tiberius, chief god of Calaban, on the other. Both the god and high lord seemed to be judging her.

The woman collected the coin greedily and flicked it into the air with her thumb. It gave a nice sharp twang as it tumbled through the air. She collected it with a snatch of her palm, nodded in satisfaction, and walked off toward the watchman without saying another word.

The woman draped her body across the watchman's lap and began to fondle his chin. The watchman made a few half-hearted efforts to shove her aside, but each successive gesture grew more limp-wristed. Finally he gave in to his base urges, threw his arms around the woman's waist, and ordered her a drink.

How men had come to rule the world was beyond Leta's understanding. She turned her attention back to the house the watchman was supposed to be keeping tabs on. It wasn't long before a man appeared on the second floor balcony. He briefly surveyed the plaza, then disappeared indoors. A few minutes later, he came shuffling out the front door. He was a young man with droopy eyes and a blond head of short-cropped hair. His left leg was bowed, and he walked with a shambling gait. An injury from the war, Leta surmised — Mayal was full of men who bore physical scars from the rebellion.

The rebel hurried down a side street that branched off the main square. Leta dared a glance at Saterius's watchman. The man was still sitting with his arm hooked around the prostitute's waist, a besotted smirk planted firmly upon his face. The ruse had worked.

The rebel headed north and Leta followed after him, careful to always stay a few dozen paces back at all times. The man periodically checked over his shoulder, but otherwise kept on like everyone else. Outwardly, he appeared like so many others — a man simply taking an evening stroll to enjoy the festivities. But unlike everyone else, who seemed to have nowhere in particular they were heading, the man walked with a purpose, setting a brisk pace even with his bowed leg.

The crowd began to thin as they left the center of town. Leta was forced to trail farther and farther behind the man to remain unseen, until finally she rounded a corner and realized she and the rebel were the only two people on the street.

A sudden fear gripped Leta's heart. What if this man meant her harm? She stopped her pursuit and leaned against a wall, wishing she could disappear into the masonry.

The man kept on as before, although his posture had become more rigid, his shuffling gait more hesitant. Finally he came to the end of the road and stopped. He had come to the entrance of the north harbor. A dock reached out into the harbor where the road ended, while a raised wooden walkway ran in either direction along the shoreline. The man seemed to be having some trouble deciding which way to go.

"Left or right?" wondered Leta aloud.

The man seemed incapable of making a decision, and each passing moment caused the knot in Leta's throat to tighten. *Why isn't he moving? What's holding him back?*

There was a copper sign hanging above the dock entrance that was polished to a mirror-like sheen. A knot formed in Leta's chest. The man wasn't hesitating. He was looking straight at the sign, using the polished metal like a mirror. His gaze was set dead upon her position. Their eyes momentarily locked, and then the man was gone, shuffling down the left walkway as fast as his feet could take him.

Leta cursed herself for being so stupid and broke into a sprint. Her feet hammered against the cobblestones, causing an echo to reverberate down the empty street. The racket destroyed any hope she had of sneaking up on the man unnoticed, but she couldn't let the man slip away, not without getting a good look at his face. She reached the wooden walkway and grunted with frustration. The man was gone.

There were a dozen storefronts and warehouses down the path, plus a pair of dark uninviting alleys. Leta sighed. It would be foolish for her to go poking around this part of town by herself. This was the kind of place where women disappeared with some regularity, kidnapped and forced to service the men who worked aboard the trading galleys that made call at Mayal's port. Her adventure in spying had come to an uneventful end. Fate had worked against her, and she couldn't help thinking that it was probably for the better.

Leta turned to walk home, and as she did, she picked up a rock and threw it at the sign that had given her away. Her aim was true, and the sign gonged like a bell as it swung back and forth on its hinges, its polished surface catching the light of a nearby oil-lamp.

"Who puts a sign in front of a dock anyway," muttered Leta in annoyance. The thought caused her to squint and examine the sign more closely. The sign read, *"Private Dock. Closed to the Public."* Only the rich and powerful had private docks, and although this one was unmarked, she immediately recognized the ship that was moored at the end of the dock.

Leta had to stifle a gasp.

There floated the Fearless Runner, the capital ship of the Elyim Fleet, and the personal war galley of Admiral Ferrus. Her blood ran cold.

The rebel wasn't going to some dockside warehouse, he was going for the Fearless Runner. *Why would a rebel be heading to meet with Admiral Ferrus. Unless...*

Leta suddenly didn't know what to do. *You didn't see this,* screamed a voice in the back of her head. *Just turn around and walk home.*

Instead, Leta stepped out onto the dock and walked toward the admiral's ship.

CHAPTER
XVII
THE RUIN OF VAS PERLOH

Emethius squinted into the darkness. The rain was coming down so hard he was forced to use his hand as a shield to keep his vision from blurring. He spied a streak of yellow and a flicker of orange against the black backdrop.

"I'm imagining things," he reassured himself. "Nothing can burn in this downpour."

It had been raining since midmorning. The first dark clouds appeared on the horizon just after dawn. They came boiling across the plains like a reaching hand, and by mid-morning the forward wedge of an anvil-shaped cloud overtook them. The sun disappeared behind a veil of impenetrable black and the rain came down in earnest. It was a soaking relentless downpour, with raindrops so large they stung.

Emethius kept at his vigil, ignoring the impulse to flinch away from the freezing rain that lashed his exposed cheeks. He had to be certain.

There it was again. The hungry leap of a flame. A red banner waving in protest against the rain.

"How far?" called Malrich, momentarily illuminated by a streak of white lightning. He was fifty feet below Emethius, standing at the base of the rock outcrop. Malrich huddled beneath his cloak, his fingers impatiently drumming against his empty canteen.

"Half-a-league. No more," said Emethius. *But they may be a great deal closer.* The rain was making it difficult to gauge distance. "Tomorrow or the next day, our paths will cross."

Malrich cursed and kicked a stone, which he immediately regretted. He hopped around on one foot for a minute, then limped off to prep the horses.

Thus begins another sleepless night, thought Emethius, as he made his descent down the slippery stone outcrop.

He hadn't slept more than a few hours in the past three days. Or was it four? Day and night were beginning to blur together. He wondered if this was how Meriatis felt as he fled across the Billowing Flats with Praetor Maxentius's grand army hot on his heels.

Emethius sneered at the thought. *I am the last*

foolish rebel fighting for a lost cause.

At least Meriatis knew who was chasing him. Emethius didn't have the slightest clue who their pursuers were, only that they were a threat. One of them had a bow, and a skilled bowman would win a battle against two unarmored men every time. Then there was the rider Emethius took as their leader. When he closed his eyes, he could still see the man standing atop the embankment, his body shrouded in a halo of light. Emethius shuddered at the vision. Of course, he wasn't even sure if the memory was true — each day Emethius seemed to recall a more twisted version of the encounter. He gave his cheeks a sharp slap hoping to drive the cobwebs from his brain.

Since crossing the Ulma River, Emethius and Malrich had pressed onward nearly without rest, spurred on by the knowledge that their followers, the men Malrich had come to call the Watchers, were never far behind. They took turns riding Baylilly to give their own horses a break, and when all three horses were too exhausted to bear a rider, Malrich and Emethius trudged forward on foot.

Emethius's rump was blistered with saddle sores and his thighs were so wobbly he had trouble walking straight. He made the mistake of taking his boots off, and with them came a great slough of blistered flesh. Now his feet were wrapped with so many bandages he could scarcely move his toes. Still they pressed on, fighting pain, fighting exhaustion. They stopped to rest when their bodies had burned through every store of energy, and even then, only for a few hours.

Despite their relentless pace, each night the campfire of their pursuers drew closer. It was a losing race, Emethius knew, and he only saw one hope. Vas Perloh.

No sensible god-fearing man would venture into the city of the damned. During the Culing War, the city had served as the last bastion of the Cul east of the Morium. It was said that the ghosts of the dead still wandered the ruined city at night. Emethius gave little credence to such superstitious fears; he had lived long enough to know that the true terrors in the world were not ghouls and shadow-wraiths, but vile outlaws and vicious Cul. An abandoned city attracted unsavory denizens like a dead horse drew flies. The detour would be dangerous, but it would test the resolve and mettle of their pursuers like nothing else. In the close confines of the ruins, Emethius and Malrich might be able to spring an ambush that would put their pursuers at a disadvantage.

Advantages and disadvantages, risks and rewards. For

now, Emethius decided to keep the idea to himself. Malrich was in bad shape, and Emethius saw no reason to place another weight on his companion's already sagging shoulders.

They rode west.

Day came, marked by a lightening of the stormy sky. The downpour eased by midmorning, then ceased altogether come noon. The rain was replaced by a thick creeping fog that chilled to the bone. Visibility dropped to a hundred paces, if that.

Emethius and Malrich spoke little, exhaustion seizing them like a drunken stupor. Malrich spent the better part of the morning with his head turned back the way they had come. He swore he kept seeing figures approaching out of the fog, but each time Emethius turned to look, he saw nothing but the depthless grays of the swirling mist.

"There it is again," whispered Malrich, giving way to a panicked delusion.

"What?" asked Emethius, trying to restrain his agitation.

"Horses," began Malrich. His face was abnormally sullen and had a yellowish hue. His eyes were so bloodshot and puffy, one would have thought he had spent the entire night crying. "I'm more sure now than before. The clatter of hooves. A soft neighing. Those bastards are not far behind us."

"Not far behind," Emethius agreed.

The road was choked with mud; it sucked at their horses' hooves. Manos stamped forward with his ears pinned straight back and his stomach flecked with filth. Etso seemed to inherit Malrich's mood and became skittish at the slightest sound. Only Baylilly trudged on without a care, content as she ever was.

"The fog may be a godsend," said Emethius, deciding it was time to let Malrich in on his plan.

"How so?"

"As you are probably well aware, there are two paths forward," began Emethius. "Soon, the road will cut north, skirting Lake Ioria by a wide margin. But in doing so, the path will take us much farther north than we need to go. Due west lies the forest of Veren Ador. I intended to avoid the haunted forest, but now that we find ourselves pursued it may be the best option. There is a road through the forest, or so the ancient maps attest, that will lead us to the banks of Lake Ioria. There was once a bridge spanning the water, although what remains of it I cannot say."

For a long time Malrich mulled over their options in silence. "I fear ghosts no more than you do," said Malrich finally. "But I expect our pursuers will be no different. They have followed us this far without apparent rhyme or reason. I doubt they will pause for a second to enter the cursed city because of the rumor of ghosts."

"We don't need them to avoid Vas Perloh, we need them to believe *we* will avoid Vas Perloh. They've had nothing but a certain choice thus far — follow the North Road. We can use the fog as a shield and slip from the main trail unseen. They may never catch their mistake."

"Or they will follow us like a hound on a scent."

"If that's the case, we set an ambush at Vas Perloh. Neutralize the bowman, and the odds won't be far from even."

"Two versus four? I like the sound of that." Malrich spit, his opinion clearly cemented. "I get the fighting part, Emethius, I always have. It's the fleeing I can't stomach. I'd sooner venture to Vas Perloh and have an end to this pursuit, one way or the other, than keep fleeing like a scared hare and wind up with an arrow in my back.

"Then you're with me."

"Always."

Emethius ran his finger along the deep gouges in his vambrace. Each represented a life that was lost because of him. Emethius was not about to add Malrich to that number. "We turn west. If it comes to blows, it will be on our terms."

Malrich grinned devilishly and patted the pommel of his sword. "The old girl's been rusting in her sheath. She'll be glad to see the light of day."

A cairn of stacked stones was all that marked the fork in the road. The path that led to Vas Perloh had vanished beneath a carpet of knee-high grass. The North Road continued onward as before, the only clear way forward. Malrich toppled the stack of stones as they departed the North Road and forged a path across the prairie.

"We follow the flight of the sun," said Emethius, gesturing to the glowing sphere of white that shone dimly behind the ceiling of clouds. *The fog is thinning,* realized Emethius with disquiet. There was nothing to be done about that.

By mid-morning, the sun had burned away both the fog and the clouds, revealing a clear bright blue sky. To the west, a line of green ran across the horizon. "That must be the haunted forest," said Malrich. Emethius grunted in agreement.

The trees of the forest — ancient oaks and elms, chestnuts and pines — pushed back against the grassland, tumbling over each other with sun-seeking limbs. Spring had yet to arrive here, and the gnarled naked limbs resembled the knotted arms of a million reaching beasts.

Emethius's unease grew as they approached the forest. There was no apparent path through the tangled mess. But as they drew near, Emethius spotted a stone sculpture set at the base of a tree. Gray and covered in lichens, the sculpture was eroded by time. Still, Emethius could see that the sculpture had once been fashioned in the shape of a bear with words etched into the chest and stomach. The markings were indiscernible, yet Emethius recognized them on sight. They were Cul runes. Whether they were set there to protect or curse, Emethius could not say.

Malrich drew his sword and hacked at the underbrush, revealing an opening into the forest. "Look here, this path is too even to be a game trail," said Malrich. "This was once a road."

As if on cue, Baylilly stamped at the ground and turned over the topsoil, revealing clay-colored bricks underneath.

Emethius chewed at his lower lip as he peered into the heart of the forest. The canopy of twisted limbs blotted out the sun. "I've never seen a more uninviting path."

Malrich did not answer, but instead motioned east. The silhouettes of five horsemen appeared on the horizon.

"I have a sickening feeling they know exactly

where we are going," said Emethius. "It almost feels as if they are shooing us along, speeding us toward our destination."

"Or driving us into a trap."

"They may be one and the same." Emethius ducked beneath a low-hanging branch and entered the forest. "Hurry now, while we still have time."

Malrich cursed under his breath and followed next, while Baylilly took up the rear, trotting along as happy as ever. The five Watchers vanished behind a wall of twisted limbs and bark. *They will be joining us on the trail soon enough*, Emethius was certain.

The forest trail was narrow, only wide enough to advance single file. The road had originally been laid in flat stone, but tree roots had long since encroached. Roots as thick as a man's leg dove in and out of the ground like serpents, twisting and overturning the stonework. The horses managed the uneven path with difficulty, and Emethius was forced to slow their pace to a crawl; if one of the horses broke an ankle, it might seal all of their fates.

Everything within the forest was still. No birds sang, no crickets or cicadas chirped. Even the tops of the trees seemed untouched by the wind. For a long time all Emethius heard was the steady clomp of horse hooves. But after riding for what seemed like hours, he began to hear the soft hiss of moving water. At first it came as a relief, breaking the silent foreboding of the timeless forest. But with each passing minute the sound grew in intensity, until by the time they reached the banks of Lake Ioria the noise had amplified into a thunderous boom.

Emethius stopped at the shore and bowed his head, realizing his mistake. On the opposite shore stood the crumbling ruins of Vas Perloh, so close, yet impossibly far. Lake Ioria was in fact two lakes, the Green Water in the north and the Red Water in the south — that much Emethius's map showed correctly. What his map failed to illustrate was the fact that the two lakes were connected by a sliver of galloping white water that cascaded down a series of impassable cataracts. No creature that walked the earth, be they on two legs or four, could hope to ford the cataracts and survive.

Emethius pointed down the bank. "There's our way across."

Malrich grunted with discontent. "Let's go investigate what remains. The Watchers will be upon us soon."

A few hundred yards downstream stood the derelict remains of a bridge. Stone pillars stood at regular intervals, thrusting from the rapids like teeth. A few of the spans were still intact, but for the most part the pillars stood naked and alone. The bridge had ceased to serve any useful purpose long ago.

"Now I fear we have come to the trap," said Emethius. But even as he spoke a smile spread across his face and he pointed excitedly. "But look, there's a way!"

Strung just above the churning water were two guide ropes bolted to the south face of the first pillar. One was set at chest level, while the other was set low to accommodate a person's feet. They spanned across the raging river, dipping below the water line at the center, and then rising back up toward the opposite shore.

"No way," spurted Malrich, not liking the idea in the slightest. "If that archer catches up with us while we're stuck in the middle we'll be as good as dead. Let's make our stand right here and be done with this."

"No," said Emethius, yelling to be heard over the roar of the water. "We cross the river and cut the line once we reach the far shore. There's less risk."

Just then, the five Watchers emerged from the forest downstream. Malrich looked from the river to the Watchers, then back again. "What about the horses?"

"We abandon them, and we go now!" barked Emethius. Without hesitation, Emethius and Malrich dismounted and began to pull everything they could carry from their saddlebags.

The Watchers advanced, not keeping their distance as they had before. The bowman drew an arrow to his string. Another shouted something that was lost in the roar of rushing water. The one Emethius had taken as their leader remained just beneath the eaves of the forest, keeping his body concealed in the shadows.

With a saddlebag slung over either shoulder, Malrich rushed over to the ropes. He gave them a tenuous test with his hands and feet. The ropes were old and stained by slippery algae, but they seemed capable of bearing his weight. He locked his hand onto the guide rope overhead, and shimmied from the shore, side-stepping as quickly as he could. Emethius was right behind him.

The ropes swayed and bobbed with each step. The water raced by beneath them, a tumble of white foam. They had not made it more than a quarter way across the river when the Watchers reached their horses.

Baylilly and Manos didn't resist being handled, but Etso bit down on the first hand that reached for his reins. The Watcher reeled back howling in agony with two of his fingers missing at the joint. The bowman rushed forward and fired an arrow straight into Etso's eye, felling the horse instantly.

Malrich howled with rage, and had Emethius not been blocking his path, he would have probably clambered back to shore and taken on all five of the Watchers by himself.

"Keep going," ordered Emethius, shoving Malrich back in the right direction.

The Watchers began to go through the saddlebags Emethius and Malrich had left behind, dumping their contents on the ground. Each piece of parchment they found was examined thoroughly before being discarded into the river.

"What are they looking for?" screamed Malrich over the roar of the water.

Emethius could only shake his head in response.

Not finding whatever it was they sought, the Watchers threw the bags into the rapids with disgust. The archer motioned out across the water, and the two able-bodied Watchers leapt on to the rope bridge and gave chase. Hand over hand, they advanced with fluid motions and began to quickly close the gap.

"Go faster!" screamed Emethius.

They were nearing the center of the river. The

rope dipped below the waterline, submerging their ankles, then their knees, and finally their waists. Emethius could feel his body weakening with every passing moment as he fought against the relentless tug of the current.

One of the Watchers drew near. He reached for Emethius, grabbing the cuff of his sleeve. Emethius kicked, trying to drive some distance between himself and the Watcher. He lost his footing in the effort and almost got swept away.

Malrich was screaming something, but Emethius couldn't understand what he was saying. Water was beating against his chest and neck. He could feel his fingers losing their hold. The Watcher latched onto Emethius's shoulder, knotting his fingers into Emethius's fox fur cloak.

"*Ehwis, vapaj veppipa!*" barked the Watcher in a commanding tone. Emethius understood enough of the old tongue to know he was being asked to surrender.

A thousand questions raced through Emethius's head at once, but the loudest was this — *who still speaks in the old tongue?* Their eyes locked, and for a moment Emethius couldn't look away. The Watcher's face was pockmarked with sores, and he was completely bald, brows and eyelashes included. Yet it was the man's eyes that bothered Emethius the most. They were the color of the setting sun.

"The Perim Lu," said Emethius in wonder.

"*Ehwis, vapaj veppipa!*" repeated the Watcher.

"*Pe,*" replied Emethius in the old tongue.

In one sweeping motion Emethius drew his dagger and hacked through the bottom rope. Their footing disappeared, and the yellow-eyed Watcher was instantly swept away by the current. The remaining Watcher hooked his elbows over the top rope and hung on for dear life. The archer, who was still on dry ground, rushed to the shoreline and leveled his bow on Emethius. Everyone was screaming, but all Emethius could hear was the thunder of the rushing current. The archer let fly. Emethius cut the hand rope.

He plunged into a frozen world. The cold water was a punch to the stomach, and the air burst from his lungs. The rushing water dragged Emethius downstream, ramming his body against submerged rocks. Emethius kicked out with his feet, blindly hoping to fend off whatever hazards lay ahead. Rocks battered his legs, forcing his body whichever way they might have him go. He felt his ankle catch between two rocks, and for a second it felt like his leg was going to snap under the strain. His lungs were screaming for air, but try as he might he couldn't reach the surface. Then, just as suddenly, his ankle twisted free and his head popped above the surface.

I'm still holding the rope, realized Emethius in disbelief. Somehow his grip hadn't failed him.

Malrich was bobbing right in front of him. He spit a jet of water from his mouth and blinked in wonder.

The rope drew taut with a stiff jerk. The current had pulled them as far downstream as the rope would allow. Emethius was shocked to discover they were only a dozen yards from the west shore. Emethius and Malrich locked arms around one another. Then mustering what little strength they had left, they pulled themselves onto solid ground.

Emethius crawled trembling from the river while Malrich retched up water. Once he caught his breath, Emethius eyed the far shore. The three remaining Watchers were not attempting to ford the cataracts, and the two that had fallen into the water were nowhere to be seen. Satisfied that they were safe, at least for now, Emethius crawled over to a bed of leaves and fell into a well-deserved slumber.

• • •

When Emethius awoke, he found himself staring into Baylilly's flaring nostrils. For a few panicked moments he thought the Watchers had somehow managed to ford the cataracts, and he frantically took in his surroundings.

Night had come, and the gray light of the moon filtered through the trees and scattered across the ruined buildings of Vas Perloh. This was the grandest city in the Cul dominion until the armies of Emonia put it to the torch. The forest had reclaimed large swaths of the ancient city — everything was overrun by vegetation. Leafy vines blanketed stone walls, turning them green. Trees a dozen feet in diameter sprouted from the center of crumbling structures. There were a thousand places to hide within this landscape of shattered bricks and twisting vines, yet something in Emethius's gut told him they were alone.

It's the aura that seems to accompany the Watchers, Emethius realized. *That feeling that a storm is just beyond the horizon.* The air somehow felt lighter. The Watchers were gone.

"Then how did you get here?" asked Emethius, regarding Baylilly in disbelief.

Baylilly answered by nudging him with her snout.

"So that's how it's going to be, huh? You want a bribe for the truth." He gave the horse a well-deserved scratch upon the neck.

Emethius and Malrich had crawled ashore at the southern end of the cataracts, and a massive expanse of water lay before him. The water shimmered silver and gold, reflecting the light of the moon and the stars. *This is the Red Water,* realized Emethius. This was the site of the most horrific battle in the Culing War. The Emoni army would have been defeated were it not for the Faceless God. She descended from the monolith of Calaban to join the fray, and with a fiery chain in hand, she drove the Cul into the Red Water and then set the lake on fire.

A place with such a wicked history should feel frightening, thought Emethius, as if the cries of the vanquished could echo across eternity and haunt the present. But in truth he felt a sense of safety. It was the silence, he realized. Save for the roar of the cataracts and Malrich's snoring there was not another sound. Emethius doubted there was another living creature for a dozen leagues.

Malrich sat nearby, slouched upright against a tree. He had failed at his sentry duties, and was snoring softly, his head bobbing with every breath. Emethius smiled at his friend's failed effort to provide security. Marlich was a faithful and trustworthy companion, even if he was a bit of a bumbling guardian.

Emethius was bundled in a warm blanket, probably Malrich's doing. "Thank you," said Emethius quietly.

Malrich jumped, startled by the sudden noise. His first instinct was to reach for his sword, but after he saw they were alone, he settled down. "Oh, it was nothing," said Malrich, finally making sense of what Emethius said. He pointed to Emethius's forehead. "You've got a cut there. Sutures would be nice, but I don't have a thread or needle."

Emethius gingerly touched his brow. It was wrapped with a bandage — a skill Malrich had mastered while caring for his wife.

"The Watchers took Manos, but Baylilly bolted the second they let go of her bridle," explained Malrich. "The stubborn old mare somehow managed to swim the rapids. Loyalty will drive a beast to do foolish things."

Emethius smiled. Malrich's words could be used to describe any one of them. "I think we are safe for now," said Emethius, propping himself upright. "If the Watchers intend to pursue us, they will have to go around the entire lake. That will take four, maybe five days."

"I've been sitting here, thinking about what they could possibly want," began Malrich. "The Watchers seemed quite content with following us, that is, until it looked like we were going to slip away. The only thing I can figure, is that they hoped we would lead them to Meriatis's allies — this Sage and Sorceress that Ftoril was so keen to tell us nothing about."

"All right," said Emethius. "Suppose this is true. Why did they wish to find the Sage and Sorceress, and how would they know about them in the first place?"

"Ftoril might have talked."

"All sound reasoning, save one thing," said Emethius.

"Oh, what's that?"

"Ftoril was taken captive by Merridian soldiers, and there isn't a Merridian alive with eyes like the men who attacked us," said Emethius. "Nor is there a Dunie or Emoni."

"Then where are they from, and who do they serve?"

"The lost sons of Fenis," said Emethius. "Do you remember the poem?" Everyone learned the nursery rhyme as a child; it was meant to scare children and keep them from wandering far from home. Emethius hummed a line and then recited the poem.

> *"Of his second love, five babes were born*
> *Of bastardly blood, by the public scorned*

Benisor heirs but without royal hue
Yellow-eyed beauties of the Perim Lu
When they had grown up from boys to men
They chose the path that the gods condemn
In hubris they entered the Great Ador
The gods often claim what people abhor
Now their souls reside in the forest boughs
And all who enter may never come out."

Malrich laughed coarsely. "We are being chased by ghosts!"

"It is not as if we were not warned. We just did not recognize the warning. Ftoril already hinted at the Perim Lu being involved when she referred to Meriatis as the Wayward Prince. No, Malrich, it is time we open our eyes. The Perim Lu are alive, and I fear they may be serving the highest caste of all."

"The gods? Now there is a fine jest."

"I do not kid. Think about the Covenant."

"Between the mortals and the gods?"

"No, Malrich. The pact that the gods have amongst themselves." Emethius paused, troubled by the implications of what he was about to propose. "The Covenant forbids the gods from directly interfering in the lives of mortals. The Calabanesi can cajole with words and sway with reason, but they may not physically intervene. So instead they have selected certain mortals to serve as their agents on earth. High Lord Valerius is one. When he sits upon the Throne of Roses he is able to communicate directly with the gods. When Valerius preaches, he is expressing the opinions of the gods, and when he commands others to act, he is echoing orders that the gods themselves have made. In effect, he is the agent of the Calabanesi on earth."

Malrich wrinkled his nose. "I'm not a historian, but I seem to recall plenty of stories about god-saints saving the lives of mortals. What of Ilmwell and Niselus, or even the Faceless God of Vas Perloh?" He motioned to the ruins that surrounded them. "Weren't they in breach of this Covenant?"

"They surely were," said Emethius. "After Ilmwell and Niselus helped the dwarves destroy the Cul in Tremel they were Sundered by the Calabanesi."

"Sundered?"

"Killed might be a better way to put it. They were banished from this plane of existence and their souls were absorbed back into the One Soul. There is no higher price a god can pay. That is why Ilmwell and Niselus are so unique amongst the pantheon of gods. They are not revered as living gods, they are martyred." Emethius motioned to the Red Water; the surface of the lake lay placid and still, smooth as a pane of glass. "When the Faceless God of Vas Perloh rescued the faltering legions of the Emoni king, she hid her face behind a veil of impenetrable mist. When the battle was through, the soldiers of Emonia flocked to the goddess, begging to know who she was. And just like that..." He snapped his fingers. "The goddess vanished into thin air. Her true identity was never revealed."

"She got away with breaking the Covenant," said Malrich, nodding his head in sudden comprehension. "That is why she is revered as the god of cunning and guile."

"The gods bend the rules whenever it is necessary," said Emethius. "They could not allow the Cul to win the war and for the Shadow to be triumphant, thus they intervened. But under typical circumstances the Covenant is upheld and the gods exact their will through intermediaries."

Malrich motioned across the water to the unseen shore on the far side of the lake. "These Watchers, these men you call the Perim Lu — you believe they are agents of the gods?"

"I do," said Emethius, growing more certain of the idea as he talked. "Most religious scholars agree that High Lord Valerius cannot possibly be the only agent of the Calabanesi walking amongst us.

The world is too vast, and the evils that need to be contested are too many. When the Wayward Prince was captured by the Perim Lu, he claimed there was an entire civilization hidden within the Great Northern Ador. If this is true, we are not dealing with the five lost sons of Fenis, we are dealing with their descendants a dozen generations removed. There could be tens of thousands of them."

"A secret army that answers only to the gods. That is a terrifying thought." Malrich paused, as if hesitant to even say the words. "I have a theory of my own."

"Oh?"

"There was a god accompanying the men who attacked us."

Emethius had already come to the same conclusion, but he had not brought it to Malrich's attention, fearful of how he might respond. "The fifth Watcher that remained within the shadows of the forest."

"The figure shrouded in a halo of light," added Malrich.

Emethius sighed. "By taking up Meriatis's cause, I fear we have fallen afoul of the gods." He looked across the lake. "This may only be a reprieve. I'm terrified by the prospect of what lies ahead."

"I'm suddenly pining for a drink," said Malrich

with a snort.

"I think we both are." For a brief moment Emethius thought he detected the flare of two yellow orbs staring back at him from the opposite shore. Emethius scowled in reply, ignoring the cold shiver that was working its way up his spine and causing all of his hairs to stand on end.

AFTERWORD

Thank you for reading FRACTURED THRONE. Other books in the series are currently in the works. For more information on my upcoming novels visit www.leehhaywood.com. There you can sign up for my newsletter to receive notifications about future sales events, send me an email, or connect with me on Facebook and Twitter. I would love to hear from you.

Also, if you enjoyed the book, please consider telling a friend or providing a review on Goodreads and your book retailer of choice. Reviews are the lifeblood of indie publishing, and your feedback can help make or break a book. Your input is greatly appreciated.

Thank you for your support!

A WORD OF THANKS

I have read again and again, that for every author, there is someone in the background carrying them through the highs and lows of authorship. That has certainly been true for me. Needless to say, if it were not for my wife's unwavering support this book would not be in your hands. She has served as a soundboard for ideas and an editor for my writing since this story was just a mere inkling in the back of my mind. She has been beside me for every step along this very rocky road to publication, and I couldn't be more thankful to have such a splendid collaborator, best friend, and wife.

A special thanks is owed to my team of betareaders; their feedback has been priceless. They were the first adventurers into the world of Elandria, and the lack of typos can largely be attributed to their discerning eyes. I am endlessly grateful.

Lastly, a nod of gratitude to my parents. They raised me to have the discipline and persistence to pursue my passion, and provided me with the rich childhood (and pile of books) necessary for my imagination to blossom. Thus, I write.

-LHH

Books by Lee H. Haywood

The Gods and Kings Chronicles

The Order – A standalone prequel

A Wizard's Dark Dominion
The Guardian
The Guardian Stone

Fractured Throne

Fractured Throne
The Wayward Prince (Fall 2018)
The Shadow Behind the Throne (Early 2019)
Empire of Madness (Spring 2019)

Available in ebook and softbound formats.

Visit **www.leehhaywood.com** for more details.